DELIVER ME FROM EVIL

AN ARRANGED MARRIAGE MAFIA ROMANCE

THE AUGUSTINE BROTHERS
BOOK 2

NATASHA KNIGHT

Copyright © 2023 by Natasha Knight

All rights reserved.

No part of this book may be reproduced in any form or by any electronic or mechanical means, including information storage and retrieval systems, without written permission from the author, except for the use of brief quotations in a book review.

This is a work of fiction. Names, characters, places and incidents are either the product of the author's imagination or are used fictitiously, and any resemblance to actual persons, living or dead, business establishments, events, or locales is purely coincidental.

Cover by Coverluv

Editing by Raissa Donovan

ABOUT THIS BOOK

I wasn't supposed to fall in love with my wife. That wasn't part of the plan.

From the moment I first laid eyes on Madelena De Léon, I felt a primal urge to protect her. Keep her safe. Her father had failed her. I would not.

She is innocent, and I have no business taking her to my bed. But Madelena and I are bonded. Our destinies inexplicably linked. As is our survival.

My past is dark. I've made many enemies and betrayal runs rampant in my world. But sometimes those closest to you are the most dangerous of all.

If I was a better man, I would let her go. I know it's the only way to keep her safe.

But any goodness I had in me vanished long ago. I am a man condemned. I want what I want.

And what I want is her.

Deliver Me From Evil is Book 2 of The Augustine Brothers Duet. Forgive Me My Sins is Book 1 and must be read first.

You can find Forgive Me My Sins in all stores!

1

SANTOS

"Where is she?" I groan, gritting my teeth as Dr. Cummings stitches me up.

"I don't know. She ran out while I was trying to keep you from bleeding out," Val tells me for the hundredth time.

"I realize that. Fuck!" Pain has me hissing. The local anesthetic is slow to work, but I don't have time to wait. I lean up on my elbows, the flexing of my stomach muscles agonizing.

"Relax, Mr. Augustine," Cummings says, signaling to Val for help.

"I've got men out looking for her," Val says as he touches my shoulders and eases me down onto my back.

I look past him, willing the doctor to hurry up. The wound looked worse than it was, although I can still see Madelena's face in that moment before I passed out. Her shock. Her horror. Does she think that I'm dead? That she killed me? The loss of consciousness was due to the crashing of my head against the floor. But there was no time to brace myself and it was either her or me.

"I need to go," I tell them both. "Now."

"A few more minutes," Cummings says, sweat slick on his forehead. For a doctor, he looks fucking queasy. "It's best for you to rest—"

"That's it," I say, sitting up as soon as he has slapped the bandage on. There's a moment of dizziness, but I shut my eyes against it, and it passes. "Get me a shirt." Val is already coming out of my closet with one, and I pull it on, wincing as I drag my arm on my injured side into it. "Where's my brother? Why isn't he here?"

"We can't get hold of him. We're still trying," Val says.

"Has anyone been to the lighthouse?" I ask, standing. Blood has crusted on the waistband of my slacks, and I know I need to take it easy for the stitches not to rip open, but I need to find her. I need to get to her before she can do anything stupid. I saw how distraught she was after what her brother—her fucking idiot brother who will be dealt with—told her.

I will also never forget the look of utter shock on her face when she saw where the letter opener she still held was lodged.

"The lighthouse? Why would she go there in this storm?"

I glance out the window as the beacon washes the

raging waves in light. They haven't found her in the building or on the property, and there's no way she could have gotten far on foot in this weather. No vehicles have left the premises.

"Because that's going to be her instinct," I say, knowing it in my gut. It's the worst fucking place she can go in the state of mind she's in. "I'm going up there. You keep trying my brother. And make sure Odin De León sticks around." The fucking asshole.

"I'll go with you," Val says.

"No cell service out there." I don't give him a chance to reply before I'm out the door. The service elevator doors miraculously slide open as soon as I push the button, halle-fucking-lujah, and I ride down along with two soldiers Val sends after me. It's faster than I could have gone on the stairs in my state.

I see in the reflection on the back of the mirrored doors how the stain of blood is spreading on the once-white bandage. At least it's a little less painful now that the local anesthetic is finally kicking in.

Once the doors open, I hurry back out of the building the way I brought Madelena in. A woman gasps when she sees me, and someone drops a tray, but I ignore them all. The two soldiers flank me. I move as quickly as I'm able out into the storm and take a moment to look at the hulking building of the lighthouse in the distance.

Wind and rain howl, and I swear when lightning strikes, I see people out on that catwalk. But the temporary illumination is gone too quickly, and it's too far to see. Besides, no one can be out there. The lock on that door is intact. I saw that myself when Caius and I went out there the night of the wedding.

Christ. Has it only been days since then? It feels like a fucking eternity has passed.

The wind picks up as we approach the narrowing neck of the cliff. One of the men curses, huddling into his coat and leaning to fight the force of the storm that seems determined to keep us away.

"Madelena!" I call out, but she wouldn't hear me over the storm.

When we reach the lighthouse, I open the door and reach in to search for the light switch. I find it but nothing happens when I flip it. I try several times to no avail.

I dig my hand into my pocket to get my phone, planning to use its flashlight, but I come up empty. It must be in my jacket.

"Give me your phone," I tell one of the men. He hands his over. I switch on the flashlight, and the other man does the same. The three of us begin the climb up the stairs. "Madelena?" I call out again, but get no answer. There's an almost eerie stillness inside the lighthouse that is opposite the chaos of the storm outside.

"There's no one here," one of the men says when he reaches the main room at the top.

I'm the last to get to the landing. I look around, but there's nowhere to hide. She's not here—not inside anyway. Shining the flashlight down, I see a spot of red at the top of the stairs. A footprint has obscured it. I crouch to have a closer look and a swipe of my finger tells me it's relatively fresh.

"She's here. She has to be!" I stalk to the door that will lead to the catwalk. My heart races because it's too fucking quiet.

When I see that the door isn't fully closed, I move.

Wind hits me square in the face the instant I pull the door open. I brace myself against it as I take in the catwalk, the damage to the railing just a few feet from me. It's the temporary rail, and it was intact when I got a look at it from inside the building when Caius and I were up here.

My heart slams against my chest.

"Madelena?" I ask, not looking over the edge, too afraid of what I'll find. Instead, I walk stiffly around the catwalk, and there's a moment of utter, indescribable relief when I see her. But that relief is short lived because she's passed out, her back against the wall, body just two feet from the edge.

I rush toward her unconscious form, my freshly stitched wound on fire as I drop to my knees on the wooden planks covering the damaged catwalk. The railing that was in place just nights ago now creaks ominously as the wind sends it swaying back and forth. What the hell happened out here?

I touch her face, seeing the bruise that darkens her jawline. Her skin is cold to the touch, icy, but when I set my fingers over the pulse at her throat, I feel the strong beat of her heart.

I exhale with relief, adrenaline leaving my system and letting me breathe again.

"Out here!" I yell to the men. "Be careful. Stay close to the wall."

"Santos!" I turn back to find not the soldiers, but Caius stepping out onto the catwalk. He's drenched, his shoes are caked with mud, and his expression is worried. He must have run from the main building.

"Caius. Help me get her inside." I slide an arm under Madelena, tilting her head onto my shoulder. When I try to lift her, though, I have to stop, sucking in a breath when several stitches rip open.

"I'll get her. Val told me what happened. Get out of the way."

It takes me a minute to clear the way, but he gathers her up quickly and carries her back toward the entrance of the lighthouse.

I'm about to stand when my gaze lands on something trapped between two planks just beyond where she was lying. It looks familiar, and I reach for it, freeing it from the crevice just as Caius peers out from inside.

"Brother?"

I look at what I'm holding in my hand then back to Caius. I shake my head, stand, and quietly tuck it into my pocket. Before I go inside, I glance over the edge just as lightning strikes, illuminating the cliffs below. The water is so high you can't see the sharp gray rocks that are visible when the tide is out.

"Santos," Caius says again, watching me as I walk toward him.

"Where were you?" I ask him before stepping inside.

"Downstairs. At the party. My phone was dead. I just picked it up from behind the bar where it was charging and saw all the messages." He looks down at my side and I follow his gaze to the quickly spreading stain of red along yet another ruined shirt. "Jesus. What the fuck happened?"

"Looks worse than it is," I say. I glance past him into the room where one of the men is holding an unconscious Madelena. "Let's go. We need to get her warm."

I move to step past him, but he sets a hand on my shoulder to stop me. "What the fuck happened?"

"It was an accident."

He glances at Madelena. "Are you sure?"

I study my brother in this half-light, and when lightning breaks, it illuminates his face and the way the shadows fall across it casts a strange, eerie look to him. We remain like that for a moment more before I hear Madelena moan.

"Let's go," I tell him and the others.

"Godforsaken place, this. We should fucking burn it to the ground," Caius says when we're down the stairs and out the door. I get where he's coming from.

The road leading to the lighthouse grows narrower and narrower. It's not wide enough for a vehicle. I'm glad when I see him take off his jacket and lay it over my unconscious wife. It's a gesture I won't forget even if that jacket is sodden. When he does, I glimpse his wrist as I slip my hand into my pocket and wrap my fingers around my find.

But then Madelena makes a sound, turning her head, and my attention returns to her.

"Get a car," I tell Caius. "We'll take her to the house. We can't carry her through the club with all those people in there. Get Cummings to follow us."

He nods. "I'll meet you at the house." He stops, puts that hand on my shoulder again, and looks at me. "I'm glad you're all right."

I nod in acknowledgement and move quickly toward one of our SUVs. We slide Madelena into the backseat and I follow her, laying her head on my lap. My gut tightens as I look at that bruise along her jaw. Fingerprints. It could only be left by a hand about my size.

Again my father's words echo, followed by Thiago's warning, as I watch her too-young, too-innocent face in her unconscious slumber.

2

MADELENA

Rain pelts us like daggers of ice. This storm will be the end of us. The wooden planks are slippery. Repairs should have been completed months ago, and we shouldn't be out here.

The scream repeats, and I'm not sure if it's my mother's or his.

Santos? No. He didn't scream.

Santos.

A hopeless keening seems to come from inside of me. I was falling in love with him all these years. Stupid, stupid me. Now he's dead, his blood still warm on my hands.

Eyes like steel bore into mine. They're so cold that I don't know if it's the look inside them or the storm that has me shivering. The skin of his neck is thickly scarred where rope bit into it. It's terrifying to see, but when I shift my gaze to his eyes, they're no less so. But he caught me when I slipped, didn't he? His hard grip was to pull me back from a certain death on those rocks, in those freezing waters.

History repeating.

Like mother, like daughter.

Someone calls my name, but I can't open my eyes. Rain beats too hard against my eyelids.

What am I doing at the lighthouse? Why did I come here?

I hear the scream again, a man's scream.

Thiago.

The sensation of falling is a terrible one, but it wasn't me who fell. Almost, but not quite.

I feel it again, Thiago's grip around my wrist—being hoisted up then crashing back against the lighthouse wall. My head bouncing off the unforgiving surface.

Then the shadow that appeared behind Thiago, the other man whose face I did not see.

"I am not your enemy... Your enemy is much closer to home. In his veins is the blood of a monster."

Thiago standing too close to the edge. A hand against a chest. A grunt. A scream.

"Madelena!" Thiago yells before he's gone.

My eyelids fly open, and I bolt upright on a gasp. It's too fast, and I regret it instantly. My head throbs and I have to squeeze my eyes shut against the too bright light, the spinning room.

No more rain. No storm. It's quiet here and warm.

I touch my head. It feels like someone is beating a drum from the inside. I open my eyes slowly. The spinning begins to slow, the blurred edges of my vision coming into focus.

The first thing I see is the richly patterned duvet. It's luxurious with its deep sapphire hue, a delicate and detailed intertwining pattern. It's expensive, I can tell. On the nightstand to my right is a glass of water, two small white pills on a pretty dish. The room itself is dimly lit, the walls papered in a deep charcoal with a subtle pattern that seems to add texture. The dresser at the far end looks like an antique. It's as intricately carved as the nightstand. Heavy floor-to-ceiling curtains draping the windows are drawn shut.

The scent and feel are distinctly masculine—not to mention familiar.

The pounding of my head becomes more concentrated. I bring my hand to the back of it and gently touch the bump, which is tender. I hit my head twice. Once by accident. Once when the faceless man slammed it against the wall.

"Aspirin is on the nightstand," comes the gravelly voice from an armchair in the far corner.

I gasp, surprised, but then a switch clicks, and Santos is bathed in the yellow light of a reading lamp.

Santos.

Santos, alive and well.

He's dressed in a charcoal sweater and black slacks. His hair is brushed back from his face, and the scruff of his permanent five o'clock shadow has grown denser, darkening his jaw. In his eyes is a look so black, it simultaneously makes the hair on my arms stand on end and sends a flush of heat to my core. Strangely, it's similar to how he looks when he's aroused.

But now, it's not arousal.

It's anger.

I lick my lips, which are so dry they feel cracked.

"Go on." He gestures to the nightstand with a nod of his head. "You hit your head when you fell."

"Fell?"

He watches me, unblinking, and I can't tell what's going on in his mind. "Why would you go out there? What was your intention?"

I stare up at him, unsure how to answer. Not because I don't know the answer, but because I can't tell him that. Can't say it out loud.

"What were you going to do, Madelena?"

"I..." I start, trailing off. What should I say?

I stabbed you. I saw you bleeding out. How are you alive?

He sighs, then rises to his feet. I feel myself cower backward as he crosses the room, never taking his eyes off me. I track him, holding the blanket against myself. Can I expect him to feel anything but anger? He probably thinks I tried to kill him.

I swallow and force myself to look up at him when he stands directly beside me. Still unsmiling and never once breaking eye contact, he picks up the aspirin and holds them out for me.

"Take them."

My hand trembles and I'm careful to pluck the pills without touching him.

I put the pills into my mouth and reach to take the glass of water he offers. When our fingers brush against each other, there's a very clear spark of electricity.

Keeping my eyes on his, I swallow the pills, drink a few more sips, then hold the glass out for him to take. He sets it aside but doesn't move back to his seat across the room. I want him to because I need the space. The air.

But he chooses to lean against the nearest wall, stealing the oxygen from the room.

"Where am I?"

"You're in my bed in the Augustine family home."

I glance around again. "How did I get here?"

"I brought you. You were passed out on the catwalk of the lighthouse. Care to tell me how you got there and who put the bruises on you?" He gestures with a glance toward my jaw.

I touch it, realizing the soreness must be from when the man gripped me to slam my head against the wall.

"You... You're... I thought I killed you," I tell him.

"I'm not so easy to kill, remember?"

Confused, I bring my hand to my forehead because I know what I saw. I remember how bad he looked as he lay unconscious, blood pouring from his side and his face bleached of color.

He lifts his sweater. Beneath it, I see the bandage on his side, the dark stain of blood. "Didn't hit anything vital. Close though." He studies me for a beat before continuing. "Hate to disappoint you."

We'd been at the dinner. Odin had come with news about Uncle Jax's death... About Santos's involvement. I'd run, but Santos had come after me, and I'd stabbed him. It was an accident, but that hardly matters.

Then there was the lighthouse. Thiago. The stranger. Me.

Thiago going over the edge.

I rub my eyes shut to clear the image. My head hurts. "Thiago?" I ask, looking up at him.

Now Santos is the one who looks confused. "What about him?"

Someone knocks on the door, then opens it. It's Caius. He peers inside, glances at me, then at his brother. "Want me to come back?"

"No, come on in," Santos says, slipping a hand into his pocket, his expression unchanging, not relaxing, as he watches his brother enter.

A hand spanned across a chest. A grunt. A scream.

The hair on the back of my neck stands on end as Caius traps me with his gaze.

"What about Thiago?" Santos repeats the question.

Caius tucks his hands into his pockets and watches me, his head tilting slightly to one side.

"He went over the edge. He..."

Santos steps toward me, that look of worry intensifying, deepening the line between his eyebrows. "Thiago wasn't there."

I shake my head, which is a mistake. The room

blurs, and I squeeze my eyes shut when it threatens to spin.

"Based on the size of the bump on the back of her head, I'd say she hit it pretty hard. Not sure how reliable her memory is," Caius offers.

"No," I say. "I remember. I know what happened."

"You're saying Thiago was at the lighthouse?" Santos asks.

I nod.

"Are you sure?"

"I'm sure."

"Brother—"

"Tell me the whole story. From the beginning."

"After..." I point to where I'd inadvertently stabbed him. "I went to the lighthouse. Thiago was already there. Out on the catwalk."

Santos glances at his brother, who shrugs.

"I didn't realize it at first, and when I saw him, I was already outside. I got scared and wanted to get away from him, but the railing broke and I..." I trail off because my stomach lurches with the memory of slipping over the edge. "He caught me and pulled me back up. But then... Then there was someone else." I look down and push my hands into my hair and for a brief moment, I have a vision of the hands on Thiago's chest. Of his body going over. I look up at Santos. "The other man pushed him."

Santos's jaw tightens. It's an infinitesimal muscle that works, but I see it.

"What would Thiago Avery be doing out at the

lighthouse? What business would he have there? Particularly last night of all nights?" Caius asks.

"I swear. I remember right," I plead with Santos. "You have to go look for him. If he survived, he'll be injured."

"No one could survive that fall. If there was a fall," Caius says.

I look at him, then at Santos, who is still watching me. "Water was high. If he was there, if he went over, his body would have washed out to sea anyway," Santos says to his brother.

"You want me to go check it out?" Caius asks.

"Best to. Take a couple men. Search the lighthouse to see if there's any evidence."

"I'm not lying!"

"I'm not saying you're lying," Santos says to me. "But you hit your head pretty hard from the looks of it."

"No. I didn't hit it. He... He slammed it into the wall."

"Thiago?" Caius asks.

"No. I..." I'm getting confused. "No." I pause, collect myself. "The other man. I hit my head twice. Once when Thiago pulled me back. Once when the other man slammed it against the wall after he pushed Thiago over."

Caius's eyebrows rise high on his forehead. He steps close to his brother and turns his back to whisper something in his ear. Santos watches me, but nods to Caius and a moment later, Caius leaves. He closes the door behind him, leaving Santos and me alone once again.

"Tell me what you remember about the other man who was out there."

"Not much. I never saw his face. It was too dark. Thiago didn't seem surprised to see him, though." I pause, remembering a detail. "He told me I wasn't supposed to be up there before the man came."

"It's all sounding very jumbled, Madelena."

"It's the truth," I tell him.

"You may not remember correctly. You were upset. Understandably."

I remember why I was upset then. What had led to the events of the night. Surveillance footage of Santos at Uncle Jax's house the night he was killed. Did my husband kill my uncle?

He comes to sit facing me on the bed and I study him, trying to glean the truth from his eyes.

"I'm glad you're safe," he says, touching the back of his hand to my cheek.

It's hard to understand how someone can possess such extreme personalities. He can be violent. I've seen the result of his violence. Yet, with me, he is so tender, so careful.

"If Thiago is somehow out there, Caius will find him," Santos says. "But you can't mention this to anyone else. No one, am I clear?"

"Why?"

"Because if he did go over the edge, who do you

think the Avery family will come after when they learn what's happened?"

"But if he's injured or worse... He saved my life, Santos."

"We'll investigate, but for now, you only talk to me, understand? Not even Caius."

That makes me look at him questioningly. Not that I'd talk to Caius unless I absolutely had to, but why would he say that?

Santos sets his hand in a particular pattern on my jaw, and I realize he's lining up his fingers with those of the man who grabbed me. His eyes narrow infinitesimally, and I'm reminded again of how protective he is of me even if I don't understand why—because I do remember what I'd realized after I'd stabbed him.

I have to keep one thing in mind, though. How I feel about him has nothing to do with how he feels about me.

"I didn't kill your uncle, Madelena," he says abruptly, taking me out of the moment. I watch him, but I don't speak. I don't know what to say. "Your uncle was dead when I got there."

"What?"

"He was already dead. Face down in the pool."

Is he lying? I can't tell. Because he has everything to gain and nothing to lose by lying.

"I asked you to trust me and you said you wanted to. I'm asking you again."

"How can I? How can I blindly trust you given what

I know, what I've seen with my own eyes? You don't give me anything, Santos."

"Have I harmed you after our oath? Have I caused you violence?"

I don't answer.

"I will protect you. I've told you that."

"It's not enough."

He studies me, face growing grave. He gets up, then walks around the room. He turns back to study me, one hand on the back of his neck, the other in his pocket. "You want something? Okay." He returns to sit on the edge of the bed. "You once asked me what it was we had on your father that made him give you up so easily."

A weight settles deep in my belly.

"Do you still want to know that?"

I feel the blood drain from my face as my heart stops beating. I shiver with a sudden chill and nod. Because even though I know I will hate this answer, I can't back out now. I can't not know.

"Your father put a hit on Jax Donovan."

"What? No." I shake my head. "That's absurd."

"Your uncle was blackmailing your father. He was going to remove your father from the business."

"Blackmailing? About what?"

"Jax had physical proof of something your father had done years ago that your father had thought he'd erased."

I'm struck mute, shocked for the second time in the

span of a few minutes. "Uncle Jax wouldn't have done that," I say, my voice barely a whisper.

"You don't know the world you come from."

"He wouldn't."

Ignoring my comment, he continues. "Your father took action."

My brain is struggling to keep up, to make sense of it all. "Took action by hiring someone to kill him? He wouldn't do that any more than Uncle Jax would blackmail him or anyone."

"He did. I can let you listen to the phone call if you like."

"What? I don't... How would you even have that?"

"I have it because he didn't realize he'd contracted the hit with my father."

My hands fly to my mouth. I know what Santos is. I know what the Augustine family is. Why is this still such a shock to hear?

"Not sure you wanted to know all that after all, are you? Truth can be a tricky thing, Madelena. There's no going back from it. No unknowing it. Remember that."

"But... No. No, it doesn't make any sense. Uncle Jax... My father wouldn't..."

He touches my face. "You're very innocent, and I like that about you. But like I said, you don't know the world you come from."

"Were you there to do it then?" I ask, annoyed at his comment and slapping his hand away. "Is that why you'd gone to the house, but found someone had already done your work for you? Because that's what you want me to believe, right?"

"There was no reason to kill your uncle. We had evidence that your father contracted a murder. We had what we needed to make him bend to our will. That's all we wanted."

"Why? Why this personal vendetta against my father?"

"That's a whole other can of worms you don't want to open," he says, pausing. He raises his eyebrows and cocks his head. "Or do you want me to tell you that, too?"

I lean away a little, my non-answer answer enough.

"Your uncle knew I was coming to see him, and we'd agreed on him turning off the surveillance cameras."

"I don't believe he'd have done that. He was obsessed with security."

He continues, ignoring me. "You having received that photo of me leaving the house, that's problematic. It means the killer knew I'd be paying Jax a visit. And he or she also knew I wouldn't fulfill the contract. So, they did, and they made sure to have footage of me arriving at the scene."

"So, you want me to believe you were hired to kill my uncle, but weren't going to, and someone else did, and they're framing you?" I remember something else Odin told me then. "Did someone frame you of murder when you landed with the Commander too?"

There's a moment when the tables turn and it's

Santos who is surprised. But it's only for a moment before a shadow settles in his eyes. "What did you say?"

"You killed a man," I push, knowing this is important, although not quite sure it's safe for me to continue. But I'm betting on the fact that Santos won't hurt me. He's never hurt me—not after making our blood oath. "You killed him over his daughter."

Santos clenches his jaw and stands. His hands fist at his sides as he turns his back to me, all the muscles in his shoulders and back going stiff, and I know this is important. This is a key to something. Santos Augustine is a man with a dark past. This is one of his secrets. I need to know it more than I need to know anything else.

"Who is she?" I ask, my heart a mere flutter of beats in my chest as I wait for his answer.

He doesn't move. Doesn't turn. Doesn't speak.

"She's important. Who is she?" I ask again, this time feeling a twinge of something I can only name as jealousy.

"Was," he says after a long moment. "Not is." He turns to me, hand still balled, jaw still tight. He doesn't speak again, not right away, as if waiting for me to process.

Was.

Whoever she was is dead. That jealousy turns to guilt.

"Who told you about her?" he asks tightly.

A knock comes on the door before I have to answer,

and I'm relieved. I know if Santos finds out it was Odin who told me, he will hurt my brother.

"Yes?" Santos barks.

Val opens the door and peers inside. "He's here."

Santos turns back to me, studies me, eyes narrowing. "Put him in the basement," he tells Val in a low tone. I shudder at the order because I know for a fact nothing good will happen in that basement. With men like Santos Augustine, that's a given.

He steps closer, and with a hand under my chin, tilts my head up. "Your brother is a wealth of information, isn't he?"

My mouth falls open, and my heart drops to my stomach.

He grins, my expression the confirmation he needs. "I'm going to teach him to mind his own business."

"No!" I leap up onto my knees and grab hold of him when he turns to leave, wrapping my arms around him and using all my power to keep him there because it's Odin he's sending to the basement.

"No?" He dislodges me easily and takes hold of my arms.

"No. Please. No!"

"Your brother told you a story and look what happened. You put a fucking letter opener in me. Then you almost got yourself killed at that damned lighthouse. Which, what the fuck were you thinking going out there? Huh? What did I tell you about hurting what is mine?"

He gives me a shake that has me clutching his shoulders as the room spins.

"Shit," he mutters, that tight grip shifting into something else, something gentler until he's simply holding me. I wonder if he realizes how much stronger than me he is. How easily he can hurt me. Break me. "Are you okay, Madelena?"

"I feel sick."

He grits his teeth, eyes intent on me. I see hesitation in them. It's all I need.

I reach to touch his face. "Please don't hurt him. Please."

"You might have a concussion. You need to rest."

When he releases me, I grip his sweater to stop him from walking away. "Please. Please. He's all I have."

"Yeah, that's the thing, Madelena," he starts, closing his hands over mine. "He's not all you have. You have me. I don't know what it's going to take to get that through your thick skull, but you have me. You have for the last five years. You just need to trust me."

Tears stream down my face, and I curl my fingers into his sweater. He shakes his head, drags my hands off but holds onto them. His expression softens, and I hear those words he just said repeat.

Trust him.

But how can I trust him?

"Please don't hurt him. I'll do what you want. Anything you want!"

"Tell me something then. Give me something like I

gave you something. Answer my question. Why did you go to the lighthouse? Why there?"

I drop back onto my heels, feeling miserable—because that's the one question I can't answer. Saying it out loud would make it too real. "I don't know."

"That's a lie."

"Don't hurt him. Please," I plead.

"Tell me the truth, and I won't hurt him."

"You're going to blackmail me?" I ask through tears.

"Tell me, Madelena. Say it."

I push my hand into my hair, shake my head. I can't. Doesn't he know that?

With a sigh, Santos turns to go.

"Thiago said something," I blurt out, stumbling to get out of the bed but getting caught in the heavy duvet. "He said something before the other man came out onto the catwalk." He stops. I hurry to get the words out, to give him something. "He said he wasn't my enemy. That my enemy is closer to home and that the blood of a monster runs in his veins."

Santos goes rigid.

"I don't know who he was talking about," I add, going to him. I stand directly in front of him and put my hands on his shoulders to look at his face, which has gone stone-still. "I will learn to trust you. This is me trying. But if you hurt Odin, anything between us is gone. That's a given, Santos."

He draws a tight breath in and nods, but I don't know what he's nodding about. He draws my hands away and releases me. Without a word, he turns and walks away, out of the room, not caring that I chase after him, not hearing my pleas. Nothing.

He only stops for a moment to tell the guard outside my door that under no circumstances am I to leave the room.

3

SANTOS

I know why she went out there, but I want to hear her say it. Maybe if she does, and we share this dark secret, just maybe she can start trusting me.

But that's not what's on my mind as I make my way down the dimly lit hallway of the mansion my father purchased five years ago. It was a defining moment for him, the physical manifestation of how far we Augustines had come.

At the time, it was a run-down, forgotten place. It had been abandoned by the last family who lived here when they ran out of money and left it to rot back into the earth. My father had put his heart and soul into rebuilding it. I take my time as I near the grand staircase that will lead to the main floor and pause once I'm there. I look at the walls surrounding me, the paintings, the stained-glass windows. I love this house. I have since day one. Caius and my mother have always made their preference for something more modern clear. I wonder if now is the time for them to move to the luxury apartments of Augustine's, for me to move back home with my wife.

My eventual family.

I shake my head. Where the fuck did that thought come from? I have about a thousand and one problems to solve before I start thinking about a family.

Reaching into my pocket, I dig out my phone and scroll to a number I haven't called in forever. My breathing grows tight when I hit the green button to make the call. It takes a moment to connect then goes directly to voicemail. There is no greeting. There never has been. Just a beep to leave a message.

I don't.

Switching to text, I type one out.

We need to talk.

The checkmark appears almost instantly telling me the message has been sent. But that's where it ends. There's no second checkmark to confirm delivery.

Of course, it could mean nothing. Thiago's never given a single shit about answering his phone or even listening to messages. Hell, for all I know, he changed his number years ago. Or maybe his phone is out of battery. But something in my gut tells me it's neither of those things.

I dial another number.

"Santos?" Addy asks when she picks up.

"Hey Addy," I say, hearing the familiar music of the strip club in the background. "How are things?"

"Not much has changed since the other night. Or did you forget you and Thiago visited?"

I turn away from the staircase—not that anyone should be listening, but I take a few steps into the dark corridor I just came from before I speak.

"Has he been back?"

There's a pause I don't like, and her tone is heavier when she responds. "Why?"

"Just need to check he's all right."

"I told you the other night he wasn't. What's going on?"

"I don't know. Probably nothing. Look, if you see him, let me know, okay?"

"Yeah. Of course. You two need to work through your shit. You were like brothers once, remember?"

I wasn't the one who forgot. "Yeah, I remember. Let me know. It's important."

"I will, Santos."

I disconnect the call and tuck the phone back into my pocket, heading down the stairs. I find Val in the kitchen eating a sandwich at the long counter as he chats with Melissa, one of the cooks. When she sees me, her smile vanishes, and she straightens up to go back to work washing dishes. Val puts the last of his sandwich into his mouth.

"Ready?" I ask.

"Born ready."

"Do you know where my mother is by the way?"

"Out for dinner."

"This late?"

He shrugs, and we make our way to the basement door. Before opening it, I turn to him. "I need you to do something for me."

"Sure. What is it?"

"Put a tail on my brother."

His forehead furrows, but he nods once. Val has never trusted Caius, but I've made clear that he is my brother first and foremost. Val has been around for a while. Dad trusted him, too, and it's one of the reasons I rely so heavily on him.

"And my mother," I add, not liking this. Betrayal is a heavy thing. I slide my hand into my pocket, and as much as I want to be wrong, I need to be sure. Because the stone I found on the catwalk is one I see every day.

I wear a bracelet with a matching set of those very stones.

When I came home after the Commander's disappearance, freed from my life of violent servitude, Dad had a gift for me. He'd created an insignia for the Augustine family, something that would be appropriate for our new standing as part of the elite of our new world. It's a heart pierced by two swords. When he'd presented me with it, he'd told me it was an old symbol he adapted with an appropriate meaning. I hadn't understood that, and I still don't. He also made a point of telling me it was for me and me alone, and that my heirs would bear the insignia as well. But only mine. Caius had very distinctly been excluded.

It was after that that I'd had the bracelets made for Caius and myself. I chose Lapis Lazuli because the stone represented truth. I wanted him to know as far as I was concerned, that no matter this strange turn with my father, he and I were brothers. Period. The end. That was all there was for me.

Yes, more people than Caius and I wear this particular stone, but the fact that I found it on the catwalk the night I found Madelena passed out there is troubling because the bracelet is also suddenly absent from my brother's wrist. Caius has worn that bracelet every day since I gave it to him.

But this isn't the time to ponder this. I have to deal with Madelena's brother now.

"How was Odin when you picked him up?" I ask as Val unlocks the basement door.

"Not surprised."

"Hmm."

Val pulls the door open, and we descend. A light is on in the large, unfinished space. It's mostly empty apart from spare furniture stored here. A single man stands guard. In the middle of the room sits Odin De Léon, elbows on the small table, his fingers steepled, his chin resting on his hands. He turns when he sees us and makes to stand, but the soldier at his back sets his hand on Odin's shoulder and pushes him back down.

He glares at me as I walk around the small desk and take the opposite chair. I lean back against it, sliding my hands into my pockets. The gesture should be casual but my fingers curl around that stone, and I'm reminded how fucked up things could truly be.

"Where is my sister?" he asks, tone hostile.

"She's in my bed," I tell him with a smirk.

He grits his teeth and although he doesn't utter a word, his eyes speak volumes.

"She's probably got a concussion, thanks to you. But she's alive and she's safe. No thanks to you on that part."

He's clearly surprised, but that surprise morphs into concern in a split second. "What the hell are you talking about?"

I set my elbows on the table and lean toward him because I'm fucking pissed. "If you're so concerned about her, why would you tell her about the surveillance footage without having any fucking context?"

"Context?" He raises his eyebrows. "What context do I need? You were at our uncle's house the night he was murdered—"

"Drowned officially."

"Bullshit."

"Agreed."

He opens his mouth then closes it. He's clearly puzzled by my shared assessment of how his uncle died because a moment passes before he responds. "You were at his house. You spent a fucking hour murdering him. Probably torturing him. Cleaning up after yourself. I have no fucking idea what you did. And then you left checking your fucking watch like you had somewhere to be."

"That's a lot of blanks you're casually filling in."

"Oh? It doesn't take a genius to fill in those blanks. Any judge and jury will see that."

"Who's seen the footage?" I ask because I have two problems here. One being the person or people who have a copy of it and sent that photo to Madelena, and the second being Odin and whoever he worked with to get his hands on a copy.

"No one," he says, shifting his gaze away.

"You're a shitty liar, you know that? Try again."

"Or what? You'll nail my hands to the table?"

"No. I'll only do that if you touch what's mine."

A beat passes. He studies me because he knows what I'm talking about. Who I'm talking about. "My sister loved her uncle. She was the one closest to him."

"Let's just get a few things out in the open here. You and I both know your Uncle Jax wasn't exactly a saint."

He keeps his mouth shut and tilts his chin stubbornly up. He knows what I'm talking about.

"And you're going to tell your sister exactly that."

"Why would I do that?"

"Because I'm the only one who can keep her safe, and I can't do that unless she starts trusting me."

"What do you mean?"

I lean back again and glance at the soldier standing against the wall. He's been with me a long time, but can I trust him? What if Caius was the stranger Madelena mentioned? What if Thiago's cryptic message to Madelena was about Caius? Because it's too similar to my father's message.

At that moment, my mind conjures up the words in the letter Dad had left to be read after his death.

I know what you did, and this is your punishment.

Was he referring to Caius? What could he have done?

"What are you talking about, Santos?" Odin asks.

"Your sister and I had an argument last night," I say, my side throbbing as if affronted that I did not acknowledge the wound. "She was upset after what you told her and didn't give me a chance to explain before she went out to the lighthouse."

"The lighthouse?" His face loses a little color. "Why would she—"

"She wasn't alone."

"What?"

"Someone hurt her, and I'm pretty sure she saw something she wasn't supposed to see." Thiago's murder. Because I know in my gut Addy won't call to tell me she's seen him. I know that text message will never be delivered. Because his phone is probably somewhere smashed on those cliffs or at the bottom of the ocean by now.

"What the fuck is going on?"

I turn to the soldier. "Leave."

He nods, and, without question, does as he's told. I take my cell phone out of my pocket and set it on the table between us.

"I didn't kill your uncle. He was already dead when I got there."

"Right." Odin snorts, leaning back in a failed attempt to appear relaxed.

"He had plenty of enemies. You know how he operated. He wasn't above blackmail."

"Like I said, tell that to the judge and jury. I'm sure they'll believe you."

I find the recording on my phone. It's a copy of the original, which is stored in the safe. I hit play, and Odin loses the last of the color on his face.

"Jax Donovan dies in three days' time," Odin's father says. "Make it look like an accident. I don't want the fucking cops involved any more than you do. I'm sending the deposit now."

There's a momentary pause before we hear my father's voice. "Received."

"You'll get the second half once it's ruled an accident," Marnix De Léon says.

"I'll get it when the contract is fulfilled."

"Fine. Just get it done."

The recording ends, and I take my phone back.

"Jesus." Odin pushes his hands through his hair.

I give him a minute to process what he just heard and double check the text I sent to Thiago. As expected, still the single gray checkbox that it's been sent but sits somewhere in limbo waiting to be delivered. What happens to those messages, I wonder, when the recipient can no longer receive them? When he or she dies. Life is fleeting. Human bodies are so fucking fragile and yet we walk through our days oblivious to the fact as though we are immortals. Gods.

I shake my head. Is he gone? Really gone? The thought of Thiago dead has me swallowing emotion I didn't know I'd feel at the knowledge. But this isn't the time for emotion. I scroll through the images on my phone to a folder from five years ago. One only my father and I know exists, and, now that he's gone, only I know.

"That doesn't prove you didn't kill him," Odin finally says albeit more quietly now that he's been confronted by evidence of his father arranging a hit on his uncle. "If anything, it helps the case against you."

"Christ." I choose one of the photos and hold my phone up so Odin can see it. "How about this, then?"

Odin looks puzzled at first. He peers closer, then turns his face away. "Jesus Christ."

"What's the time on the clock say? It's incidentally logged on my phone as well in case you think I arranged that." He keeps his gaze averted. I signal to Val, who takes hold of Odin's head and forces him to look back at the phone. I get that he doesn't want to look. I'm zoomed in on the photo of his uncle floating face-down in the pool where the clock on the wall clearly shows the time. "If you've seen the rest of the surveillance footage, you'll know I let myself in about three minutes prior. Hardly enough time to drown a man, dry myself off, and take a fucking picture, don't you think?"

Odin looks up at me, confused. "Why don't you show Maddy that? Then she doesn't have to know what her uncle did."

"You think her seeing his body floating in the pool is a good idea?" Is he for fucking real? I could have shown her this from day one, evidence that what I was saying was true. But no way I was doing that to her. Hell, if it were up to me, she'd never have found out the kind of man Jax Donovan was, but there was no other way—or if there was, I didn't think of it.

"She's never going to find out about the existence of this photograph, understand?"

He nods.

"And you're going to tell her what Uncle Jax did. How he was blackmailing your father, among others, and left him with no choice but to remove himself from the company or face prison time."

He grits his teeth.

"Now tell me. Who got you the surveillance footage?" Because it's not supposed to exist. We made sure it was erased at the top level of the security company.

"No one."

I raise my eyebrows and study him, giving him the opportunity to find the right answer without me having to beat it out of him. I'm doing this for my wife.

"I have it. It's hidden," he finally says.

"Where?"

"Home."

"We're going to go get it when you're done talking to your sister. Now who got it for you?"

He shifts his gaze away, jaw set stubbornly again.

"Is it your boyfriend?" I ask, because I do know a

few things about Odin De León. One of them is that he's not interested in girls. I don't give a fuck about his sexual preferences, but Marnix De León does. Odin has been forced to keep this hidden from the society of Avarice and is expected to marry a woman of equal standing. Madelena is aware and keeps his secret with him. It's one of the reasons Marnix is so disappointed in his son.

What I do care about is that his boyfriend, Rick Frey, is some sort of computer wizard. He's the only person I can think of who could hack into the security company's database and find what was supposedly destroyed years ago.

Odin tries to keep his expression neutral, but I see the flicker of emotion in his eyes, see the line form between his eyebrows. I give him a minute and sure enough, he faces me, eyes welling up with tears.

"He won't talk. He's not like that. He's trustworthy."

"Well," I push the chair back and stand. "After you talk to your sister and we've picked up that surveillance footage, you and I will pay him a visit and I'll decide then how trustworthy he is."

4

MADELENA

Santos is sitting in the same armchair he'd been sitting in when I woke up. He's watching me with an expression I can't quite name as Odin confirms what he told me, that Uncle Jax was blackmailing our father. He, too, however, declines to give me more details, and I know it's bad.

My gaze vacillates between my brother and my husband as the façade of the world I've always known is chipped away, exposing an ugly truth beneath. As I numbly listen, I remember the overheard conversations, the distrust going back years, as far as when Mom was alive. No, not just distrust. Hate.

"I'm sorry, Maddy," Odin finally says.

"You've known all these years."

"What could I do? What would have been the point in telling you?"

I wonder if he suspected my uncle was murdered because he knew about the blackmail. He knew he had enemies. But does that mean he'd suspected our father? No, on that he seems as dumfounded as me, as stunned.

But he does confirm that Santos couldn't have committed the murder—not based on the timeline of his arrival and the fact that our uncle was already dead by then. There's photographic evidence to prove it.

I don't ask to see it because this is enough for one night. Hell, it's enough for a lifetime.

A man I'd thought honest and upstanding wasn't. My brother has known the truth for five years and shielded me from it. I understand he did it to protect me, but it doesn't feel good.

And then there's the fact that my own father is capable of murder.

Odin looks defeated when it's over. He turns to Santos as if to ask what's next, and Santos dismisses him. Val is right outside the door, as usual. Santos tells him to take my brother downstairs and he'll be down soon, and once again, I'm left alone with Santos, who comes to sit on the edge of the bed.

"You can just go. I'm tired."

"We have business yet, sweetheart."

"If you want to gloat, can you maybe hold off until tomorrow morning? I don't think I can process a whole lot more tonight."

"I'm not going to gloat. Believe it or not, it doesn't make me happy to see you unhappy. I didn't want you to find this out."

"No, I know. I asked for it, right?" I shake my head,

push my hand into my hair. "I'm tired." I meet his dark forest gaze. How many more secrets does he keep that will unravel me? Will I ever know all there is to know about this man?

"You need to learn to trust me. Because without me, you're not going to survive."

"Is that a threat?" I ask, my voice barely above a whisper.

He gives me a half smile. "No, Little Kitty. It's advice you should take."

"Great, thanks. I'll consider it. Can you go, please?"

"Like I said, we have business between us." He takes a breath in, gets up, crosses the room and locks the door. I sit up on alert and watch. He turns back to me, rolling his sleeves up to his elbows as he returns to the bed.

Something about the ominous gesture sends some message that bypasses my thinking brain and hits at my very center. My stomach flips as, unable to hold his gaze, I look to his hands, his exposed forearms. He's wearing the ring I remember from our first meeting on his right ring finger, and on his left is our wedding band. On one wrist is an expensive watch and that beaded bracelet. The olive skin is dusted with dark hair and watching his muscles work and flex has a strange power over me—like there's something in me that has no choice but to submit to this man, that *wants* to do just that.

Santos Augustine is raw, animalistic masculinity. He is all alpha male, and my body is very aware of his.

Our connection is undeniable, the feelings he stirs inside me wrong to my thinking mind and yet so very real.

He sits down on the edge of the bed and draws the blanket that's covering my legs back. I'm dressed in a T-shirt. One of his, I guess. It's huge on me. He must have put it on me when he brought me here from the lighthouse. I'm sure my dress was ruined.

I watch as his gaze slips to my bare legs. He rests one hand on my thigh, and I'm reminded again of the difference in size between us.

The difference in strength and power.

Even that does something to me.

When I look up, he's watching me. I swallow because his eyes have gone dark, the pupils dilated. I find I'm licking my lips in anticipation of a thing I shouldn't want.

"Take off the shirt," he says.

I tilt my head in confusion because I think I was expecting him to kiss me.

"Go on."

I reach for the hem of the shirt and pull it off over my head. He takes it from me and sets it aside, then lets his gaze skim over me. My breasts are bare, but I'm still wearing my panties. My nipples pebble as his gaze moves over them in and it takes all I have to keep my arms at my sides.

He shifts his eyes to mine.

"I know what happened was unintentional, but you

should never have picked up that letter opener and brandished it like a knife."

"What?" I ask, confused. This is not where I thought this was going.

"And I'm going to punish you for it now." I barely register his words before he continues. "Lay across my lap. Face down."

"Excuse me?" I instinctively reach back to grab hold of one of the carved wooden rungs of the headboard because I think I know what he's intending.

"You heard me. Lay across my lap." He takes hold of my wrist and gently uncurls my fingers from the rung even as I try to pry his off me.

"Let go!"

"It will go easier if you don't fight me," he says calmly, like this is a remotely normal conversation.

"You're fucking insane if you think I'm not going to fight you!" In a minute, we're in a full wrestle. Well, I am. I'm giving it my all. I'm up on my knees and he's got my wrists while I try to shove him away. He easily overpowers me, but I see what it costs him when he winces. It must be the wound on his side. That would make me pause, and maybe it does for a moment, but I know what he's intending and I have to fight.

"One more chance, Little Kitty," he says, shifting my arms to my back and holding onto both wrists with one hand. "Lay yourself across my lap and take your punishment."

"Go fuck yourself!" I start to tell him, but before I've even gotten the words out, I'm face down over his lap, my wrists trapped at my lower back. He uses the elbow of the arm holding my wrists to keep me down as he peels my panties off of me with his free hand.

I kick my legs, and he spanks my ass so hard, I lurch forward, gasping for breath. It takes my brain a moment to process what just happened. I squeeze my legs together as my back goes ramrod straight, and I clench my cheeks and grit my teeth so as not to cry out.

He rubs the spot he just spanked then smacks it again, making me yelp as I make fists with my hands. Once again, he rubs, then leans over me, so his mouth is at my ear.

"Here's a tip. Try to relax. It'll hurt less," he says, spanking again.

I turn my head so I can see him from the corner of my eye. "Fuck you, and fuck your tip!"

A wide grin spreads across his face, and I feel exactly what spanking me is doing to him when he shifts my body slightly and his hard cock presses against my stomach. I renew my fight, kicking, wriggling. But he just laughs it off, restraining me with one hand while he rains down hell on my ass.

"You're fucking hurting me!" I finally cry out, hating to because I don't want to give him the satisfaction as tears sting my eyes.

He stops spanking for a minute and I look over my shoulder at him.

"If I don't punish you, you won't learn," he says, no joking in his tone. He spanks each cheek again, and I cry out. "You ever try anything like that again, you ever raise a weapon against me or yourself again, and you'll realize how easy I'm being on you tonight. Do you understand me?"

"Easy? You're a sadist!"

He spanks. "Do you understand?"

"Yes, asshole! Stop!"

"Those are not the words of someone who understands," he says, punctuating his words with more smacks.

I grit my teeth, determined to take the rest of his punishment in silence—determined not to give him the satisfaction of my cries, but it's fucking impossible.

"Stop. Please. It hurts," I finally beg.

"That's the point," he says, then hauls me up and sits me on his lap. His slacks chafe my raw ass. He keeps my wrists at my back, and I can't wipe the tears from my face. Santos brushes them away, and that hand that just spanked the crap out of me is so gentle that I wonder again how one man can have so many contradictory parts to himself. "Are we clear, Madelena?" he finally asks again, tone level. But that is Santos. Controlled. Even this spanking was controlled, and I know in my heart of hearts that this was him going easy on me.

"Yes," I force out through clenched teeth, feeling not only the pain of the spanking but the embarrassment of it. He loosens his grip on my wrists, then releases them altogether. My face burns with humiliation, and I am quick to rub away any remaining tears, hating that he has conquered me. "I hate you."

"You don't," he says, cupping the back of my head gently, careful of the tender spot. He pulls me to him and kisses me, and my heart races with confusion, blood pounding in my ears. My breath hitches when his tongue touches mine, and I don't understand why I'm allowing this. Why I'm kissing him back.

It's wrong. I shouldn't feel this way, especially after what he did, but my body is not my own when he touches me, and I want him. I want this, and I want him.

How the fuck am I turned on?

He undoes his slacks and shifts his grip to my hips to lift me so I'm straddling him. I pull at his sweater, needing to be flesh to flesh with him. I'm clumsy, and he helps me tug it off. I glimpse the bandage on his side but I'm quickly distracted when he grips my hips, fingers kneading flesh, and meets my eyes before he pushes into me.

That thrust has me crying out, the pain intense, the pleasure creeping along its edges almost unbearable.

I close my hands around his shoulders as he takes me, fucking me from below while kissing me and kneading my sore ass.

"Fuck, Madelena," he says against my lips, biting them before he shifts our position, flipping me onto my back on the bed. Again, I see him wince, but he just groans, pushing through the pain he must be feeling and climbing on top of me. His thrusts build in intensity as he rises and crashes against me, rocking into me.

I whimper and cling to him, release so close. I close my eyes and bite my lip.

"Open your eyes," he says. "I want to watch you. Open your eyes and look at me."

I do, and our eyes lock, and I don't know what it is about this moment because I should fucking hate him. After that humiliation, I should despise him. But as I look into those dark eyes, all I can think is that I want him. I want to be here beneath him. I want to feel his strength around me. His weight on top of me. I feel so strangely close to him, closer than I've ever felt to another human being.

"I'm going to come," I cry out.

"Come, sweetheart. Come for me." He bites my lower lip and, eyes open, I come undone, watching him as he watches me. He thickens inside me and a moment later, he's coming too, and I cling to him because I want this. There's nothing else in the world right now but this. Us like this. Him and me with nothing between us.

When it's over, I lay boneless on the bed. We lie in silence for a long moment as we catch our breath before he retreats to the bathroom to return with a warm washcloth. He cleans me, then lifts me to lay me down so my head is on the pillow.

I lie on my back while he props his chin on his elbow and looks me over. When one hand slides down over my stomach toward my legs, I think he's going to cover us, but he doesn't. His face grows serious as his gaze follows his fingers. I hold my breath and watch the top of his head.

He nudges my legs apart a little, fingertips coming to trace the fine lines cut high on my thighs.

I close my hand over his to stop him. "Don't."

He meets my gaze but then, ignoring my plea, shifts his attention back to my thigh and continues.

A tear slides down over my temple.

"What does this do for you?" he asks.

I swallow hard. How do I explain this? It makes no sense. So, I shift my gaze away instead of answering.

"No, Madelena. Look at me. Don't hide from me." He touches my cheek to turn my face to his. "Tell me."

I shake my head, suck my lower lip in, feeling my face burn. Feeling exposed.

"Tell me. I want to understand."

"It concentrates everything," I hear myself say. "Makes it manageable. I guess."

He is quiet for a moment. I think he's processing. "When was the last time?" He must see there are no fresh scars.

"A while ago. Two years maybe."

"Good," he says with a gentle smile. "When you feel like you need to cut, you come to me, understand?"

I wipe away tears. "So you can spank it out of me?" I say half-joking, half I don't know what.

"Maybe." He grins, pushes my hands away, and wipes away the tears himself. "If it ends like this, why not?" He kisses my mouth, then the tip of my nose before reaching to turn out the light. He draws the blankets up to cover us. "I'm glad you're safe, Madelena."

"Thank you for coming to get me," I say, meaning it. Feeling it in my chest.

If you can hear a man smile, I think I hear it. "Good night, my sweet Little Kitty."

I curl into him, tucking myself against his chest, not minding the nickname as he wraps powerful arms around me, and I find there's nowhere else I want to be right now. As I listen to the beat of his heart and feel the heat of his skin, there's nowhere but here. There's no one but him.

5

SANTOS

I'm sitting in the living room, watching the fire blaze in the fireplace. I turn the insignia ring over and over on my finger as time ticks by on the antique grandfather clock.

After Madelena fell asleep, I slipped out of the bed and went to get the surveillance footage with Odin. He'd had it hidden in Madelena's old bedroom under some floorboards. I found an old diary in there but left it alone. I want Madelena to tell me her secrets. I don't want to take them from her.

What happened between us up there was unexpected. At least what happened after I spanked her was. Spanking is an easy, harmless punishment, one that will make her think twice next time she considers doing something stupid that will harm either her or me. But the fucking afterward was unplanned.

I was aroused by spanking her. What man wouldn't

be? But I hadn't intended on fucking her. It confuses the message.

Then after that came our conversation about the cuts. I don't know what made me ask or what made her answer.

Her revelation about why she does it is interesting. She had no control over traumatic events of her life, and they just kept coming, a snowball growing into a fucking avalanche and taking her under. Not that her trauma was ever snowball-sized. She wasn't that lucky. Cutting she could control. Pain she could control. I'm not sure I fully understand that infliction of pain on oneself when it's not punishment, but it makes sense in a way, too.

If I think about the cuts I sliced over my arms and shoulders, that was different. I did have control, to a degree. Those were to inflict pain for punishment. It's different than Madelena's cutting to center the pain, give it a focus, make it manageable by concentrating it.

I take a deep breath in and sigh it out. That chapter is closed now for her. That's what matters. That, and the fact that she gave me that little piece of herself. She let me see her.

And she thanked me for coming to get her. As if I wouldn't. Still, the memory makes me smile, at least momentarily until my attention shifts to the pierced heart of my ring. Two swords. Was my father marking some betrayal? He was a strong man, and every strike against him only made him stronger, made his skin thicker.

Made him less forgiving.

Commotion in the hallway has me checking the time. It's almost one in the morning. I hear my brother's voice asking one of the guards where I am, and a moment later, he enters the living room.

"Anything?" I ask.

He shakes his head. "If he was there, there's no physical evidence to prove it."

"Good," I say because this will be important for the Avery family.

He crosses to the bar to pour himself a whiskey. "Want one?"

"No, thanks." I'm not sure why he always asks. He knows I won't accept it. Not that I don't want to. I just can't have it.

He leans against the bar and sips. "Do you believe he was up there?" he asks me as I study him, thinking about what Madelena told me Thiago said.

"I don't know why she'd make that up. She was pretty shaken up about it."

"Well, good riddance, I say, right?" I don't respond and he sips from his glass, eyes locked on me. "Don't tell me you're going to miss him."

"He didn't deserve to die like that."

"But he's dead. I mean, if it's true. And that's what matters. One less person to cause trouble."

"I'll go to the Avery house tomorrow to see what's up."

"I'll come with you."

"No, actually. I need you to do something."

"What?"

"I'm moving back into the house with Madelena."

"Oh?" His eyebrows rise up in surprise.

"It'll be better for her to be away from the lighthouse."

"And you care about that why?"

"Because tormenting her gains us nothing."

"But it is fun."

"Don't be a dick."

He shrugs a shoulder. "Just messing with you. It'll be easier to watch her here anyway. Especially once she's pregnant."

My jaw tightens, and it takes me a minute to speak. "I want you and Mom to move to the apartments at Augustine's."

He's mid-way to bringing his glass to his lips but stops. "Why?"

The front door opens then, and we both glance toward the hallway where we clearly hear our mother's voice. I stand, shove my hands into my pockets, that bead burning a fucking hole in my brain. "Easier. You don't like it here anyway," I tell him as I listen to her heels clicking along the floor.

"That's true, but you're kicking us out for her?"

"Who's kicking whom out?" comes my mother's voice as she enters the living room. She's wearing a dress I haven't seen before. I wonder which designer but can guess the price tag.

"Mom," Caius says, swallowing the contents of his glass. "Drink?" He moves around the bar to make a vodka martini for our mother and pour himself another whiskey. She studies me as he carries her drink to her. "Santos wants to move back in here with his wife. And he wants us out."

She takes the glass and turns back to me, eyebrows furrowed. "Why would you want that?"

"Which part?" I ask.

"Don't be a smartass," she tells me. "If you want to live here, that's fine. I wanted that anyway, especially as we move into phase two."

I take a deep breath in and force myself not to comment on that *phase two*.

Caius watches us, and when I open my mouth to answer, he comes to stand beside me. "I have good news," he says.

She raises her eyebrows, surprised at the interruption.

"Thiago Avery is dead," he tells her, saving me from having to answer. Because the answer is that I want to keep my wife away from them. I feel that in my gut.

"What?"

"I think that's one of the reasons my brother wants to move his wife here. She went out to the lighthouse last night after they... had a disagreement."

"You mean after she stabbed him," Mom says, surprising me but also not. Cummings must have told her he patched me up. So much for doctor-patient confidentiality. "I heard tonight. Let me see."

"It's nothing. Flesh wound."

Caius snorts.

"That's not what Dr. Cummings said. That girl is dangerous, Santos."

"What were you doing with Cummings?" I ask.

"That's my business, isn't it? Your father has been dead for two years. I won't answer to my own son."

"Hey you two, knock it off. Infighting is no good, remember?" Caius says casually. "Don't you want to know about Thiago's unfortunate accident?"

"Tell me."

"Apparently he was at the lighthouse doing devil knows what, and he *fell* over the edge." He puts air quotes around "fell."

It takes her a minute, and it's like she's forgotten about the stabbing. She cocks her head, and a small smile begins to creep along the corners of her mouth.

"I'll go to the Avery house tomorrow, get a feel for what's going on there," I say. "In the meantime, no one mentions he was at the lighthouse. I don't want anyone to know that."

"Hmm," Mom murmurs, sipping her drink, thinking. "That's a pleasant turn of events, isn't it?"

"A man is most likely dead," I remind her.

"Most likely?" She looks to Caius for clarification, not me.

"No body," Caius fills in. "But the water was high in that storm. He was probably washed out to sea. I just got back from checking the lighthouse and the perimeter. Nothing."

"Well, that's not a fall anyone can survive. Do you still think your little wife is harmless after she stabbed you and murdered Thiago Avery?" she asks me.

"Christ. She didn't murder anyone. How would Madelena murder a man Thiago's size? Think." I tap my skull.

"You're very defensive. I'm just trying to help. And besides, I'm worried about you," she says.

"Well, no need. I'm fine." I push a hand into my hair. "I'm going to bed. I'll arrange for someone to move Madelena's and my things out of the apartment. There's not much."

My mother studies me, then turns her gaze to Caius. "What do you think of moving out?"

Caius shrugs a shoulder. "You and I never really liked this house much anyway, right?"

"That's true." She swallows her drink and sets the glass on the mantle. "But it's late to make this decision now. I'm going to bed, and we'll discuss it tomorrow." She turns to walk out of the room.

"Decision's been made," I say in no uncertain terms. "You'll start packing tomorrow and be out by the end of the week."

She stops, glances back at me, expression unreadable. She then turns to Caius and gives him a smile. "Guess it's you and me again, kiddo."

He smiles that charming smile of his. "You and me."

6

SANTOS

My mother is put out over being asked to move, even though she's had designers to the apartment to refurnish it entirely to her liking. I love my mother, but I also know her. Evelyn Thomas came from nothing. She had Caius when she was in her late teens and scraped by working any job she could find to support herself, her baby, and her parents, whom she never speaks of. As far as I know, they died years ago.

When my father met her, Caius was still a baby. He was smitten upon first sight, and I understand. My mother is a very beautiful woman. But she is also a woman comfortable with manipulating every situation to best serve her wants and needs, and she is incredibly protective of her first-born son.

I get it and hold no grudge against my brother. The two of them are bonded in a way she and I will never be. I had a father who loved me from day one. My father adopted Caius because he wanted my mother. I believe she loves me, but when my father set Caius aside and cut him out of his will, things changed, and I understand the ferocity of her instinct to protect him.

These last few days that she is at the house instructing the staff on her packing, she makes sure to show me how much of a sacrifice she is making for the comfort of myself and my wife, the enemy.

I go along with it because it's temporary and it's easier this way. Besides, I have more important things to deal with at the moment.

Val and I pull up to the gates of the Avery property along the edge of town late in the afternoon two days after the incident at the lighthouse. There has been no contact from Thiago. That message I sent still sits undelivered in outer space somewhere. Two more calls to Addy have turned nothing up.

Val slows the car as we pull up to the gates. The security cameras on either pillar zoom in on our faces, and I'm surprised when the gates ease open before we have to announce ourselves to the two armed soldiers approaching from the guardhouse. We drive toward the entrance of the opulent home while I take in the grounds, seeing in my periphery the closing of the gates and the two men standing just outside of the guardhouse watching, automatic rifles slung over their shoulders.

The house itself is a French style stone structure. It is beautiful, certainly, and I imagine the interior to be just as luxurious as ours. I'm sure Bea Avery wouldn't have accepted anything less than the very best. They can afford it. The Commander was a very wealthy man—the kind of wealth one can only acquire in the line of work he was in. The line of work my family is in.

We are all criminals, no matter how we try to scrub the blood from our hands.

"Wait here for me. I shouldn't be too long," I tell Val once he pulls the SUV to a stop.

"You sure?" he asks, peering to look toward the front entrance, the door of which has just been opened.

"I'll be fine," I say, watching Camilla and her creepy brother step outside.

I climb out and take note of the armed guards at the door, who step forward as I climb the stairs.

"Search him," Camilla orders.

"That's not necessary. I'm unarmed."

"We don't believe you," she says, folding her arms across her chest like she always used to do because she's still a fucking brat.

Before I have a chance to respond, Bea Avery appears. She's wearing a black dress, and her long blond hair is loose down her back. She's still attractive, but she must be aware that her daughter's beauty has surpassed her own.

"Don't be a child, Camilla," Bea says. She brings the cigarette she's holding in its vintage silver engraved cigarette holder to her mouth, and her gaze moves over me. "Santos. What a surprise. Come in."

She stands back, and the twins move into the

house so that I can pass through the door. I notice another soldier inside the house. The Commander never had so many armed men so visibly present. Thiago wouldn't have either.

This is because he's gone.

Once we're inside, Bea Avery leads the way to a formal living room and takes a seat on an armchair by the fireplace. She doesn't invite me to sit while Camilla and Liam perch on the couch. That's fine. I don't intend on staying long. Besides, this is like old times. To them, I am a servant. One who deals in blood, but a servant nonetheless.

"I'm here to see Thiago," I say flatly and watch them closely. I see how Liam glances to his sister for a clue on how to react, see Camilla's eyes narrow accusingly, and watch Bea Avery's cool gaze not wavering from me once.

"Are you? Well, I'm sorry to say he's not here."

"No? When do you expect him home? I'll come back."

"Why? What business do you have with him?"

"That's between us."

She studies me as she takes a drag from her cigarette. "Any business you have with my son is business you have with me."

"As far as I know, Thiago is the head of this family since the Commander's unfortunate absence." I add the last part in with a grin I don't like the feel of and a glance toward the twins.

"You mean since his murder?" Liam asks.

"Shut your mouth," his mother chastises him, exhaling cigarette smoke as she speaks and looking like the fucking dragon she is. "My son was on his way to dinner at your club two nights ago, but sadly he never arrived, and we haven't seen him since. He seems to have vanished off the face of the earth, in fact. You wouldn't know anything about that, would you?"

I raise my eyebrows. "Oh? Has he called in?"

"Of course not. I'm not stupid, Santos."

"I hope he hasn't disappeared like Father. You do have a knack for making people disappear, don't you?" Camilla asks in a sickly-sweet tone that grates on my nerves.

"I learned from the best," I tell her.

She flips me off.

"Well, if you could let Thiago know I came to see him when he's back, I would appreciate it."

Bea is twirling a long strand of hair around her finger. I always wondered about her. Despite knowing exactly the kind of man her husband was, she was devoted to him in a strange, unnatural way. They had a dynamic between them that was pure hatred at its core, but neither was willing to let the other go, as if the other's suffering took precedence over their own happiness. I never understood it. I saw with my own eyes how he treated her and she knew well how many women he took to his bed.

I also saw what happened to those he was particularly fond of once his wife got wind of it.

Bea Avery grins, and I wonder if my face gives away

my revulsion at the memory of what she is capable of. "Camilla, see Santos out."

"Yes, Mother," Camilla says, standing. She hates her mother, but she's also afraid of her. I think that fear and Thiago are the only two things that keep the little psychopath in line.

"I can see myself out."

As if she doesn't hear, Camilla steps toward me, standing too close. She smiles, then slides her hand into mine. When I take mine away, she weaves her arm through mine and holds tight as she leads me out of the living room and down the hallway toward the front door. Her familiar perfume is cloyingly sweet, and I hold my breath because it reminds me too much of the past. Of my life when I lived with this family. Of the kind of man I became during those years.

Just before we get to the front door, though, she turns to another that a guard is standing in front of, and she nods to him to open it. He does.

I raise my eyebrows.

"I don't want to be interrupted, understood?" she tells him in a tone that is neither bratty nor at all like her usual tone. I study Camilla Avery, wondering how the power dynamics of the family will shift now that Thiago is gone.

"What do you want, Camilla?" I ask when she closes the door and we're alone in a small library.

She lets her gaze move over me, then brushes non-existent lint off my shoulder. "You look good, Santos. You're aging well."

I roll my eyes. "Good to hear. Now if you'll excuse me." I head toward the door.

"I know where he was going," she says.

I glance back, keeping my expression more amused than anything else. "Excuse me?"

"Your wife is pretty," she starts as soon as she knows she has my attention. She crosses the room to plop herself casually down onto an oversized armchair. She slings her long legs over one arm and lets one spiked heeled shoe hang off her toes. "Do you fuck her, or do you let your brother do that like you used to with the gifts Daddy sent you?"

Gifts.

Women.

Human beings.

But this family has never been bothered by such distinctions. I know one of the reasons being around them impacts me so viscerally is that for a time, I became like them... and that's a terrifying thing to see in oneself.

I narrow my gaze, my jaw tightening, but I don't respond. She knows I never fucked any of the women her father sent as my rewards. She also knows that Caius did. Camilla always had a way of finding things out, almost like she had her own spy system all those years. I wonder if we all didn't underestimate her.

"I hope you don't mind my asking. I'm so curious." She lets her gaze slide suggestively over me.

"You're out of line."

"Am I? It's just a question. You know I used to

wonder if you couldn't get it up, but then I'd hear you some nights." I should walk out. "Choking the life out of your dick when I'd happily have pleasured you with my mouth. Or any other hole."

I try to hide my surprise at her crudeness, which is so opposite the perfect good-girl look she has going on. "My dick would have shriveled up and died once your poison tongue touched it. Excuse me."

"I bet she likes taking it from him," she says innocently. "Do you watch?"

I've just put my hand on the doorknob, and although I should know better, although every instinct is to walk away, I react. Because something about the thought of Caius touching Madelena makes me fucking insane. Before she can utter another word, I'm on her, and have her on her feet, my hand around her throat.

"You don't talk about my wife. You don't think about my wife. Thoughts of her never cross your sick mind. Understand?"

She claws at my forearm, her face growing red, eyes too wide. I loosen my grip then release her altogether before I fucking kill her.

One corner of her mouth curves upward, and she licks her lips in that way a predator licks his before closing its jaws around the throat of its prey.

"You mean thoughts about your wife in general or thoughts about your brother fucking your wife?"

My fists clench at my sides.

"Caius is pretty talented with his tongue. I'm sure

she's enjoying—" She cries out when I take her by her throat again and this time, thrust her against the wall.

"You are your father's daughter. It's no wonder he was so fucking proud of his little psychopath brat." I give one more squeeze, hear the strangled sound she makes before dropping her onto the floor and turning to go.

"Thiago got a call before he left," she says, tone scratchy and not quite as composed as it was moments ago.

I pause, then decide to keep walking. She's playing with me.

"Something about a meeting at the lighthouse," she adds.

That does make me stop and squeeze my eyes shut. Because fuck.

"Did you know that when I'd listen to you jerk off, I'd finger myself and imagine it was you fucking me?" she asks, all sweetness again.

I glance back at her. She's up on her feet and twirling her hair like her mother was moments ago. "I heard him. He was going to meet someone at the lighthouse. And now he's gone. Was it you he was going to meet? Did you make him disappear like you made Daddy disappear?"

"You're lying."

"I think you know I'm not. But there's a more important question you should be asking me, don't you think?"

"What's that?"

"How do I know just how good Caius is with his tongue?" She watches me closely as she grins like the fucking predator she is. She slides one hand over the peaked nipple beneath her blouse and down her stomach to the waistband of her jeans. "I'll tell you something else too. He's even better with his cock."

7

MADELENA

The next few days pass quietly. I spend a lot of the time sleeping. I don't know if it's because that night at the lighthouse took its toll or because of the bump on my head—or it could be the fact that Caius and his mother are around packing, and I'd just rather avoid both of them. Santos is apparently moving them out of the house and to the apartment at Augustine's, and he and I will be living here.

I admit, I like the idea of not being near the lighthouse. Just like when he'd sent me away to college, it's a relief to me. Moreover, I like this house. I remember it from when I was little. It had belonged to the Valerian family years ago but had fallen into disrepair when they lost their money and eventually the last of them disappeared. There was no shortage of rumors about what happened to them, either.

As far as the house, there were always stories that at least one of the disappeared members of the family had been murdered in it and still haunted the place. It's an old, gothic style behemoth and something I've always found beautiful even as it fell into decay.

I expect Santos to give me my own room. I assumed I was sleeping in his until one was made up for me, but the housekeeper who came to help me unpack informed me I was to unpack my things here. I'm surprised but not unhappy about it. I feel safer with Santos close by and strangely anxious when he's not. I know what happened between us the other night has a lot to do with that, especially his question about the cuts. It was in the way he asked. He seemed to genuinely want to understand and, in a way, telling him helped me to understand.

The spanking, too, was intimate, although I'm still not sure how I was turned on. Feeling a blush creep up along my neck at the memory, I shift my attention to the task at hand.

I've left the bedroom door open a crack so I am sure to hear him when he gets back. He's paying a visit to the Avery family to get a read on what they know. The image of Thiago going over the edge still haunts me and whenever I close my eyes, I see that hand on his chest, hear the grunt of breath, the scream.

The night Caius went to the lighthouse to look for anything having to do with Thiago, he returned with the news that there was no evidence of his having been there and certainly nothing of his demise. He didn't tell me this, but Santos relayed it to me.

Regardless, I know what I saw.

Thiago didn't deserve to die like that. No one does —and I won't forget the fact that he saved my life. I don't know if Santos believes me or if he thinks I somehow imagined it, like Caius does, but I don't care. I won't forget it.

I'm unpacking my toiletries in the bathroom when I hear the bedroom door close. Assuming it's Santos, I hurry out, but stop short when I find Caius standing in the bedroom. He sets a box down on the bed and turns to take the other from the man carrying it.

"Knock-knock," he says to me then dismisses the other man, who closes the door behind him once he's gone.

I'm tempted to walk over and open it, but Caius is watching me, and I don't want to appear weak. So, instead, I take a deep breath in and put my hands into my pockets to have something to do with them. "What are you doing here?" I ask.

"Delivering the last of your things." He gestures to the two boxes. Sticking out from one is the locked box I found when I was going through Santos's closet at the apartment on our wedding night. He follows my gaze toward it. "That shouldn't be here," he says, lifting it out and setting it on the bed. "You recognize it?"

"No," I lie and walk over to my nearly empty duffel bag, picking it up and busying myself with the notebooks left inside. I wasn't going to unpack my sketchbooks from those two years at college, but I need to have something to do until he goes. I stack them on the table and zip up the empty duffel.

Caius surprises me when he comes to look at them. "Sketches, right?"

I put my hand over the stack when he reaches for one. "They're nothing. Just schoolwork."

"You're pretty good," he says.

I glance at him from the corner of my eye. "How do you know?"

"My brother showed me some of the ones you'd sent him." Ignoring my obvious attempt to stop him from picking up one of the books, he does just that.

"He did?"

"Yep." He flips through the pages. "They made him smile," he says, glancing at me momentarily, then returning his attention to my book. "He doesn't do that often enough, but you've managed it."

He pushes his hair back when it flops forward and for some reason, seeing it, seeing his big hand, has me taking a step backward. I don't know why I do it, but he notices. He looks at me, eyebrows raised in question. He smiles with one corner of his mouth and that dimple forms on his cheek. He's so different in appearance from Santos, equally handsome but disarmingly so in a harmless boy-next-door way. Although I know in my gut, he's anything but harmless.

"Do I scare you, Madelena?" he asks, taking a step toward me. "Or is it something else?"

"What would it be?" I ask, standing my ground.

"So, I scare you then."

"No. That's not what I meant." I clear my throat. "I

don't like anyone looking at my work. It's not really meant for that."

"Oh? Then what's it meant for if not to be seen?"

I shrug. "It was just school."

"Didn't you go to school to study art to become an artist? Or am I missing something?"

"Can I have that back?" I gesture to the notebook.

"You know which ones are my favorites? The ones of you flipping my brother off." He holds out the notebook. I reach to take it, but he keeps hold of it, forcing me to look at him.

"Why do you like fucking with me?" I ask him outright because fuck him.

He grins, then lets go. "I like you. You're fun. And believe it or not, I think you're good for my brother."

"I don't think you do like me, Caius."

"Then maybe you should take some time to get to know me, and you'll realize your error."

"How's Ana?"

His eyebrows rise. "Ana?" He shrugs a shoulder. "Fine, I guess. Tell me something. You sent those sketches to him once a month. Why?"

Did Santos really tell him all of this? Did he show them all to him? What else has he told his brother?

"Well, he wanted letters," I answer truthfully because it really doesn't matter. I'm not even sure why he's asking, but if I know Caius, he's got an agenda. "I had little choice in the matter and controlled what I could. So, instead of letters, he got sketches."

"See," he says, pointing a finger with a smile like he

and I are sharing some inside joke. He moves backward and sits on the edge of the bed. "This is why I like you. You don't do as you're told exactly. Not without a little sass."

Caius's gaze moves to that locked box and I see how his expression darkens, his bright eyes going a little darker, growing a little sadder.

"I'll take that downstairs and get out of your hair."

"What's in it?" I ask before I can stop myself.

"He's sentimental, my brother," he says, fingering the box. "Likes his pen pals. You wouldn't know it looking at him."

"What do you mean?"

"Nothing that's any of my business. I'll take it to his office."

"But you made it your business, and you clearly brought it up to send some message so just go ahead and get it over with," I say outright because Caius Augustine is a manipulative son of a bitch—and I do mean bitch. There's no way that box just got up here by accident or coincidence. There's no such thing where he's concerned.

Caius's expression shifts, then grows serious. He studies me for a long minute before a little gleam brightens his eyes. "Fair enough," he says. "You want me to be direct? Okay, I'll be direct. He cares about you, which means you can hurt him, and he has been hurt enough for a lifetime. Clear enough?"

"Is that some sort of threat?"

He sighs. "What would threatening you gain me?"

He shakes his head, then walks around me to get to the box, knocking my shoulder on his way even though there's plenty of room to get by. "You know we're half-brothers right?" he asks. He picks up the box and heads to the door.

I follow him. "What does that have to do with anything?"

"Let's just say I'm the unwanted half."

The way he says it makes me stop. This isn't what I'm expecting at all.

"All my life I've dealt with people not wanting me. Not trusting me. Not being good enough for anyone," he starts with his back to me, then faces me when he reaches the door. "When people keep assuming the worst of you, you grow a thick skin. Problem is, that makes you a little less human. And I think that less human part is all you see when you look at me. It's a shame." He gestures for me to open the door and continues before I move, "I am the result of collective disappointment, Madelena. Can you relate?" Another pause. "But my brother has always been there for me. He's never judged me, thought anything of me that he wouldn't tell me to my face. That means a lot to me, and I am loyal to him and very protective of him."

"I wouldn't hurt him," I say feeling defensive.

"You know about the Commander. But you don't know what put Santos firmly under that bastard's thumb." I hold my breath and wait and a long enough moment passes that I'm not sure he's going to continue so I'm surprised when he does. "He wasn't even eighteen when he found the girl he loved murdered, the word *whore* written in her own blood across her stomach."

"What?" I find myself covering my mouth with one hand and my stomach with the other.

"She was stripped naked, legs spread wide. Staged that way after her death as if the killer had meant for him to find her in that degrading position."

I lean my weight against the wall. "Oh, God."

"Her father had killed her the night he found out…" he pauses, shakes his head. "Santos was hours too late and blamed himself. And then he took his revenge."

"He killed her father."

Caius nods. "Then you know something."

"Only that."

"That one act caused his life to change forever—hell, all of our lives to change forever—because the Commander intervened."

"What happened?"

"Those next five years are too ugly for your ears, I'm afraid. If you open the door, I'll go."

"Why did you tell me this?" I ask, blocking his exit.

"Open the door, Madelena."

"Why?"

He sighs. "Because he's not going to. He wants to protect his innocent little bride. But you should know how damaged he is. That, what I just told you, is the tip of the iceberg. And he didn't deserve any of it. Not one little bit. He used to be good. I should have done more to protect him from the Commander. I was his older brother, after all. But I didn't. Like Santos himself, I, too, failed. But I won't fail again. So, I guess the reason I'm telling you is so you know where he's coming from, the damage that's made him what he is."

"Like I said, I wouldn't hurt him."

"Good. Because if you do, I'll hurt you."

8

SANTOS

After confirming Caius is on his way to Augustine's, Val and I head there. I find Mom standing in the middle of what was once an uncluttered living room looking at various swatches of fabric for new curtains she's apparently having made.

"What was wrong with the old ones—which, by the way, were brand new?"

"Nothing. Just not my style. You want me to be comfortable, don't you? Since you're moving me out of my own home."

"Of course I do," I force myself to say. I am running out of patience with this poor me routine. "Where's Caius?"

"I'm not his keeper, in case you haven't noticed. He's a grown man."

"He was supposed to be here."

"And he's not, but I am. I'm happy to see you, by the way. Aren't you happy to see me?"

With a sigh, I walk into the kitchen and help myself to a can of seltzer from the refrigerator.

"You're in a mood," she says. She turns to the designer, who is making notes into her laptop. "Go get the fabrics in the bedroom situated, will you?" she asks the woman.

"Yes, Mrs. Augustine," the designer says, taking the hint.

Once she's gone, Mom walks toward the counter that divides the kitchen from the living and dining rooms. "How was your visit to the Averys?"

Before I answer, the door opens, and my brother walks in. He pauses on the threshold, and I'm not sure if he's surprised to see me here or if it's the state of the place that halts him.

"Christ," he mutters, taking off his coat and hanging it in the closet before stepping inside, making a point of taking exaggerated steps around various boxes and pieces of furniture the designer must have brought. "Is there room for me?" he asks in a teasing tone. He walks into the kitchen and opens the refrigerator. "I'm hungry. Anyone want a sandwich?"

"No, thanks," I say while my brother takes out the makings of a roast beef sandwich, which he begins to assemble.

"Santos was just about to tell us about his visit to the Avery house," Mom says.

"How did it go?" Caius asks as he smears mustard

onto his bread, then picks up the sandwich and takes an enormous bite. "Mmm. You guys sure you don't want any?"

"Wipe your mouth." Mom hands him a napkin. I'm pretty sure he does it to annoy her.

"You and I need to talk," I tell Caius.

"Hold on," Mom interrupts. "What happened? They suspect something?"

"Well, Camilla apparently heard Thiago arranging a meeting at the lighthouse."

"Of course it would be that little bitch to hear it," Mom says.

Caius mutters a curse through his giant mouthful. "So, they know he was out there?" he finally asks after swallowing.

I shake my head. "Only Camilla overheard the conversation, apparently, and it doesn't sound like she's told anyone."

"Not yet," Mom says. "I'm sure she has a plan. Waiting for the perfect moment to do the most damage."

"If I know Camilla, she is going to see how this plays out for her," Caius says. "Thiago and Bea are the only people capable of keeping her in line. She may want Thiago out of the way as much as we do."

"What do you know about Camilla?" I ask, stuck on that.

Caius turns to me, confused. He studies me for a beat too long before responding, "Apart from her being a fucking psychopath, you mean?"

"He's right," Mom chimes in. "She'll wait. Bide her time. I want to see what Bea does. She's the one to watch for now. It won't serve her to spread her version of history, not right now, not without Thiago to handle the consequences. We just need to make sure she and Camilla know exactly what those consequences would be sooner rather than later. We can't give them a chance to regroup."

"What would the consequences be exactly, Mother?" I ask.

She gives me an exasperated look. "Isn't that your area of expertise?"

"My area of expertise?" I ask, feeling my eyebrows rise as I wonder about her meaning. Is it because of what I've done, what I'm experienced in doing? The violence I've committed?

"I don't know. Men's work, I mean. Isn't that what your father used to say?" she backtracks.

With Thiago gone, the Avery family will be vulnerable—at least until they figure out he's not coming back and reorganize themselves. I have no doubt Bea Avery will be able to move into the role of head of household, but it will take time. She works better behind the scenes. Camilla is young, immature, and spoiled. For her, anything having to do with me is personal. But I saw how she commanded that soldier earlier, and I think she's one to keep an eye on because she may be the most cunning of them all... not to mention the most dangerous.

"Go take care of your curtains," I tell her. "Caius.

Let's talk."

I turn to walk toward my study. Well, Caius's study now, I guess. He follows and I see Mom's face just before he closes the door.

"What the fuck is up your ass?" Caius asks.

"I'm going to ask you a question, and I expect an honest answer."

"Because I usually lie to you?" he asks, tone sarcastic.

I face him. "Have you ever touched Camilla Avery?"

It takes him a minute, and he looks almost like he's been physically struck. His eyebrows practically disappear into his hairline, and he stares at me in utter disbelief.

"What the fuck did you just ask me?"

"If you ever touched her. Did anything with her."

"Camilla Avery? You're asking me if I fucked Camilla Avery?"

I nod, jaw tight, hating this.

"I can't fucking..." He shakes his head, muttering the last part. He pushes his hand into his hair. "No, I never touched that bitch. She's fucking poison. Why in the fuck would you think I did?"

"Are you sure, Caius? Because she mentioned something."

"What did she mention?"

"If you did anything with her, anything at all, now is the time to come clean."

"I'm not sure how many times I can tell you no. Oh, and by the way, fuck you!" He turns to the door. "I don't have to stand here and take this, you fucking asshole. All I've ever done was have your back and what? You go over there, and she spews some poison, and you eat it up? Are you that gullible or am I that untrustworthy? Is that how little you think of me? Of us?"

"Push up your sleeves and hold out your arms."

"What?"

"Do it. Push up your sleeves and hold out your arms."

"You're fucking insane, you know that?" he says. Shaking his head all along, he does as I say, pushing up the sleeves of his sweater. He holds out his arms.

And fuck me.

Because right there, right where it's fucking supposed to be, is that bracelet.

9

SANTOS

Blood rushes in my veins, the sound a roar in my ears as I stare at that fucking bracelet for a fucking eternity. I scrub my face, wrap my hand around the back of my neck and turn away, slamming my fist against the desk so hard, everything on top of it rattles.

"What the fuck, Santos?"

I shake my head. How could I think it was Caius? How could I fucking think it was my own brother up there? That he lied to me.? That he killed a man and brushed it off like it was nothing?

I should know better. I should remember that I'm the only one in our family capable of that. He's never gone that far.

He slaps his hand onto my shoulder. "I think you owe me a fucking explanation, don't you?"

"I need a goddamn drink." I look around the room

but all I see are boxes and boxes and more fucking boxes.

"Let's go to the bar. I can't find shit up here," Caius says.

I walk stiffly alongside my brother. My hands are buried inside my pocket, that damned stone right there. Right fucking there. We don't talk on the elevator. The lobby is moderately busy with men coming for card games or board meetings and ladies on their way from some luncheon to some charity event or tea or whatever it is the idle rich do to fill their days.

Caius leads the way into the dark, elegantly appointed bar. A fire roars in the large limestone fireplace set at the center of the back wall. Booths with high backs along the walls offer privacy. The mahogany bar itself spans the length of one wall. Crystal cocktail glasses hang upside down just above, and behind them, glass shelves illuminated from above carry every liquor known to man.

Caius gestures to the barman and leads us to the farthest booth. I slide in across from my brother, push a hand into my hair, and think what an asshole I am. How could I have suspected my brother of murdering Thiago Avery?

Because that's what this comes down to.

I meet his eyes. We don't speak until a bottle of whiskey and two tumblers are set before us and the barman leaves. Caius pours for us both and I swallow mine before he's picked his glass up.

"Okay, what the hell is going on?"

I can't tell him. Not about the bead, not that I suspected him of murdering Thiago.

"Camilla. She said some things."

"Yes, you've mentioned. Start from the beginning."

"She suggested you'd been with her. Sexually."

"Oh, she suggested that? She's a fucking liar, but that's not news to you, is it? I wouldn't touch that woman with a ten-foot pole." He reaches over and pulls the back of my head toward him. The gesture is aggressive, violent almost, and I deserve it. "And you fucking know that. So what the fuck else is going on?"

When he sits back, I pick up the bottle and pour myself a second glass, the burn of the first having disappeared too fast.

"Jax Donovan was dead when I got there."

"Already knew that."

"The security footage was erased."

"Again, old news."

"Except it wasn't. There's video of me at the house."

That stops him. "Shit."

"Yeah, shit."

"That was destroyed," he says.

"Apparently not. The person who has that footage, who most likely killed Jax Donovan, sent a still of me coming out of Donovan's house to Madelena right before the wedding. It's why she was so out of it. So upset. She thought I'd killed her uncle."

"If she saw you coming out of the house the night he was killed, I get it."

"Well, lucky for me, I have a copy of all of the footage now."

"Why lucky for you?"

"There's one thing the killer doesn't know." Caius's eyes narrow as he waits for me to take my phone out of my pocket and scroll to the image I'd just shown Odin. I turn the phone toward him. "When I saw Donovan's body in the pool, I snapped a picture. It's time stamped. It was three minutes after I got inside."

"Oh?" He takes my phone, zooms in. "Good. This was smart. It'll at least prove you couldn't have done it." He hands the phone back. "You don't know who sent the photo?"

"No."

"Who would have something to gain by this? If they don't know you have the time-stamped photo of Donovan dead, who would have something to gain by sending that photo to Madelena?"

I shake my head. I'm fucking tired. Too many fucking questions.

"I can think of one family," he says, answering his own question.

He means the Averys. "How would the Averys be involved? Why?"

"I'm sure Thiago or Bea or fuck, Camilla even, could have been having you followed. Maybe they somehow knew the plan."

"I don't fucking know."

"Is it possible Thiago was going to meet with whoever has that footage?"

"I can't see how that makes sense."

"Or maybe give that footage to someone. De León maybe? I mean, he is the reason you were there in the first place."

"De León is not strong enough to push Thiago off the catwalk," I say, voice lowered. "He has no use of his dominant hand, remember?"

"Not the old man, but Odin maybe? If he had enough reason to? I mean, he could use it to blackmail you and save his sister."

I shake my head. "I don't think so."

"Because you can't imagine him being violent? Are you—*you*, brother—surprised to learn how far people are willing to go to protect themselves and those they love?"

"I'm well aware but it's not him. I know because he'd never have left his sister out there. Besides, he's not capable of murder."

"I wouldn't be so sure."

"I'm getting a fucking headache." I inhale a deep breath in. "Between that footage coming to light, Thiago, finding Madelena passed out up there, and what Camilla said today, it just got to me."

"You really considered I was the stranger your wife was sure she saw up at the lighthouse?" I look at him for a beat too long because he shakes his head and smiles a disappointed smile. He swallows more whiskey.

"No, I don't think that, brother," I finally say. "But I believe there was someone there. And I don't think

Camilla was lying about Thiago's call. He'd have no other reason to go up there. Madelena couldn't have pushed him. She's just not strong enough."

"If he was off balance and she was scared…"

"No. It doesn't fit. I know it, know it in my gut."

"But you thought I could do it," he asks, sounding hurt. I scrub my face. "Why did you ask me to roll up my sleeves?"

I look at him, consider, then reach into my pocket and set the stone on the table between us.

He looks at it and I look at him. I can't believe there was a moment I gave credit to Camilla. That I believed he may have been with her sexually. That I believed he murdered Thiago.

"I'm sorry, brother. I was wrong," I say.

Caius drags his gaze from that stone to me. One of the staff puts another log on the fire. It hisses and swells casting a shadow that obscures my brother's features momentarily, but I see the set of his jaw well enough. "Let's just agree to trust each other going forward."

I nod, feeling ashamed. Without another word, I get up and leave.

10

MADELENA

I can't stop thinking about what Caius said, can't stop hearing his threat like it's on repeat in my head. The way he looked at me when he spoke those words, the way his eyes went flat, I have no doubt that he would hurt me if Santos didn't stand between us. That bullshit about him liking me, I don't believe it, not for a second. He must think I'm completely gullible and I am, often, but not on this. Although, I also think I understand him.

The relationship between the brothers must be difficult. Santos was favored by his father. Caius was set aside once Santos came along even though Brutus Augustine had officially adopted Caius as his son. I think the brothers do love each other but there has to be jealousy too, on Caius's part, and with Santos, guilt maybe?

The story about Santos finding the girl he loved murdered that way, though, that's the vision I keep seeing. Why did Caius tell me that in so much detail? To pique my curiosity about that box? He has. But he also put space between Santos and I because he knows I'm not going to ask Santos about the murdered girl.

Once I'm sure Caius is gone and the only people in the house are a handful of soldiers and staff, I make my way out of Santos's bedroom and down the stairs, taking in the dark paneled walls and the stained-glass windows of the foyer that span the full three floors of the house. They filter in the quickly fading sunlight, shining beams of light that look almost otherworldly.

I take a minute to look down from the top of the stairs into the grand entrance of the house. It was restored to look like it had at the height of the Valerian family's standing in Avarice, back when they had the means and the desire to maintain it. There had been an article in a local architecture magazine about it along with an interview with Brutus Augustine. I remember how annoyed my father was about that.

As I descend the stairs, I hear the kitchen staff working. The large fireplace in the grand living room that usually has a roaring fire is still dark, though. They won't light that until just before dinner. Mrs. Augustine usually likes to have a cocktail in there beforehand. Although now that she and Caius have moved out, I'm not sure if they'll be back for cocktails or dinner or how formal Santos will be if it's just the two of us.

I pass the living room on my way to Santos's study, which used to belong to his father. I make a point of taking the long way just to make sure the coast is clear, and once I know I won't run into anyone, I push the door open. I'm glad to find it unlocked, but at the same time, I'm looking over my shoulder as I hurry in. I feel like a criminal for it.

Once inside, I stand with my back against the door and take it in. The lamp on the desk is on. It casts a soft yellow light, and although it's not bright, it's enough for me to get a look around.

Boxes waiting to be unpacked are set against the walls and at the foot of the leather sofa against the wall opposite the desk. The bookshelves are only half full. I assume the books that are here belonged to Brutus Augustine because I don't think Santos has been home to unpack.

At the thought of Brutus, I look up at the portrait hanging over the mantle of the fireplace. It's about half the size of the one in the living room but in no way small. Brutus Augustine stands staring down at me from his place high above, his gaze no less penetrating than in life, no less threatening. It sends a chill down my spine, and I turn away because I need to get to work.

I assumed Caius would have laid the box he carried down on top of the desk or on a bookshelf, but he hasn't. I have to pull back the tops of the moving boxes to search for it. I find the lockbox in one of those and carry it over to the desk, looking underneath to see if Santos might have taped the key onto it. That would be too easy though, and he's smarter than that.

I reach into my pocket for the hairpins I carried down. I'm not bad at unlocking simple locks. It's how I got in and out of my locked room at college. The girl who had the second room in my building, the only two rooms in the original mansion, was also locked in at night—but she'd had a cell phone. So I'd get out myself, then unlock her door in exchange for the use of her phone.

I never learned the reason for her confinement, but I know she hated her family and in those two years, she only had visitors a handful of times. It's not like she and I became friends though. Neither of us wanted the other in our business. We had an arrangement. I let her out. She let me use her phone. Once I was finished calling my brother, she'd leave the building. I don't know where she went, if she managed to get off the property or what, but I didn't care. It had nothing to do with me.

I kneel down to examine the lock, twisting the pins to ready them as I do. It shouldn't be too hard, and I wonder what I'll find in the box. Caius made it seem like it was important enough to have a look, although part of me is afraid they'll be pictures of the crime scene. I don't think Santos would keep those though. Why have a reminder of how someone you loved was murdered?

Caius had mentioned pen pals. I am assuming I'm going to find letters between Santos and the girl, and there's a part of me that wants to see those. I want to know the girl he loved so much he committed murder to avenge her death and set into motion what happened next.

I push the pins into place and begin to manipulate them. It's been a while since I've done this, but it's like riding a bike. You don't forget once you've learned. A light touch is best.

But this lock is more sophisticated than the old ones on our bedroom doors at college. After a few minutes, when I still don't have it, I hear my name. I don't recognize the voice, but it's a woman and she very clearly tells whoever is asking that she'll take them up to my room.

Shit. Shit. Shit.

I glance around, I'm not sure what for, but I hear more footsteps so I rush to the door and set my ear against it. I wait until the steps recede, and once it's quiet, I open it a crack. I hear footsteps on the stairs and slip out of the study just as one of the staff comes around the corner. She stops, clearly surprised to see me, and I smile and head toward the kitchen like I was headed there all along.

My heart hammers. The staff is busy cooking when the woman who saw me in the hallway follows me inside.

"Can I help you, Mrs. Augustine?" she asks. "I believe you're wanted upstairs."

"Oh? I didn't realize. I was coming down for a snack."

"You didn't pass them on the stairs?"

I clear my throat and I'm sure it's obvious I'm lying.

"Dinner is in an hour," she says, saving me from having to answer. "What would you like?"

"An hour? I can wait then. Who's here to see me?"

"I'm not sure, ma'am. Perhaps you should go up."

"Yes. Good idea. Thank you." I walk out of the kitchen and hurry up the stairs to find two people standing in the open door of Santos's bedroom.

"I thought she'd be here. I'm so sorry, Doctor," the younger girl says.

"Are you looking for me?" I call out, pasting what I hope looks like a relaxed smile on my face.

"There you are," the girl says.

"I'm Dr. Fairweather," the doctor says, walking toward me and extending his hand. "Your husband sent me."

I shake it. "He did? He didn't mention..."

"No?"

"I mean, I'm fine. Dr. Cummings said he didn't think I had a concussion so I'm not sure why Santos would have called you."

"Oh, this isn't for that," he says, glancing at the girl who is hovering. "Perhaps we should step into the bedroom to talk privately?"

I nod. "Thank you," I tell the girl and invite the doctor in.

"It's a beautiful house, isn't it?" he asks, looking around. "I remember this place from before it was abandoned. It was something else. It's so good to see it's been rebuilt with such care. It's important to preserve our history. Avarice is a special place." It's a strange thing to say but I don't comment as he sets his bag down and smiles at me.

"I'm sorry, but I don't know why you're here."

"Mr. Augustine has asked me to provide you with a birth control shot."

It takes me a minute. "He what?"

"Is he here? Perhaps I've misunderstood."

"No. No, you haven't. I just didn't realize he'd arranged for you to come all the way here," I quickly make up, not wanting to miss the opportunity even though I'm wondering why he didn't ask Dr. Cummings or just give me back my pills.

"I didn't mind. I wanted to get a look at the house, honestly."

I smile, trying to process this.

"I'll need to examine you and ask you a few questions first, but it shouldn't take too long. If you're ready?"

I nod. "Anything you need."

The exam takes about twenty minutes, and, in that time, he asks me questions about my cycle and explains how the shot works. I wish he were a woman, but if the end result will be reliable birth control, I'll take it. He's just preparing the injection when the bedroom door opens, and we both turn to find Santos standing in the doorway. He looks impeccable in a bespoke three-piece suit in deepest blue.

My heartbeat picks up and I feel my face begin to burn with guilt for what I did. Does he know? No. How could he? But his expression is dark, and I see the smile he puts on for the doctor is forced as he enters and closes the door behind him.

"Mr. Augustine, you have a lovely home."

"Thank you, Dr. Fairweather. I appreciate you coming out on such short notice," he says, the words forced.

"Like I told your wife, my reasons were not entirely unselfish."

Santos smiles a tight smile.

"Well, I don't want to intrude on your evening. And I'm almost finished here." The doctor unwraps an alcohol swab and cleans the injection site. It's hard to hold Santos's gaze, so I look at the needle instead—which is not a great idea either, so I stare at the far wall. "I was just explaining to be on the safe side you'll want to use contraception for the next week or so but after that, this should protect you for the next three months. I'll leave a packet with more details, and you are always free to call my office. Ready?" he asks me.

I nod and wince when the needle penetrates, but then it's over and he's packing up his bag.

Someone knocks on the door, and Santos opens it. Val stands in the doorway.

"All done," the doctor says, snapping his bag shut.

"Thank you, Doctor. Val will see you out." Santos steps aside and extends his hand to shake the doctor's, his message to leave clear and just this side of rude. I don't think Santos cares much about being rude though.

They shake hands and after the doctor says goodbye to me, he's gone.

I stand up, adjusting my blouse and buttoning the top buttons as Santos closes the door and turns to me. He shoves his hands into his pockets, nothing forced on his expression now. No smile. No softness. Just the look of a man who knows what I've done.

But that's not possible. That's just my own guilt, I tell myself.

"I didn't realize you'd arranged for the shot," I say, my throat dry.

"I must have forgotten to mention it with all that's gone on." He is quiet, gaze scrutinizing me. "You're happy with it?"

I nod.

He momentarily lifts his lips into a smile that doesn't go near his eyes. "Good."

"Dinner smells good."

"They told me you'd gone down for a snack."

I clear my throat, glance at the open bathroom door and nod. "I'll just wash my hands quickly." I don't move though, because the way he's looking at me has me trapped. It's not accusing. That would be easier to handle. It's something else. Disappointment.

"You were busy today," he says. He slides one hand out of his pocket, and my blood turns to ice when I see the small bent hairpin he's holding. I must have dropped it in my haste.

I open my mouth to speak, to say what, I don't

know, but it doesn't matter because it's like I've swallowed sand.

There's another knock on the door then. He doesn't turn as it's opened, but I watch Val enter, carrying that damned box.

"On the dresser, please," Santos says, never taking his eyes off me.

Val does as he's told and then he's gone.

"Santos, I can explain," I start, finding my voice.

"I'm not sure you can," he says, that non-smile once again appearing and disappearing. When he takes a step toward me, I jump, let out a small scream, and lunge for the bathroom. It's pure instinct, fight or flight. I'm not thinking because if I were, I'd know how stupid it is to try to run from him. Besides, I don't get far. Before I've reached the bathroom, he catches me with an arm around my waist and tugs me to him.

"Is this how you trust?" he asks, holding that pin out for me to see.

I twist in his arms. "I just… I…"

"Were your words just lip service to save your brother from a beating he deserved?" he asks, throwing me onto the bed so hard I bounce before I flip over to scramble off the other side.

Again, he catches me easily and has me flat on my stomach in a second, dragging me toward him. Once my legs are dangling off the edge of the bed, he pins me with the flat of his hand against my lower back.

"What are you going to do?" I ask twisting to get free as he tugs at my blouse, the sound of it ripping off me making me scream. My leggings are next. He strips those off, along with my panties, and I'm left bent over the bed in just my bra.

I hear the unbuckling of his belt, twist my head around to watch.

"You are not trustworthy, Madelena," he says. He tugs the belt out its loops, the whoosh it makes registering. What he intends to do registering.

"Santos," I ask, blood draining from my head as I recall his warning when he last punished me.

He doubles the belt, gripping the buckle in his palm and even though he's not holding me down anymore, I don't move. When he meets my gaze, his face is a tight mask, his jaw clenched. In his eyes I see the fire of betrayal.

"Santos," I start, my voice a whisper.

"Do I have to make a prisoner out of you? Lock my doors in my own house?"

"No. No." I shake my head, closing my eyes as he drags the belt over my thigh, slapping it lightly against it. "Please!"

"What have I done for you to distrust me?"

"I'm sorry. I'm sorry!"

"Answer me!" he demands, cracking the belt across my ass this time, the contact making me cry out as pure fire stripes my butt.

"Nothing!" I should run. Try to get away. I don't, though. I remain bent over the bed waiting, hands fists, every muscle tight. Because I deserve this. I have earned this, haven't I? I close my eyes preparing for the next lash.

"Then why would you deceive me?" he asks, voice more broken than anything else. "Why?"

"I'm sorry. I'm..."

"I found your diary under the floorboards in your room, did you know that?" he asks, no lash follows the still-burning first.

"What?" I'm confused by this turn in conversation. I look back at him, afraid of what I'll see, but needing to at the same time.

"I didn't take it, though. Didn't look through it. Because what's inside it is not for me to take," he says and I don't know what I expect to see, but it's not the face of a monster. Not at all. "Those are your secrets to keep or to tell as you choose. You don't have the same respect for me though, do you?"

Guilt settles deep and heavy in my belly.

"I'm sorry. I am. I shouldn't have done what I did."

"Sorry is easy to say," he says, tone strange, dark but also heavy with something else. Something that doesn't have to do with me, with us. I feel it. He shakes his head, drops the belt and steps backward. When I sit up, he doesn't stop me. "Question is, do you feel it, in here?" he asks, pressing one hand to the center of my chest, the other to my head. "Do you understand it here?" And even though he is right to be angry, he is gentle, and in his eyes, I see despair and betrayal.

I drop my head in shame.

"I'm not a monster, Madelena. And whether or not

you believe it, I don't like hurting you. The opposite. I'd do anything to protect you."

He shakes his head and walks to the door.

"What are you doing?" I ask.

"Walking away." He reaches for the doorknob and I don't know what it is about those words that has me panicking. That has made my heartbeat irregular and twisted my stomach in knots.

"You can't walk away!"

He doesn't answer.

"Wait." I swallow. Am I going to do this? "Don't go. Please!"

He looks back at me. He's waiting for me to make the next move. He won't hurt me. I know that. I've always known that. He will go to great lengths to protect me.

And I betrayed him.

So, without another word, I pick up his discarded belt and cross the room to hand it to him.

He takes it, watching me wordlessly.

"You're right. The only reason I stopped was because I was interrupted. Otherwise, I'd have opened that box and looked inside it. I would have taken your secret." The words are a weight in my stomach. Guilt and dread. I've disappointed him. I feel my face fall, feel the tightening in my chest. "I don't like hurting you either, whether or not you believe it. And I am sorry."

I walk back to the bed and drape myself over it, my weight on my elbows, unable to look back at him, tense as I submit myself to his punishment.

It takes him an eternity to move. Or maybe that's just my dread stretching time. But when I do hear his approach, my heartbeats accelerate. I brace myself for a lashing, one I deserve, but what I feel isn't his belt. It's his fingers on what I'm sure is a thick stripe of red across my ass. My nipples pebble as he traces it, and I take a ragged breath when I hear the belt drop to the floor. That's when I turn my head to look at him and watch as he grips my ass and splays me open. When he drags his gaze to mine, his eyes are burning black coals.

Something rattles in his chest. I watch from my position as he strips off his vest, his shirt, eyes locked on me, before reaching to open the drawer on the bedside table and taking out a bottle of lotion.

"I'm not going to whip you," he says, shifting his gaze momentarily to squeeze a generous amount of lotion onto my lower back. He meets my eyes again as the fingers of one hand begin to smear that lotion into the crack of my ass. Every muscle tenses and my anxiety builds as he circles the hole he hasn't yet claimed and I understand what he means to do.

I swallow hard.

With this free hand, he undoes his slacks, takes himself out. He's hard and I can't help my glance at his cock as my mind tries to process how exactly I'm going to take him there.

"You're not going to come," he tells me as he smears lotion over his length, dragging his palm back and forth, back and forth. He shifts his focus to my ass, to spreading me wide and pushing his fingers inside me. To my surprise, I meet the intrusion with a moan even as my body tightens, every muscle tensing.

Santos is unrushed, lubricating me from the inside, readying me. By the time he removes his fingers and brings his cock to my ass, I'm not sure if I'm more aroused than scared.

I arch my back to take him, my breath quivering when I feel him at my entrance. He isn't rough when he enters me, but he isn't exactly gentle either, and he's big. I let out a whimper, claw at the bed, but he keeps my hips in place. Sweat drips down my forehead as he pushes in, all the way in, a low, guttural moan coming from deep inside his chest.

He sucks in a ragged breath. I look back to watch him and I can't look away. He's beautiful and powerful and my submission in this moment, this offering of myself, it's like a sacrifice at an altar. The feeling of giving myself over to him, it's indescribable and somehow freeing and more. So much more.

Because whatever this is between us, I don't want to lose it. I don't want to lose him. In spite of everything.

His eyes are black as he shifts his gaze to watch himself. He grinds my ass against himself, pushing impossibly deeper before he begins to draw out, biting his lip and taking his time, before pushing in with another moan.

"You don't come." He reminds me, pushing my legs wide, lifting my hips just enough so my clit is no longer in contact with the bed before he begins to fuck me and when I try to slide my hands between my legs, he takes my wrists and pins them to my sides, keeping hold of my hips as he does.

I understand the torture of his punishment. I understand that fine line between pleasure and pain and feel the coiling of tension so tight I'm desperate for release. Desperate for it as he takes his pleasure from me, using me, denying me.

"Please!" I cry out, needing release as his thrusts come harder, deeper, sensations like nothing I've ever felt before. Sweat drops from his forehead onto my back and when he releases one hand to slap my ass, I slide my fingers between my legs. The instant they come in contact with my clit, I moan out my release, not caring that it may earn me another punishment. Not caring about anything at all but this orgasm.

Santos groans, spanking my ass again before closing his fingers over mine, orgasm intensifying as he thickens, laying his body over mine and thrusting once more until I feel the throbbing of his cock, feel his release inside me, his full weight on me, all while my own body is pure sensation, pure pleasure, my vision blurred with it.

When it's over and we're both panting, I draw in a shivering breath. He lifts off me and I miss his weight, his heat. He draws out of me, lifting me. My body is limp, my eyelids too heavy.

"I told you not to come," he says as he lays me down under the blanket and settles close behind me, his arm across my belly.

I nod, sleepy. "Next time."

He chuckles, draws the blanket over us and holds me tight.

I drift off, feeling drunk. It's like the orgasm, the intensity of it, has me floating between worlds. "I love you." I hear the words slip off my tongue, recognize my voice. They're a whisper in a dream as I let myself melt into the warm embrace of Santos Augustine's arms feeling protected. Feeling safe.

11

SANTOS

I love you.

I hold her, her body surrendered to me in sleep, her breathing quiet, skin warm and soft.

Did she mean to say those words? How can she feel that way? How can she love me? The thought of it, the idea of it, is so foreign and strange that I can't quite process it. I care about her. I meant what I said about protecting her. But love?

A half-sleep steals me away, but I'm restless. The day has been long, and my brain won't switch off. It keeps going over everything that's happened, giving me flashes of images—some of which I've seen, while some it's making up along the way.

Camilla with the two-pronged tongue of a snake as she sows seeds of doubt about my brother.

Thiago sitting across from me at the strip club, his head smashed in, his face a partial skull. The whiskey he's drinking is pouring out of the open gash in his neck where the rope has sliced through to bone.

Thiago telling me I can trust no one.

Caius's face swims before my eyes. He smiles, dimples making him look five years younger than he is. He pats my back and ruffles my hair and all the while, he has a hand in his pocket and his head is cocked to the side. His tell when he lies.

"You know what you did. This is your punishment," my father says as if a voice over commercial.

The Commander the way he was at the end. On the last night of his life. Laughing at us. Stance casual and relaxed. Until Thiago strikes. Until I do. A life lived in violence ended in violence. We each reap what we sow.

Madelena at the lighthouse. Madelena pursued, running out onto the catwalk. Madelena in Thiago's place too close to the edge. A hand on her chest. She catches the wrist of that hand but she's not strong enough to hold on when she's pushed and she goes tumbling. A thousand little blue stones bounce onto the catwalk, raining down on her as she falls, falls, falls, hair a dark halo around her, arms reaching, grasping at air, at nothing, her mouth open on a scream.

My eyelids fly open, and I bolt upright. Sweat covers me from head to toe as I gasp for breath. My chest feels like someone is sitting on it and I can't breathe.

"Santos?"

I blink, then shift my gaze to Madelena. She looks

up, sleepy, and smiles. She closes her eyes and stills again.

Just a nightmare. Just my mind working overtime. She's here, at my side, in my bed. She's safe.

I know one thing for sure. I know it in my heart, in my head. I caress her hair, slip out of the bed, and tuck the blanket around her. I lean down to kiss her forehead and whisper the same words into her ear that she'd whispered to me in her half-sleep.

"I love you, too."

I look at her for a long, long moment before straightening. I pull on my pants and on my way to the door, I glance at the box. One of the kitchen staff mentioned to Val that she'd seen Madelena emerge from my study. With a quick look around, I'd found the bent pin on the floor in front of my desk and put two and two together.

I slide my hand into my pocket to take out the key, ignoring the smooth, hard bead of the bracelet I'd thought belonged to my brother. Sliding the key into the lock, I turn it, then open the box. I glance inside and find the feelings that usually come with looking at the contents of this box are different... not so powerful, suddenly.

Leaving it like that, I grab my shirt on my way out of the bedroom. Down the hall, I choose an empty guest room. There, I shower so as not to wake Madelena and put on the same clothes I'd worn earlier. I go downstairs to the kitchen, where a whole roasted chicken sits wrapped in the refrigerator. The dinner we missed.

I find some bread, make myself a chicken sandwich, and carry it into the study. The house is quiet; the staff all went to bed hours ago. I close the door behind me and switch on the overhead light. Setting the plate on the edge of my desk, I pick up the sandwich and take a bite, looking around at the boxes that need to be unpacked. It's not too bad. Most of what I keep is electronic, and anything pertinent to have on paper is locked up in the safe only I have the combination to.

The chicken is good, and I'm hungry. I eat the sandwich and look up at my dad's portrait.

"What did you mean leaving that letter, old man?"

Once I've finished the sandwich, I set the plate aside and move to sit in my chair. I swivel around and slide open the cabinet door to unlock the safe. Inside are stacks of cash—which are always handy—and some personal documents. There are also several USB sticks containing five years' worth of highly sensitive information on too many high-ranking officials to count, including the Avery family, all of it collected during my time with them.

But those aren't the things I'm interested in.

I take out the envelope I want and swivel my chair back around to set it on the desk. I take out the single sentence letter inside. I look at my dad's familiar writing, the pen pushing a little too hard:

I know what you did, and this is your punishment.

"What did you mean? Who did you mean?"

There's a soft knock on the door, and I look up as it opens. Madelena stands in the doorway, her hair wet from a shower. She's wearing an oversized T-shirt that comes to mid-thigh, and I realize it's one of mine. Probably the one I'd put her in after bringing her home from the lighthouse. In her arms, she's carrying the box.

"You should sleep," I tell her, setting the letter on the desk and getting up to take the box from her.

She closes the door as I walk the box to my desk, and when I turn around, she wraps her arms so tight around me it catches me completely by surprise. When I hear her sniffle, I find myself wrapping one arm around her waist, cupping the back of her head with the other and pulling back to look at her.

"What is it?" I ask, wiping her tears.

"She was pregnant with your baby?"

I study her eyes, the golden brown so warm, so full of emotion. So honest. "It was a long time ago now."

"What was her name?"

"Alexia." I take her hand, then move around the desk to sit on my chair with her on my lap. "Her father killed her the night he found out she was pregnant. And I killed him for it."

"I'm sorry," she says.

"Like I said, it was a long time ago." Her gaze moves to my empty plate and her stomach growls. I smile while she blushes. "Come. I'll make you a sandwich."

We stand and when I reach for the letter, I see her scan it. "What's that?"

I put it back into its envelope. "My father's cryptic letter to us, read by the executor of the will."

"Who's it intended for?"

I shrug. "My mother or brother. Hell, maybe me. No one knows."

"Or they know and they're not saying."

I nod in agreement. That is the most likely scenario.

The image of Madelena's face in my dream as she plunges toward those cliffs, the waters of the raging ocean, flashes before my eyes, and I have to close them for a minute.

"What is it, Santos?"

"Nothing." I set the envelope back into the safe and remember the stone in my pocket. I take it out, turn to Madelena. I open my palm so she can see it and I watch her, wondering if it will jog a memory.

She looks at it and tilts her head, forehead creasing. She looks up at me. "Where did you get that?"

"Do you know it?"

She pushes a hand into her hair. "It makes me think, makes me remember, the hand on Thiago's chest. And then hearing the popping sounds like when a necklace or a bracelet breaks and all the beads scatter, the sound they make." She shakes her head. "It makes no sense."

"Actually, it does. I found it on the catwalk when I found you."

"Wait." She takes my arm and pushes my sleeve up. She touches the bracelet. "You and your brother have them." Her expression changes like she's just realized something. "Oh my God, it was him?"

"No, Madelena. It wasn't. His bracelet is intact. I saw it." I take a minute because I'd thought the same thing.

"But..."

I turn to put the stone into the safe along with the letter and lock it. "Let's go get you a sandwich." I take her hand to walk her out of the study and into the kitchen.

"You kept all my letters."

"I wouldn't call them letters," I say with a wink, switching on the light and pulling out a chair at the counter. "Chicken sandwich okay?"

"Sounds great, actually."

I take out what I need and begin to assemble a sandwich, then set it in front of her.

She picks it up but doesn't bite into it. "My mom's memorial service is next week. It's been sixteen years."

"I know."

She meets my eyes. "I want to go. There's a ceremony at the church, then my dad hosts a lunch in her memory."

"Do you think I'd say no?"

"It's at my father's house."

"It's the anniversary of your mother's death, Madelena. Of course you'll be there, and I'll be at your side."

She smiles. "I'd like that. You being with me, I mean."

"Can I ask you a question?" She nods as she eats a bite of her sandwich. "You said once you wouldn't have a baby." Alarm has her stop mid-chew. "Don't worry, I'm not talking about now. I was just curious because you said, if I recall, you wouldn't have one *ever, not with anyone*."

She swallows the bite in her mouth and puts the sandwich down.

"Why not?"

"Santos—"

"I just want to know your reasons. That's all."

Her face flushes, and her eyes fill up with tears. "Isn't it obvious?"

"Tell me."

Her eyes grow darker, and she doesn't hold my gaze as she answers. To hear her say it, to watch her muster up the strength to, makes my chest tighten and my throat close up.

"What if I hurt her?" she says so quietly I almost can't hear her.

"Madelena—"

She shakes her head. "You couldn't be sure. I could be sick too, you know? Damaged goods. Hate to break it to you," she adds, trying for a smile but shifting her gaze down to pick at the bread of her sandwich as a tear drops onto the countertop.

I walk around the counter to take her face in my hands. "You're not damaged goods. And you'd never hurt a child, not yours, not anyone's. You are incapable. It simply is not in you. Not at all."

12

SANTOS

The next week passes strangely peacefully. My mother and Caius stay away for the most part as they settle into life at Augustine's. Thiago is still absent, and the Avery family is quiet. But it's not as though they would call the police or file a missing person's report. I'm sure Bea Avery has been in touch with the Commander's old friends, but if they couldn't find the old bastard's body, they'll never find Thiago's because I have a feeling it's at the bottom of the ocean by now.

The thought bothers me, but I shove it aside as Madelena comes down the stairs dressed in black from head to toe, which is her usual, except that today it's more elegant. Not so contrary. She's winding her hair into a loose braid as she heads down and doesn't notice me. I'm happy to say I think the move to the house was a good idea. She looks better, not glancing over her shoulder all the time.

What she told me that night in the kitchen a week ago, though, upsets me. Does she truly believe she could have the same mental illness as her mother? Is the thought of it on her mind more often than I realize? I have been doing some reading on the matter. While it's a fact that these things do run in families, I don't like that she's worried about it, that she's already decided, probably at a far younger age than I even realize, that she will never have children just in case.

"You look nice," I tell her.

"Thanks. Shit." She begins to undo her braid and shakes her hair out to start again.

"What is it?"

"I keep messing it up."

"It looked fine."

"My mom used to braid my hair like this when I was little. She'd do hers too, tell me we were twins."

"It looked good, Madelena. We should go." I check my watch.

After finishing the braid, she takes a deep breath. She takes my wrist and checks the time because she doesn't wear a watch and I haven't given her a phone yet. I plan on giving her a new one. It's probably paranoia on my part that the old one could somehow have been tampered with, her location or conversations tracked, but I am not taking any chances.

"Few more minutes. I like to get there last."

"Why?"

"I don't want everyone staring at me."

I nod and take her arm to steer her into the living

room for privacy. "I wanted to mention something anyway."

"What?"

"Dr. Fairweather's visit is between you and me. No one knows about that, and it has to stay that way."

"Okay?" she says it like a question.

"Not a soul. It's very important. Not even your brother."

"That's fine. I mean, I wouldn't anyway; contraception is a weird conversation to have with one's brother, don't you think?"

"Good."

She checks my watch again. "Now we can go."

We head out to the chapel where the ceremony will begin. It will end at the De Léon house. From what Madelena told me, they're expecting almost seventy-five people.

Once we arrive, I see how well Madelena has timed it. Most of the pews are filled, everyone standing to watch the altar boys and priest on their procession toward the altar. Their candles flicker as somber organ music winds down, and incense fills the air.

I breathe through my mouth to block the images that smell conjures. The memories of all those Sunday masses I had no business attending, not after the things I did.

Odin, who is sitting in the front pew, turns to glance at the entrance. He looks relieved when he sees his sister. Madelena raises her hand in a subtle greeting. He's seated beside his father and there's enough space for one more person on the other side of Marnix De Léon. I know it's intended for his daughter, but she won't be sitting in it for two reasons—one being he neglected to save a space for me, and two that Madelena will want to disappear along the edges of the crowd rather than become its centerpiece.

I look at those who've come, recognizing some faces. I'm just scanning the pews across the aisle from where the De Léons are seated when I do a double take.

"You're fucking kidding me," I mutter. People in the back pews turn to look. I guess I said it louder than I thought. I couldn't give a fuck. The organ quiets and pews creek as the dearly devoted are seated.

"What?" Madelena asks, stepping backward into the shadowy corner of the baptismal font.

I gesture with a subtle nod toward Bea, Liam, and Camilla Avery, who are settling into their pew, second to the front. Liam is flipping through pages of the bible like he's never seen one before. Bea's eyes are on the altar. Her lips are moving as she says the rosary. In the five years I spent with the Avery family, I don't think she or the Commander missed one Sunday mass. They'd make us all go with them, too, and throughout, they'd mutter their prayers as if those words could cleanse them of their sins.

But I don't care about Bea Avery. It's Camilla that has me sliding my hand up my wife's back and wrapping it around the back of her neck to tug her closer, a move the little viper doesn't miss. She smiles wide and even raises her hand in a schoolgirl-like wave.

"What the hell?" Madelena mutters.

Why the fuck would anyone attend a memorial service for someone they don't know, have never met, have zero connection with, and couldn't give a flying fuck about?

"Ignore them," I tell her as Camilla, satisfied with herself, turns to face the altar where the priest is just beginning the service.

Marnix De Léon checks his watch and glances back at the door. I assume he's looking for his daughter. When he sees us, he gives me an angry glare and whispers something in Odin's ear. Odin gets up and walks along the center aisle toward us. I watch, noticing how he still limps. Although it's better than it was when I first met him, it will never really go away.

"Maddy, Dad wants you to sit with us." He glances at me, the invitation very clearly for one.

People turn to look, and I see the whispers that begin as soon as they spot her. I want to tell them to fuck off and mind their own business.

Madelena shakes her head. "I can't."

I study her in profile, and I don't think I realized how hard this day is for her. I knew it wouldn't be easy, but after sixteen years, her pain is more intense than I'd imagined.

Odin takes her hand. "I need you," he tells her. He does. I see it in his eyes.

"Go. For your brother," I tell her. "I'll be here when it's over."

Odin glances at me. I guess he's not expecting that, but when his sister acquiesces, he exhales and takes her hand to guide her through the center aisle to her seat. As they walk up, the priest momentarily stops the mass. I don't know if it's in annoyance at the disruption or simply to watch as if he, just like his flock of sheep, enjoys the spectacle of the suffering of another human being.

Asshole.

As soon as he resumes the service, my phone buzzes in my pocket. I take it out to silence it, but when I see what it is, I do my second double take of the day.

I watch Madelena settle into her seat. I see the glance she sends back as if to make sure I'm still here, like I said I would be. Once she looks forward, I walk deeper into the unlit corner and look at the screen again.

Because the text I sent to Thiago Avery's phone days ago has just been delivered.

It's been read.

And the three undulating dots signaling a message is being composed have me holding my breath.

13

MADELENA

I try to block everyone out as I sit between my father and brother and listen to the priest saying mass. He's the same priest who buried Mom sixteen years ago.

Sixteen years.

I don't remember the funeral itself, but there's a feeling to this day. A darkness. Today is a day to get through, because today my life is on display. After sixteen years, they don't expect tears anymore. Not that I ever gave them tears, not even when I was little. I think I was too numb for tears.

People would whisper that I didn't understand what had happened, and I'd just remained silent holding my brother's and my uncle's hands. Not my father's. He offered no comfort. Ever. But when the adults around me would talk about how pitiful I was, how sorry they were for me, how evil of my mother, I just stood like a little porcelain doll. Emotionless. Glass-eyed.

Once those public displays were over, I pretended not to have heard any of it. I locked all their words away, all their eager glances too. I learned early on how much people like to watch the pain of others. Like watching it happen to someone else somehow lessened the chances of it happening to them.

The mass is long, over an hour. I look at the photograph of Mom on the altar. She was so pretty. So young.

Odin squeezes my hand, and I squeeze back.

When mass is over and the priest leaves the church, we stand and follow. The people who have come to the service wait for us to go before leaving their pews out of respect.

I can see the Averys from the corner of my eye and think of Thiago.

How he saved my life.

How he lost his in the process.

I glance over at them. I can't help myself. Mrs. Avery's face is stony. Liam's is bored. But Camilla has her eyes locked on me. The way she's grinning, I wonder if she feels anything at all—if she is worried about her brother, or if she even wonders about his whereabouts.

"You'll ride with us to the cemetery," Dad says without bothering to look at me. "Your husband can meet us at the house since you insisted on bringing him."

I search for Santos as we near the back of the church. I wonder if he's already outside. The incense is suffocating in here.

But when we get outside, our car and driver are already waiting for us. At a quick look around, I only see Val. He nods to say he's seen me, but when my dad ushers me into the backseat of our sedan, Val simply climbs into his vehicle. It's an SUV, but a different one than the one we came in. He merges into the line of cars that will head to the cemetery.

Did I miss Santos? I turn to look out of the back window but only see Val in the driver's seat. The passenger side is empty, and Santos wouldn't sit in the back if it was just the two of them.

"Can I have your phone?" I ask Odin. I need to push Santos to get my phone back.

Odin hands it to me and I type in Santos's number to send him a text.

> Me: Where are you?

My message sends and delivers but the checkmarks remain gray.

I send another one.

> Me: Santos where are you?

Again delivery, but that's it.

Dad takes the phone from me before I can stop him. He's sitting between us in the backseat. "It's not the time for texting." He tucks the phone into his pocket. "Glad it's not raining. She hated the rain," he says, and I wonder if he misses her. If he thinks about her. If he loved her. But then I smell whiskey on his breath—or maybe it's just coming out of his pores because he drinks so much—and I think I'm probably giving him too much credit.

"Why are the Averys here?" I ask.

"Everyone who wants to remember your mother is welcome."

"They didn't know Mom."

He gives me a nasty look and shifts his gaze out the front window as the car slows once we pass through the cemetery gates. Once we arrive at the grave site, Val comes to stand at my side, ignoring my father entirely as he tries to step between us.

"Santos will meet you at the house," Val says.

"Where is he?"

"Something came up."

"For God's sake, this is your mother we're talking about," Dad finally says, taking my arm forcefully and leading me to the grave, gripping the flowers the driver handed him in his other hand. He's holding them so tightly the stems are smashed.

I don't like coming here with him, but I know the drill. I just have to get through this.

We will leave the flowers, have a few moments of silence, then go back to the house, where he'll pour himself a whiskey. I hate that part most because it requires socializing. I was hoping to get out of it or at least have Santos at my side. I'm disappointed he's not here, but Odin needs me, and I won't let him down.

In less than half an hour, we're pulling up to the house. I haven't been here in a long time, but it looks the same as it used to. The grounds are pristinely maintained, the house grand and looming. It smells the same, too, I think when we enter. Even with all these people already here, the subtle scent of wood polish mixed with whiskey sends me back in time.

People come to greet us, reminding me that we don't have relatives left apart from us. Odin is the last De Léon. What will happen to our name? Will the line end with him? Maybe it should.

A few minutes after we're in the house, the front door opens. Val slips inside and, after locating me, he stands against the wall. My father notices too, and I don't miss his nod to a man I don't recognize. I guess he hired security. I don't know. But Val can manage himself.

Robotically, I assume my role as the porcelain doll with the glass eyes. I stand between Odin and my father and, with my arms at my sides, I accept people's hugs, ignoring their pitying eyes, their empty words. I try to remember if my mom had friends, but I was too young to know that. She and I were together a lot, and we were mostly on our own. Odin and Uncle Jax were the only two people I remember being around.

Uncle Jax.

Another wave of sadness steals over me, and I wish again that Santos was here. He'd know how I was feeling. He'd be the rock at my side. But irritation creeps along that thought as I wonder what could have been so important that he abandoned me like he has once before.

"Excuse me," I say. My father halts his conversation momentarily, but I slip out of reach before he can stop me walking away. Odin, too, watches as I hurry through the crowd in the living room toward the stairs. I just need a few minutes alone, so I head to my room.

Voices carry, following me up. The lights are out up here though—my father's subtle sign for guests to keep to the ground floor. I'm grateful for it.

My room is at the far end, just past Odin's. I hurry to it, open the door, and slip inside. As soon as I've closed it, the sound of voices dies down to a murmur, and I take a moment to exhale.

Except that even before I've released that single breath, I hear the sound of water running and turn to find the bathroom door opening. I realize then the room isn't pitch black. The light on the nightstand is on. And I watch in disbelief as Camilla Avery steps out of my bathroom, not startled to see me, or hiding it well if she is. She smiles, carelessly tosses the towel she was wiping her hands on to the floor, and steps into my bedroom.

"I hope you don't mind. I had to use the little girl's room." She winks at me like we're old friends, her gaze remaining on me a beat too long before it scans my bedroom.

"What are you doing in here?"

She cocks her head and crosses the room to meet me. "I just told you. The line for the bathroom was so long downstairs. Don't you hate that?" She picks up my braid, studies it, then drops it again. She walks toward the window and looks out over our back garden. "It's not a bad room. But didn't you take anything with you when you moved in with Santos?" she asks, planting herself on the edge of my bed and picking up a tube of lip balm. She opens it, sniffs at it, and for a minute I wonder if she's going to use it.

Recovering myself, I walk to her and snatch the lip balm out of her hand. "Get out of my room!"

She giggles, stands. "Touchy. I was just seeing what scent it was."

"What do you want, Camilla? What are you even doing here in my house? At my mother's memorial service? Why would you come to something like that?"

She shrugs one shoulder. "Mom. She thinks we need to show our faces, especially with my brother missing. Integrate. You know." She rolls her eyes. "Oh, my condolences." Not remotely bothered, she runs her fingers over the spines of the books on my bookshelves. "Where is Santos?" she asks, facing me again.

I hesitate too long because I don't get to make up an answer before she speaks again.

"Did he disappear? He used to do that a lot when he lived with us. Had all these jobs to do." She puts jobs in air quotes. "Can I borrow this one?" she asks, holding up a book she slips out of my bookshelf.

I cross the room and take it from her. "No. Get out."

"That's rude."

"No, what's rude is you coming into my room clearly to have a look around. Maybe take something."

"I don't need to steal from you." She gives me a flat smile.

"I'm glad to hear it. Now get out."

"I'm trying to be friendly here, Madelena. I mean, you're married to a man with whom I'm very close."

I laugh outright at that. "Close? He can't stand you."

She sulks. "That's not very nice. And besides, I think it's more that he's probably a little afraid of me."

"Why would he be afraid of you?"

"I know things." She shrugs again.

"What things could you know that would scare a man like Santos Augustine?"

She studies me curiously, and I wonder what I just gave away. "Things about what he did."

I force a grin, pull out my desk chair, and sit facing her. I prop my elbow on the desk, rest my chin in my hand and yawn to show her I'm bored. "You clearly want to deliver some message, so just go ahead and deliver it so you can go. I realize you may not understand this, but today is a hard day for me, and I'd really like to *not* be with you."

"There you go hurting my feelings again." She pushes her lip out, sulking. What is wrong with her? Santos called her a psychopath. I assumed he was exaggerating but I'm wondering now. "But I forgive you because I get it. I mean, you were five when your mom killed herself." It takes all I have to keep my face neutral as her words hit their mark. "Now if it were my mom, I can tell you one thing, I wouldn't be as sad as you if she jumped out of a lighthouse," she says, her words so ugly I almost can't believe I heard correctly.

"Jesus." I rub the back of my neck, feeling exhausted and wanting badly to lie down.

"Anyhow, listen, you seem sweet and innocent, Madelena. You really do. Santos doesn't deserve you."

"Good to hear. Is that it?"

She comes to sit on the edge of the bed again. She's just a few feet from me. Facing me as she is, I study her face as she studies mine and for a moment the bitch mask slips, and I see a line form between her eyebrows. See how dark her eyes grow. She reaches out a hand to touch my knee.

I tug it away and she looks hurt once more. It's an act, and she's very good. I open my mouth to tell her to go for the last time, but she speaks first.

"I used to watch him when he'd get home from the errands Daddy had him run. His *jobs*."

I bite my lip and wait for more. It's what she wants, I know, but I can't help myself.

"He was a wreck afterwards. I mean, not always. Daddy was... Let's just say he was all about an eye for an eye, a tooth for a tooth, but like multiplied by a million gazillion. He never forgot anything. Never forgave anything. It's how he got to the top, right? He was ruthless. Even Thiago was afraid of him. Did you know that?"

I shake my head.

"Liam too, but he'd never admit it. Not me, though. Daddy loved me the best. Anyhow, back to your husband." She emphasizes that part. "Some of the jobs he'd do, the people were bad, you know? They deserved what they got. But some of them had wives and kids and families, and I know he hated that part so much."

"What do you mean?"

"When he'd have to hurt them. You know he did that, right?" she says with a pitying look, her lip curled like the thought of hurting anyone is unpalatable to her. "Well, sometimes he'd have to make an example, you know? So others would know if you crossed my daddy, you'd have to deal with the consequences. Between Santos and Thiago, let me tell you, not a lot of people went against my father. I mean, imagine, Thiago and Santos together beating the crap out of your kid while you watched. Doing terrible things to your wife or daughter." She turns away. "No father wants to see that."

"Get out, Camilla."

"Those cuts on his body, that's how he kept a tally."

I'm about to repeat that she get the hell out, but that makes me stop.

"They're the innocents. That's what he called them. He'd cry over them some nights. I'd hold him but he didn't want comfort. Caius, now he took all the comfort Daddy sent, all those rewards. But not Santos. I guess if you can be good in this world, he's it. I mean, if you can overlook all the damage he did. I get it, too, you know?

What happened to Alexia, poor thing. Murdered so brutally. It broke him. Made a murderer out of him."

I push my hand into my hair and take a deep breath. Someone knocks quietly on the door then opens it, and we both turn to find Liam standing there. He looks at me, then his sister.

"We're leaving," he says to his sister. "Finally."

"Just a sec. Close the door behind you, Liam," she tells him, very clearly dismissing him. When her brother obediently leaves, she looks at me. "Just be careful with him. Everyone who cares about Santos Augustine disappears or dies. Alexia. His father. Thiago. Like I said, you seem sweet. Watch your back."

With that warning, Camilla gets to her feet, smiles down at me, then reaches to the desk to take the book she'd asked to borrow.

"Mind? I'll return it. Promise."

"Take it. Just go."

"Aw, thanks!" She looks down at her prize and I rub my forehead, a headache forming. Without another word, she's gone.

14

SANTOS

The text I receive is an address four hours out of town. When I enter it into Google Maps, it comes up with a motel that looks about as inviting as the Bates Motel. As much as I hate leaving Madelena at the memorial service, I have no choice. Val will be with her, though, and I've instructed him to bring her home as soon as she's ready.

My mind is racing. Did Thiago survive the fall? The cliffs? The water was high. It's possible—if you're very lucky. But he'd have to be a hell of a swimmer, and I can't remember that he was... and he was never lucky.

Could it be that he didn't have his phone with him when he was up at the lighthouse? Does someone else have it, and are they sending me on a wild goose chase? Or have they accessed his account and are sending the messages from another source? It's a possibility. It could be a trap. But I can't ignore the message.

I pull up to the parking lot of the motel in just

under the four hours my GPS predicted. It looks to have fifty rooms spread over two floors. About a third of them are occupied, based on the number of cars.

I double check the message and park the SUV at the far end of the lot. Room nineteen is what I was sent and that's on the second floor.

First, I text Val to ask about Madelena. They're still at the house, apparently, which surprises me, but he's got eyes on her.

Taking the revolver from the glove compartment, I double check that it's loaded and tuck it into the back of my pants. I hadn't brought a weapon to the memorial service, so I don't have my shoulder holster.

After a glance around, I climb out of the SUV and walk to the stairs.

A beige SUV is parked a few spaces down and beyond that is a run-down white Toyota with duct tape holding the rear bumper in place. Cigarette butts are crushed into the asphalt. On the highway in front, cars fly past. Behind the motel, the forest of trees is dense. At the bottom of the stairs, I step over a broken whiskey bottle. I pass six doors to nineteen.

From the large windows, I see that each of those rooms is empty, the beds made. The curtains of room nineteen are drawn shut. I take hold of my revolver and keep it at my side. When I reach the door, I realize it's not closed all the way. Readying the gun, I push the door open, letting the fading afternoon light fall across the unmade bed inside.

I don't need the light, though. The bathroom door

is open, and the blinking fluorescent light is bright enough to illuminate the hotel room. I step inside, peer into the bathroom. It's empty. I return to the bedroom. Whoever was here is gone, and they didn't leave anything behind. I sit on the edge of the bed, the mattress too soft with overuse, and set my pistol on the nightstand. I reread the text.

This is the address.

I try calling the number, which I have tried multiple times. It goes directly to voicemail, as it has every single time. I type out a text.

Me: Who is this?

Because I'm thinking more and more that this is not Thiago but someone with access to his phone's messaging app. Why would Thiago send me on a wild goose chase? It's not like him.

The first checkbox appears. Message sent. Second one appears. Delivered. And that's where it ends.

With a deep sigh, I stand. I will head down to the front office to see who stayed in room nineteen, although I have a feeling there's no paper trail.

But when I pick up the gun to tuck it away, I notice the nightstand drawer is half-open. I pull at it. It's cheap and sticks and when I get it open, it jerks so hard whatever is inside rolls to the back.

Inside I find a bible. Standard. Beneath it, however, is an envelope. I take it out, slip my finger under the flap to unseal it. In it are two sheets of paper, one with charred edges that flake off on my fingers, the other a torn half-sheet.

Carefully, I unfold the one that looks like it was snatched out of a fire. It's almost impossible to make out what it says, I'm holding less than half a page in my hand. The edges are black, what remains of the yellowed paper badly damaged. It looks like some sort of report. There's nothing handwritten on it.

There is one thing, however, that makes me stop, that tells me this was left for me to find. Because I see a name I recognize. Evelyn Thomas. Thomas is my mother's maiden name. In addition to that, I can just make out a watermark repeating throughout the damaged piece of paper.

What the hell would Thiago Avery or whoever is impersonating him have that has my mother's name on it?

Nothing good.

I refold it, set it carefully on the nightstand, and look at the torn piece of paper. I know what it is instantly. I clench my teeth together in anger, an old pain burning my eyes.

It's a torn off piece of the police report detailing the coroner's findings after Alexia's autopsy. I automatically scan the text I can recite by heart. I memorized it years ago. I wonder if this is the same sheet I kept with me for those five years I served the Commander. My secret torture worse than any other. My failure to keep her safe.

But this is only one paragraph of the pages-long

report. One paragraph that has been especially selected. Is it to torment me? Again, not Thiago's MO. The report doesn't even start on a full sentence, as if the start of it was purposefully torn away.

...victim sustained several wounds from a sharp object, seven in total to the stomach and chest area. These were inflicted in a manner consistent with a right-handed perpetrator. Both hands of the victim were wounded, indicating the victim tried to shield herself from...

That's where it ends.

This I don't carefully refold. This I crush in the palm of my hand and shove into my pocket.

The vision of how I found her is still as vivid as if it was yesterday. How her father must have posed her after death. How can a father do that to his daughter? Spell out whore in her own blood along her torn apart stomach? Spread her legs to disgrace her in death?

I swallow hard. Before I left to kill her murderer, I made sure no one would find her in so degrading a position. In the madness of the moment, I tried to care for her, even knowing I was far too late.

I force a deep breath in to banish the image, the memories, and reach into the back of the drawer to get whatever it was that rolled back. My heart races as I wrap my hand around the objects and draw them out, and I don't need to see them to know what they are. I've become very familiar with their texture. But I look anyway.

Three more blue stones. Three to match the one I found on that catwalk.

My gut tightens. The hair on the back of my neck stands on end.

I turn to look over my shoulder through the slight split between the curtains, but no one can be watching me. No one could see inside.

I turn back to the beads in my hand and from under my sleeve, see the few of mine that peek out. An exact match. But it doesn't mean anything. Caius's bracelet is intact. I saw it with my own eyes.

So, I tuck the beads into my pocket, put the burnt sheet of paper into its envelope and walk out of that room. I look around as I go toward the front office, taking in every model of car, every person I see, all the while feeling like I'm being watched.

A bell over the door chimes as I enter the front office. Someone is getting change for the laundry machine from the attendant, who can't be more than seventeen. When the man leaves, I walk up to the counter.

The kid looks me over, confused. "You need a room?" I must not look like his usual clientele.

"No. Question for you. Who was staying in room nineteen?" I ask, taking my wallet and slipping some bills out, looking like I'm counting them.

"Oh. Um." His gaze moves from the bills in my hand to his computer. "Aaron Anon," he says. "Dude checks out tomorrow. Asked not to be disturbed."

"Aaron Anon. That's what his ID said?"

The kid flushes. "Might have forgot to check."

"How did he pay?"

He hits a few buttons, although it's for show. He and I both know the answer. "Cash."

"What did he look like?"

His gaze falls to the bills in my hand again and I slide some of the cash toward him.

He takes it. "Big guy. Baseball cap, hoodie. Kept his head down so I didn't really get a good look."

"Hm. Did he have any scars? On his neck, maybe?"

"Came in late a couple nights ago. Couldn't see him all that well."

"Do you remember what kind of car he drove?"

"I know a taxi dropped him off."

"Checks out tomorrow, you said? Did he have a bag with him?"

"Can't remember. Maybe. I don't know, man. I'm not supposed to talk about our guests."

"I bet. Thanks for nothing." I walk out. That was useless, and there's no sense in waiting for Aaron Anon, aka Aaron Anonymous, to return. He won't be back. He just wanted to give me enough time to find what he left me.

I take my phone out of my pocket to look at my exchange with Thiago or whoever has access to his messaging app. I hit the call button one final time and I think I know what I'm going to get—and I'm right.

This time, the phone doesn't ring, doesn't go into voicemail. A recorded message comes on to tell me that number is no longer in service.

The afternoon sun is setting in the horizon. I stand outside in that parking lot and watch it descend. I've found what I was meant to find. I won't have any more messages from Thiago's number.

The parking lot lights flicker on as I cross to my SUV. Val texts me as I climb in. He tells me he's taking Madelena home. I ask him to let her know I'll be back in a few hours and start the long drive back to Avarice, but I'm not going home just yet.

It's a little after ten at night when I get to Rick Frey's house. Rick Frey is Odin's boyfriend and the same man who was able to hack into the website of the security company Jax Donovan used to access files that were supposed to have been destroyed years ago. He lives in a modest apartment with his mother. I walk into the three-story building and make my way up to the third floor. It's quiet inside when I ring the bell, then remember from the last time Odin and I were here that it's broken and knock on the door.

The first time I paid Rick Frey a visit, Odin was at my side. If he hadn't been, I'm pretty sure Rick would have had a heart attack. He's skittish, one of those people whose IQ is so high they pay the price socially. I wonder how he and Odin met, actually.

I knock again, louder this time, and hear someone hurrying to the door.

"Who is it?" Rick asks.

"Santos Augustine."

A moment passes where things go completely still. It's like a kid closing his eyes, thinking he's safe if he can't see the danger.

"Open the door, Rick. I need your help."

I wonder if he is calling Odin when I hear his panicked voice on the other side, but when I bang again, the lock clicks and he opens the door as far as the chain allows.

"Seriously?" I ask. Does he think that ridiculous chain will keep me out?

"What do you want?"

"I need your help. Please."

He hesitates, but closes the door and I hear the chain slide before he opens its gain. Rick stands there in a black T-shirt and dark jeans, his phone in his hand. He looks like he's had too much coffee and not enough sleep, like he had the last time I was here.

"Odin's on his way!" he says, backing away as if that might mean something to me.

"Relax. Like I said, I need your help." I push the door open and walk in, taking in the tiny apartment, the tired but neat furnishings. The smell of burnt coffee comes from the kitchen.

"My mom's asleep," he says. "She doesn't like visitors so late. Can you, um, maybe come back tomorrow—"

"No, afraid not. Let's go." I gesture to his room, which is where he has his computer. "Take it easy, Rick. I'll pay you for the work."

At that he stops. "You will?"

"If you can help me."

"Um. Okay." He moves toward the front door, keeping a wide berth around me. He locks it but doesn't put the chain on and walks toward his room.

"Rick? Who is it?" A woman calls out from behind a closed door.

"Just a friend of Odin's, Mom. It's fine. Go back to sleep." He turns to me. "She loves Odin."

"Does she."

He closes the door behind us and sits on the chair in front of the computer. The room is small and crappy, everything old and used up, but it's neat and tidy. Again, I wonder how he and Odin De León met. What Marnix would do if he knew this was the guy his only son, the man who should carry on the De León name, is in love with.

"What do you need?" Rick asks.

"This," I say, taking the letter out of the envelope and holding it out for him to see. "I need to find out what this logo is. What the report means. And I need you to keep this between us."

"Yeah, yeah, man. I haven't said a word about the other thing."

"Good." I did pay him to keep his mouth shut so I expect that.

He takes the letter. "Pull it out of a fire or something?"

"Or something. Can you figure out whose watermark that is?"

He sets it on his desk, puts on his glasses and peers close, then starts typing using both pointer fingers. He types at a pace that is much faster than I'd expect, considering. He glances back at the sheet of paper and keys keep clicking as I look around his room. It's not only tidy but weirdly clean almost to the point of being obsessively so. They're poor, that's obvious, but doing the best they can with the little they have.

I sit on the edge of the bed and wait as he works. I try not to think about the stones or that crumpled sheet of paper in my pocket.

Fifteen minutes go by, and he's still at it. He's so focused on his work, in fact, that he doesn't react when someone enters the apartment. I get to my feet to check who it is just as Odin opens the bedroom door. He's still wearing the suit he had on for the service, minus the jacket.

"What are you doing here?" he asks me, then turns to Rick. "You okay, Rick?"

Rick looks up and smiles at Odin. "Yeah. I panicked. Sorry, man."

"No problem." Odin turns to me. "What are you doing here, Santos?"

"I needed Rick's help."

"You can't come here. He doesn't need your kind of trouble."

"It's okay, Odin," Rick says, patting his arm. "It's fine."

Odin looks from him to me. "Where did you go, anyway? She needed you."

I take a deep breath in feeling guilty.

"Why aren't you home with her now?" he continues.

"I'm going home as soon as Rick gives me what I need."

As if on cue, Rick swivels his chair, that letter in his hand. "That logo is for a private firm called Illuminate." He points to his computer screen.

"Illuminate? What do they do?"

"Genomic research mostly."

"What does that mean? Like DNA?"

"Yes and no. A genome is an organism's complete set of DNA. It's mostly research for medical purposes, disease and treatment, I believe."

"Disease?"

"Cancer research for one, I'd guess."

Cancer? I see my mom's name on that piece of paper again. But that makes no sense.

"That's one thing. They do a whole lot of other things."

"That sheet looks like a report of some sort. Can you tell what it is?"

"Not yet but see this up here? Looks like it's a patient number maybe. Give me a few days and I'll see if I can figure out who it is and if I can access the files."

"I need to know sooner. Like a couple of hours."

"I have work. I don't think I can—"

"Call in sick." I take my wallet out and slip out the bills that are left over after paying the useless idiot at the hotel. "Call me as soon as you know. Odin has my number. And don't fucking lose that," I say, pointing to the charred report. "I want it back."

"All right, man. No worries."

I look at Odin who is watching me, still looking pissed off but also concerned. "You call me as soon as he has something. I don't care what time it is. Understand?"

"Yeah."

"And not a word to anyone. Not even your sister."

"What's going on?"

"Nothing."

"Right."

"Not a fucking word, clear?" I ask, stepping right up to him. "I don't want her worrying."

"Yeah. Fine. Clear. I already called her before I came here so she knows you're here."

"Why the fuck would you do that?"

"Because she's my sister and you left her on her own when she fucking needed you, asshole," he says, not backing down. I find I respect him more for it.

Gritting my teeth, I walk out the door.

15

MADELENA

I'm sitting in the dark in the living room watching the dying embers of the fire when I hear the front door finally open, and Santos and Val's voices as Val tells Santos where I am. Probably also how pissed I am. Two sets of footsteps approach, and I turn to watch Val walk on while Santos, looking a little worse for wear, stops at the arched entrance of the living room. He makes a point of checking his watch as he tosses the suit jacket draped on his arm over the back of the sofa.

"Madelena."

I get to my feet, drop the throw I'd had on my lap to the floor and go to him. I'm barefoot, so I have to crane my neck to look up at him which is irritating. Setting my hands on his chest, I shove him, managing to nudge one shoulder backward but apart from that not moving him.

"You disappeared! Again!"

He draws a deep breath in. "It couldn't be helped."

I snort, then shove at him again. But again, I can't budge him. I'm so angry, I can't think straight. My conversation with Camilla, the things she told me about what he did, what those scars are, the thought that she knows that about him, knows more about Alexia than I do... it's too much. That he'd told her about someone so important to him at all is mind boggling.

Then there's the fact that for the second time since I've known him, he has disappeared when I've needed him most—and when he did come back to town from wherever he was, he didn't come to me. He went to find Rick to solve some new mystery.

"What the hell, Santos? I'm going to need more than that? What couldn't be helped exactly?"

"Madelena—"

I put my hand up to stop him and shake my head, so angry I can't formulate my thoughts into sentences. "You know what? Never mind. It's not worth it." I walk past him, but before I'm two steps away, he has me by the arm and is tugging me backward.

"It's not worth it? What does that mean? This isn't worth it?"

"Let me go!"

"It's been a long fucking day—"

"You always seem to have long fucking days!"

"For fuck's sake!" He shakes his head, exasperated, and takes a breath before continuing. "You're wrong. It is worth it. I'm sorry I left you on your own, but it couldn't be helped."

"What couldn't be helped?"

His lips tighten and he takes a moment. "I can't say. I need to figure it out first."

"Not good enough, Santos. Let me go." I try to shrug out of his grasp, but he doesn't let go.

"Tell me about the service. Tell me—"

"If you cared so much, you should have stayed to see it for yourself. Let. Go."

He walks me backward into the room, and only when I'm backed into a corner does he release me, setting his hands on the wall on either side of my face to cage me in.

"I do care. Don't you know that yet? Do you get that part in here?" He pokes a finger at the side of my head, and I raise my arm to slap him. Mid-swing, he catches my wrist, never even taking his eyes off me. "Don't."

"You'd hit me back, wouldn't you?"

He shakes his head. "Really? Do you really believe I'd do that to you? Christ, Madelena. Did you hear what I just said?"

I did, but I'm angry and I have a right to be. Unshed tears blur the sight of him. I try to get free, but he doesn't let me go. I search his face, the forest green of his eyes that are still a mystery to me. That may always be a mystery to me because he can't seem to let me in. Can't seem to let me see him, truly *see* him, even though he's seen me at my most vulnerable.

But when we're this close and I can feel the heat

between us and inhale the scent I love so much, the scent that's become a refuge over the years, I feel my resolve crumbling.

"Damn you, Santos!"

"Madelena," he starts, tone different, not so angry. I look away. I don't want him to watch me cry. But he releases my wrist and touches my jaw, turning my face to make me look at him. "Tell me you know that I care about you."

"Just let me go."

"Tell me."

Only when I meet his eyes does he drop his hand from my jaw.

"Then why did you leave?" I ask, slipping under his arm and hurrying around him, not sure why I'm running, where I'm going to go. Not sure why I'm afraid of this. I vaguely remember last night, remember falling asleep in his arms and hearing my own voice as I spoke those three little words. I thought they were a dream. I hoped they were. But I know better.

"Come here, sweetheart." Santos's arm wraps around my waist and he draws me back. Setting the flat of that hand against my stomach, he searches my face, wiping a stray tear, then kisses me deeply. "I heard what you said," he says, as if reading my mind. He draws back just enough so we are looking at each other.

I blink, shifting my gaze to his mouth, his shoulder, anywhere but his eyes.

"Don't you know," he starts, that hand on my

stomach sliding to my thigh, into the waistband of the leggings I'd put on when I'd gotten home. As he lowers himself to his knees before me, he draws them down, my panties with them. He kisses my belly button, my stomach, lower.

I suck in a breath, my fingers creeping into his hair. I mean to pry him off, but I don't.

"Don't you know I feel the same," he whispers, breath warm against my clit. "Don't you know that yet?" His eyes hold mine as he kisses, then licks, then takes the hard nub into his mouth. I'm gasping, knees trembling. "I am on my knees before you, my Madelena. All you have to do is open your eyes and see," he breathes against me. I moan with pleasure, fingers woven in his hair as he makes love to me with his tongue. Because that's what this is. This is Santos Augustine making love.

When I come, it's a slow, deep orgasm that lasts and lasts. I become pure sensation, a heart beating too hard, too fast, blood rushing in my ears. And when it's over, my legs are too weak to carry me.

Santos stands, holding me up, and kisses me hard on the mouth. He presses himself against me, lifting me, carrying me to a side table against the wall. He sets me on the edge of it, kissing me again as he pushes my legs wide. I fumble with the buckle of his belt, his slacks. He pushes my hands away to do it himself and I watch as he tugs me forward and pushes inside me.

"Say it for me. Say the words," he says against my mouth, cock driving into me as I cling to him. The table rocks, unsteady beneath us. He draws out, turning me. I brace myself against the wall as he pushes into me from behind. "Say the words," he tells me, his chest pressed to my back, one hand on my hip, the other coming around to hold my jaw, to keep my face turned to him as he drives into me. "Tell me again that you love me, Madelena. Because I love you and I need to hear you say it. Say it now."

I do. I tell him I love him, and he swallows the sound, his thrusts coming harder, deeper. He moans into my mouth, the fingers of one hand dig into my hip as he nears his release. "I love you," I tell him again, and he sets his hands over mine on the wall and closes his teeth over the curve of my neck, muttering a curse as he stills, throbbing inside me, the beats of his heart powerful against my back.

When it's over, when we've caught our breath, he draws out.

I turn to watch his beautiful face, the softness in his eyes after he comes, the way he looks at me in those moments. I love that too.

After tucking himself back into his pants, he turns me to face him and slides my panties and leggings back up. He kisses me.

"Do you understand?" he asks seriously. "Do you understand that I love you?"

My heart flutters, missing a beat. "Why?" I hear myself ask. What a stupid question.

He looks momentarily confused. "I forgot you are

unaccustomed to being wanted. Being loved. That ends here and now."

Before I can process, he lifts me in his arms and carries me upstairs to the ensuite in our bedroom. There, he runs a bath, and as it fills, he strips off my clothes and his and we slide in together. I sit with my back to his front, his long legs cradling mine. He wraps his arms around me and holds onto my hands. I take in the differences between us, my pale skin against his olive tone, his muscle against my softness. I twist in his arms and face him because I need more so I sit on his lap to study his face. When I lay my hands on his shoulders and he captures my wrists to stop me, I shake my head.

"Let me see you."

"Madelena," he starts, sounding older.

"Camilla told me what they were," I cut him off. "I need to hear from you."

"Camilla?" He stiffens. "Why would you talk to her?"

I meet his eyes. "I didn't have much choice when she ambushed me in my bedroom."

"She came to your house?"

"Along with everyone else after the service. But it doesn't matter. She doesn't scare me." I shift my gaze to his scars, those precisely drawn lines. I slide the tips of my fingers over them and when I subconsciously start to count, I stop myself. I don't want to know the number.

"Tell me what they are." I meet his eyes. "What you did."

His lips tighten into a line, and I watch his throat work as he swallows. He searches my face, then touches my cheek.

"Tell me, Santos."

"After Alexia's murder, after I killed her father, the Commander made a deal with my father. I'd work for him for five years rather than spending the rest of my life in prison. He could arrange for that. He made sure my father and I both knew the extent of his power." Santos sighs deeply, and I know it's taking a great effort for him to hold my gaze. "The work I did for him was ugly work —the kind that leaves your hands stained forever no matter how much you scrub at them. Thiago and I, we were his enforcers. We... *I* hurt a lot of people, Madelena. Maybe if you knew what I was capable of, you wouldn't be here like this now. You certainly wouldn't let me touch you, not with these hands I hate so much."

He turns his face away, but I turn it back. "I'm here, aren't I?" I bring those hands he hates to my lips and kiss them. "And I love these hands that make me feel so safe."

He looks confused. "I don't deserve you. I know that."

"Are *you* so unaccustomed to being wanted?" He just watches me, eyes so full of tenderness. "Tell me the rest, Santos."

He takes a deep breath in. "There were criminals

we dealt with, of course. But these lines are for the others. The innocent ones. The pawns in the games of evil men. Every night I came back to that wretched house after I hurt one of the innocents, I would carve out a line in my skin. I did it to feel their pain. Their terror. To keep a part of them in my own skin because they deserved that, at least, and I deserved to be made to remember."

I hold his face in my hands and lean toward him to kiss him softly on the lips. I then shift my position to lay my cheek against his chest as he cradles me.

"It doesn't change anything," I tell him. "The Commander was responsible."

"No, sweetheart. I could have chosen a different path. The one that would have landed me in prison."

"He'd have found someone else."

"Doesn't matter. I chose selfishly. I can admit that. I try to make amends now, financial amends. It won't bring anyone back, but I try. And he can't hurt anyone anymore. Thiago and I made sure of that."

"You made him disappear."

"What's the saying? Live by the sword, die by the sword? When my five years was up, he decided to add another five. He could do that. He held all the power. But he made a mistake. Overreached. You see, Thiago was as trapped as I. Alone, he and I would still be the Commander's dogs. But together, we were stronger than him. I knew there could always be another five years, and another after that, and another after that. And I was finished."

"I'm glad he's gone." I look up at him. "Was Camilla in love with you or something?"

He looks down at me, one dark eyebrow raised. "You give her too much credit. A snake cannot feel emotion. It only wants to sink its venomous fangs into its prey. What else did she say?"

"Doesn't matter. Nothing important. Are you going to tell me where you were?"

"Madelena—"

"We're learning to trust each other, right? Tell me."

He hesitates but then nods. "The message I'd sent to Thiago the night you told me he went over the catwalk finally delivered. And I got a reply."

"What?" I sit up so fast water splashes out of the tub. "He's alive? Thank God!"

"No, sweetheart. At least, I don't know. It's unlikely. I think someone is playing a game with us. And I don't like it."

16

SANTOS

At lunchtime the following day, my phone rings. I see Odin's name on the display and answer.

"Rick figured out what that report is," he says without greeting. He sounds off.

"Well, what is it?" I ask after a long pause on his end.

"I think you should meet us."

"Why?"

"Just..."

"Fine. Where are you?" I ask, dread settling in my gut.

"At a bar called Brady's outside of town. It's off exit fourteen on highway 85."

"I'll be there in twenty minutes."

I disconnect the call, grab my coat, and head out of the house. I know the bar from passing it but have never been inside, and I'm concerned why they chose that location to meet. Clearly, whatever Rick found is delicate.

I get to the bar, park and enter. Inside, the place is dimly lit, the windows tinted dark. It smells of stale beer and cigarettes smoked a decade ago. Country music is playing, and disco lights turn the empty dance floor various shades of red. Rick and Odin are sitting at a table at the far end of the bar, and I walk over, looking at each of the few patrons and recognizing no one. But Avarice's upper class wouldn't frequent this place. Hell, they wouldn't be caught dead here.

I pull out the only empty chair at the table, take off my coat, drape it over the back and take a seat.

"Can I get you something?" a waitress asks.

"Club soda," I say, raising my eyebrows at the two of them.

They each have a nearly empty beer in front of them and they order another round. Rick looks nervous, and Odin swallows what's left in his glass.

"What did you find?" I ask when she's gone.

Rick opens his backpack which is on the floor next to him and hands me the envelope that contains the burnt sheet of paper. Along with it, he holds out another one, this one thicker.

"What is this?" I ask, not wanting to take it.

"The report. The full report."

That feeling of dread I'd felt since Odin called worsens. It's the way they're looking at me. I take the envelop but don't take whatever is inside it out.

"I told you what Illuminate does as far as the

public is concerned. But they also provide discreet DNA testing," Rick says.

The waitress brings our drinks. Rick stops talking, and I don't miss how Odin is watching me.

"Spill it, Rick," I say once the woman is gone.

Odin continues when Rick doesn't. "That is a copy of the report that was burnt," Odin says. "Rick was able to access the file."

"What's on it?"

"It's Caius."

"Caius?" I ask, confused.

"Open it." Odin gestures to the envelope while Rick picks up his glass with sweaty palms and loudly drains the contents.

I take the papers out, unfolding them. I recognize the watermark that repeats throughout. I can see a similar table to the charred one, though this sheet is pristine white, the edges not having been turned to ash, the paper not yellowed with age.

I read my mother's full name on it. Evelyn Thomas. She's in the column labeled Mother. Under the column labeled Child is Caius's name.

A cold sweat breaks out over my forehead, under my arms. I drag my gaze to the column labeled Alleged Father and my world goes sideways.

I've never known who Caius's father was. Mom never talked about him. Dad never did. I was never sure he even knew.

"This can't be right," I tell Rick, turning the paper over, turning it back to see the date of the report. It's eleven years old. Caius would have been almost twenty-one then.

"It's right, man," Rick says. "These things are like 99.999999% right."

My hand turns into a fist. I'm crushing the report in my palm. "Can't be." I push my chair back noisily and stand, then need to grip the edge of the table because it's like I stood up too fast.

"Are you going to be okay?" Odin asks, getting to his feet.

I look at him, then at Rick. I lean toward him, take him by the collar. "If you're fucking wrong—"

"I'm not," he says, looking terrified.

"He's not, Santos. You may not like the outcome, but he's not wrong."

"I need to go." I start to walk out.

"Wait." Odin rushes to my side. "I need to talk to my sister. Is she at the house?"

"You can't tell her. You can't fucking breathe a word of this. I'll fucking kill you if you do."

"I won't. It's something else."

I don't answer his question. I can't think about anything but what's in that report right now.

"Your coat. You forgot your coat," Rick says, shoving my coat into my hands.

I walk outside in a fog, climb into my car, and drive, and drive with that damned report on the seat beside me, constant in my periphery. I don't want to see it. Think about it. I don't want to know it,

Because if what's on that thing is true, it changes everything.

17

MADELENA

I found the library a few days ago, but today is the first day I'm able to explore it. This house is almost like stepping into the past. I never know what I'm going to find when I walk down a corridor or open a door. The gothic style suits it, and the Augustine family has spared no expense.

The library is one large room that spans two floors. Bookcases line three of the four walls. Where the second floor should be is a catwalk, and on the ground floor is a sliding ladder to access the books on the higher shelves. It's like something out of a fairy tale. The iron clad windows and what look to be antique leather reading chairs along with the smell of the place all scream history.

I will ask Santos how much of the room was intact when his father bought the property. I can see that some of the bookshelves are slightly damaged and have been repaired. I think they may be original to the house.

Santos left a while ago but said he'd be back for dinner. I am sitting in one of those chairs with a sketchbook in my lap, looking out at the early evening light, bracing myself. What Santos had thought was a diary hidden under the floorboards of my room is actually my first sketchbook. I brought it home with me after the memorial service.

I touch the front cover. It's a cheap spiral notebook, nothing special, and the light blue cover page has faded over the years. I open it, my heartbeat hitching up as I do and see the first sketch. I was young when I drew it, and it's childish but not bad. I don't know why I drew this particular thing but I remember doing it. I was at the club alone after school while Dad attended a meeting. My nanny had been sick, and Dad was forced to take me along.

I still remember the moment clear as day even though it's been years. As I sat at that table and tried not to see the lighthouse, I made a choice. I opened my notebook and from my pencil case, I took out a Hello Kitty pencil and sharpened it. Then, I made myself look at the hulking building in the distance. It terrified me. It always terrified me. But I made myself do it. I sketched the lighthouse.

That was the first time.

I drew it again and again and again over the years.

Every page you turn in this notebook is another sketch of the same subject. You can see my progression over time, but that's not what I'm interested in. What is so powerful about this notebook is that I can remember all the feelings I felt when I drew each of these. It's why I'd hidden it away as soon as the last page was filled up. I couldn't look at it for a long time. But now, I find I want to.

A knock on the library door startles me, and I straighten as Jocelyn, the same woman who caught me coming out of Santos's study the other night opens it. I don't like her even though I know she'd just been doing her job when she reported that I'd been in the study.

"There you are," she says. "You have a visitor."

Odin comes in before I can ask who it is, and I stand as she retreats.

"This is a nice surprise." I go to hug him, and he hugs me back, then takes in the room.

"Wow."

"I know."

He looks me over, eyes catching on the notebook at my side. He knows what it is and doesn't mention it.

"What are you doing here?" I ask, leading him in. "Everything okay?"

"Yeah. I needed to talk to you about something."

"Okay. You want something to drink or eat?"

He shakes his head as we each take a seat on an armchair. "I had a meeting with Mr. Jamison. Do you remember him?"

"Should I?"

"I guess not. He was Uncle Jax's attorney and

executor of his will."

This is not what I'm expecting.

"You turn twenty-one soon," he says.

"I know."

"Mr. Jamison couldn't reach you since you have no phone, which if your husband doesn't take care of that, I will."

"He'll get me one. What about the meeting?"

"Uncle Jax's house has been in trust all these years. I didn't know. I assumed Dad took it over, although I did wonder why he never sold it."

"I'm still not following."

"Well, according to the lawyer, Uncle Jax left it to you."

"What?"

"Yeah. When you turn twenty-one, it's yours. Mr. Jamison said Uncle Jax has made sure that the house should be held in trust for you if anything happened to him."

"Why did he leave it to me?"

Odin shrugs a shoulder. "I'll inherit our house. Maybe he knew that and wanted to make sure you were taken care of."

"I'm not sure I want it. He died in it."

"I know. It's a lot to process. There's one more thing. It's weird although I guess not, now that we know. Uncle Jax had left specific instructions that Mr. Jamison was only to deal with you or me. Not our father. No matter what. I wonder if he always knew things could go badly with Dad, and considering..."

He doesn't finish. He doesn't have to, and I don't want him to. "What happens now?"

"This is his card," he says, reaching into his pocket to hand over a business card.

"He arranged for a meeting on your birthday," he says. "I'd like to be there with you."

"Of course. I don't want to go without you. But what am I going to do with it?" I haven't been inside since he passed away.

"He wanted you to have it. You can decide what you'll do with it later."

I nod and tuck the business card into my pocket. "Did Dad know?"

Odin hesitates.

"Tell me."

"He tried to take control of it with the excuse he'd look after it until you came of age, but Uncle Jax's will was very specific to protect against that."

"God. I don't like thinking about this."

"Then don't. Not yet. You have time to process. Is Santos here?" Odin asks.

I shake my head. "No. Why did he go to Rick's house, by the way?"

"Oh, nothing." Odin doesn't quite hold my gaze, but comes clean in a minute because we have never lied to each other. We can't start now. "I'll let him tell you."

"That sounds ominous."

"It doesn't really have anything to do with you or me." I raise my eyebrows and open my mouth, but

Odin stands up. "I'm hungry after all. Can we get something to eat?"

"You're trying to distract me."

"Is it working?" He holds out his hand, palm up. "Just let him tell you, Maddy. I think it's up to him."

I place my hand in his. "Okay."

We walk out of the library and as soon as we turn the corner, I stop dead in my tracks. I hear Odin mutter a curse behind me. He sets his hand on my shoulder as if to draw me back.

"There she is," says Caius. He's standing just inside the foyer talking to Jocelyn—or more accurately, listening to her do the talking. He straightens, then steps away from her. He looks me over, shifts his gaze beyond me to Odin, and smiles. He dismisses Jocelyn with barely a nod. She walks away, obedient. I guess she still feels like she works for him since he used to live here.

I remember our last conversation, two distinct pieces of it coming to mind. One was where he'd made the comment about becoming less human. The other, his threat that he'd hurt me if I hurt Santos.

"Caius," I say, forcing a smile and walking toward him.

Odin falls into step beside me.

"Good to see you, Madelena," Caius says. He kisses my cheek and I shudder at how cold his skin is. Although it's a rare sunny day, it's below freezing. "Odin." He shuffles the package and what looks to be mail around to shake Odin's hand.

Odin hesitates, and I remember something else Caius had said about not being good enough. Not being wanted. I watch my brother-in-law's face and I find I can't feel sorry for him. I don't know what it is about him, but I can't. Although I am grateful when they shake hands and it's not awkward.

"Where's my brother? Brought some mail that came to the apartment." He gestures to the letters and package he's holding.

"He's not here. I'll take it," I say, and he hands it all over.

"Couple of things are addressed to you."

"Oh?"

"Mind if I come in? I wanted to grab some more things from my room."

"Go ahead," I tell him, then turn to Odin when Caius goes upstairs. "I'll be right back. I'll just drop these off in the office."

"Sure," he says, gaze following Caius up the stairs. He doesn't like him any more than I do.

I carry the things into Santos's office and set them on the desk, casually glancing through them. I find a box addressed to me. When I open it, I see it's an iPhone. Santos came through. I take it out of its box and push the button to switch it on. As the welcome message flashes on the screen, Odin appears in the doorway.

"Hey. What is it?"

I hold up the phone and walk out into the hallway. "The phone Santos ordered."

He smiles wide. "I'll help you get it set up over lunch."

"Someone say lunch?" Caius asks, hopping down the stairs with a duffel bag.

Odin and I exchange a glance.

"Oh, come on. Don't be that way. I miss the cooking here." He drops his duffel at the door and walks toward us. "Besides," he starts, stepping between us and setting his hand at my lower back to guide me toward the kitchen as if I were an invalid. "I could use some company. Ana and I broke it off this morning."

I look up at him. He has his free hand over his heart like he's hurt. He's not. I can hear it in his cool tone.

"Did you?" I ask, stepping away and folding my arms across my chest.

He grins. "She's very clingy and possessive. Never did like that kind of woman. And she has a thing for you, Mad Elena."

"Why are you such an asshole?" I walk away from him.

He catches up, takes my arm, and spins me around. "That was in poor taste. I'm sorry."

"Fine. Let go."

"She's a bitch," he says. "You were right about her."

"I never said she was a bitch." I tug free. And as far as being a bitch, she is, but I never told him that, did I?

"But you think it, and she is. Just being honest. Let's eat. I'm starving."

18

SANTOS

I stalk into the private room of the spa that caters to Avarice's elite and find my mother relaxed in a chair with four attendants around her. Two are polishing her fingernails, the other two her toenails.

"Santos." She sits up from her leaning position, clearly surprised.

"Out. Everyone. Now," I command.

The four attendants glance from me to my mother to each other.

"I said out!"

"Go," Mom tells them as they're scrambling to their feet, tripping over each other to get out.

Once the door is closed, I pull up a chair and sit facing my mother, looking at her confused expression as she waves her hands in the air to dry the nails.

"I wish I could say it's nice to see you, but that was simply embarrassing."

"Embarrassing you was the furthest thing from my mind."

"They're going to have to start from scratch," she says with a glance at her fingernails. "I hope you have a good reason for this."

She's barely finished when I slap the report Rick printed for me on the table in front of her. It's a flimsy thing, and it rattles, an open bottle of blood-red nail polish flying over the edge and landing on its side. It doesn't break, but varnish begins to pour out of it.

But my mom doesn't even look. I'm not sure she even heard the crash. Her eyes are glued to that report, and her face has gone deathly white.

"Does he know?" I ask, my voice sounding foreign. The betrayal feels like a fucking knife in my back.

It takes her an eternity to look up at me, and when she does, her vivid blue eyes swim in tears.

"Where did you get this?" she asks, the first of those tears catching on her eyelashes.

"Does he know?"

She shakes her head, wiping away her tears with the backs of her hands, careful not to smear still-wet polish on her cheeks.

I exhale. Because I'm relieved. If Caius knew and kept it from me, that would have been the real knife in my back. Because my brother and I, it's always been us. No matter what. He's always been at my side through everything, and I need him.

"Where did you get it?"

"Did Dad know?"

"No. No one did."

"How about Commander Avery?"

She watches me, studying me, her eyes clear again. They bounce between mine as if she's trying to figure out how best to answer.

"It's not a hard question. Did Commander Avery know that Caius is his son?"

To hear it out loud, it's like a slap to the face both to me and, from the looks of it, to her. She shakes her head slowly.

I get up, push my hand through my hair, and pace the room once, twice. "I don't understand."

"Santos, sit down."

I shake my head.

"Sit. I'll explain it, but just sit. Give me a minute."

I look at my mother and see something I've never seen before. Fear. It's in her eyes. If she didn't keep regular Botox appointments, I think her forehead would be creased with wrinkles. So, I sit.

She pushes her hair behind her ears, something she never does because she's so hyper-aware of the scar along her temple. She picks up the glass of white wine beside her and drinks the whole thing like it's water before she faces me and takes my hands.

"I worked for them. I was a kid. Barely seventeen."

"You worked for the Avery family?" Shock is obvious in my tone.

She nods, and I think back to the few times my mother has been in the same room as them. If she was barely seventeen herself, Liam and Camilla wouldn't have been born yet. Thiago would, although he'd have been too young to have any memory of her.

But Bea would remember her.

"It's why I couldn't show my face when he came to take you. I was afraid he'd recognize me."

"I'm not following."

"I worked as part of their household staff. I'd only been there a few months when he... noticed me." She shifts her gaze down and I see something else I have never seen in my mother. Shame.

"Mom?"

"He had a taste for certain young women. Women who are under his control. Who can't refuse. That can't come as a surprise to you."

It's not. But fuck. My mother?

She swallows hard and looks up, and I see the effort it takes her to meet my eyes. "He doesn't take no for an answer. You know that better than anyone." She's trying to hold back her tears, but a sob breaks from her throat. She wipes furiously at her eyes.

"Jesus." I'm up on my feet again. Pacing. Jesus. Fuck. No. Not this.

"I needed the work. My parents depended on me. I couldn't leave. And he knew it." She takes a minute to pour herself another full glass of wine and drinks that, too. "It went on for six weeks. When I learned I was pregnant, I left. I ran away before he could find out. Because I was damned if I was going to let him get his hooks into my baby."

"Did Bea know?"

"As far as she was concerned, I was willingly going to his bed. But it wasn't ever a choice."

"How did you manage to get away from him?"

She puts one hand over her mouth, slides it up to her forehead. She holds her hair back so I can see the scar fully. The skin is paler than the rest of her face, and bumpy.

"She *helped* me."

Bile rises in my throat.

My mother snorts, an ugly laugh accompanied by tears. "Although I suppose 'helped' isn't quite the word," she continues. "She found the pregnancy test and came to me with a solution. She wanted me gone as much as I wanted to be gone, but it's not like you can walk away from that man. That family. So, she made me an offer."

She picks up the bottle of wine, but I take it from her and set it aside. I hold onto her trembling hands.

"Tell me."

It takes her a long time to continue. "She offered me a way out. Money. A means of disappearing." She says all this with her eyes lowered, and when she turns them up to me, I see how dark her usual sky-blue is. How clouded in shadow. "But there was a price. I had to be punished first."

"She did that to you." It's not a question.

She nods. "It could have been worse. She could have taken an eye. She was always a jealous bitch, jealous of any woman her pig husband looked at twice. As if any of us wanted his attention." Her voice is bitter at the end but stronger for it, more like the woman I know.

"Acid?"

"Her specialty. And I know I'm lucky, Santos. I've seen what she's done to the unlucky ones."

"Dad never knew?"

"No. Never."

"The Commander coming for me, after Alexia... How did he find *me*?"

She studies me for a minute, then shakes her head. "I'm sure he heard what you did and who your father was, what your father was. Back then, Brutus was a low-level thug, and the Commander must have thought you'd be just like him. Why not have a young, strong man who is indebted to him be his enforcer? If he could do it to Thiago, his own son, why not you?"

I process this, trying to make sense of it. The world is full of people. Why did I catch his eye?

"Did he take me to punish you?" I ask.

"What? You think I'd—"

"It's a strange coincidence, don't you think? That he'd harm our family not once but twice?"

"Do you think I'm lying?" She pulls her hands out of mine.

"I'd forgive you. You know that. And I'd rather he punished me than you a thousand times over."

"But you think I'm lying."

I shake my head, guilt creeping in. I don't believe in coincidence though. Never have.

"You think I had a choice and let him take you?"

she asks. Her eyes are saucers and tears spill freely from them.

"No. No, I don't. I'm sorry, I didn't mean to infer that. Stop crying, Mom. I don't want to make you cry. This is bad enough." I take her hands again.

"It's actually a relief that someone besides me knows."

"But you're sure Caius doesn't?"

"He can't know, Santos. I don't want to think what that would do to him. Where did you get the report?"

"Doesn't matter. I will destroy it."

My mother's cell phone, which is sitting beside the bottle of wine, rings. She looks at me before answering. I glance at the screen. It's Cummings. "Go ahead," I tell her, getting up and turning my back to give her some privacy.

She sniffles, steeling herself I suppose, and answers. She sounds like herself, not at all like the woman who just broke down before my eyes. She tells him she's delayed and she'll be there soon.

"You two dating or something?" I ask once she disconnects the call.

"He's not a bad man."

"If you're happy, then I'm happy for you. Go ahead. Go on your date." I walk to the door.

"Santos?" she calls, standing.

I turn.

She walks to me, hugs me. "You're a good son. I'm lucky to have you and Caius both."

I hug her back. "Thanks, Mom."

19

MADELENA

Odin, Caius, and I sit at the kitchen counter. Caius is the only one of us who seems to be enjoying himself as he digs into a sandwich even though it's late afternoon.

"Settling in all right?" he asks.

"I am, thanks. You and your mom?"

He takes a bite of his sandwich. "To be honest, we both prefer it. A little more lively than this place. More people buzzing around."

"Hmm."

"What?"

"I don't get the impression you like a lot of people, Caius."

"Oh, I don't. But it makes things interesting." I hear the ding of a text message, and he reaches into his pocket to retrieve his phone. When he reads the text, his easy smile vanishes and his jaw tightens.

"Ana?" I ask just to taunt him. "Does she want you back?"

He doesn't even look at me. Instead, he sets his sandwich down and types out a reply before tucking it back into his pocket. He slides off his stool and wipes his mouth. "I have to run," he says with a tight smile.

"Run where?" Santos asks. We all turn to find him standing in the entrance of the kitchen. He entered so quietly none of us noticed. His hair is standing up in places like he's been running his hands through it repeatedly, and his expression is tired. That line between his eyebrows seems to have settled in permanently.

"Hey, brother," Caius says.

Santos walks into the room. He studies his brother, and I can't read the expression on his face.

"Where are you running to?" Santos asks.

"Some issue with a delivery to the apartment. I guess Mom's not home to take care of it."

"She's out with Cummings. Let someone else handle it. Stick around. I'll join you."

Caius's phone buzzes again. He doesn't take it out but reaches into his pocket, I assume to silence it. "Later. Come by the club. We'll have a drink." He glances at me then back to Santos. "Bring your wife. It'll be an early birthday celebration. Twenty-one soon, right?"

I nod, confused he's noted the date.

He turns back to Santos, who is standing like a statue, eyes fixed on his brother. "Everything okay?"

Caius asks him. He sets a hand on his shoulder and Santos glances at it, then back at his face.

"Yeah. Fine. We'll see you later."

Caius nods, pats his brother's arm, and he's gone. Santos watches him leave and only when he hears the front door close does he turn back to Odin and me. Odin, as if taking some unspoken hint, gets up.

"I need to head out, too. Call me later," he tells me.

"I will." I get up to hug my brother, and he, too, leaves. Santos takes a deep breath in when it's the two of us. "I got my phone. Thank you." I hold up the brand new, latest model iPhone.

"Good. I'm glad it got here. You can set it up?"

"No problem. Your number was already programmed in it, so I assume you have mine."

He nods.

"Are you okay?" I ask, going to him.

He looks distracted. That's what it is. He's distracted, but also sad, like he's carrying a new weight on his shoulders.

He takes my arms, then pulls me close to hold me for a long minute. "Let's get out of here." He draws back to look at me, squeezing my arms gently. "Let's just go for a little while."

I nod because something is wrong.

He takes out his phone and types out a text. I hear the ding of a reply moments later. He leads me up the stairs to the bedroom, where we throw clothes and toiletries into a duffel. He leaves me at the front door to talk to Val for a few minutes, then he and I are outside.

"Where are we going?" I ask as he climbs into the driver's side of the SUV and starts the engine.

"North. There's a place I know." He glances at me. "You'll like it."

"What's going on, Santos? Why this sudden trip?"

His eyebrows furrow together, and he keeps his gaze out the front windshield. "I want to take you away, have you all to myself for a change. Can't I do that with my wife?"

"Of course, but you told your brother we'd meet him."

"It's fine. I'll call him later." He smiles at me as we merge onto the highway. "Your birthday is coming up. This can be an early present."

"I don't need a present. You gave me a phone. Are you sure you're okay?"

He nods.

"Odin told me something today."

"Odin?" he turns his dark gaze on me.

"About my uncle's will."

It takes him a moment, but he relaxes, and I explain about Uncle Jax's will. "That's unexpected. You had no idea?"

I shake my head. "Dad apparently did and was trying to get his hands on the house at least until it transferred to me. Not sure what he'd have done with it."

"Just like him."

I settle into the seat, hyper aware of Santos, who is

lost in his own thoughts with his hands tight on the wheel and his entire body tense.

We drive in silence, and by the time we pull into a town by the name of Hells Bells, I'm hungry and ready to stretch my legs.

"I've never heard of this place. Cute name."

"Lesser known town than the ones surrounding it. I hope it stays that way. Tourism would ruin the place."

Santos drives a few more minutes until we come up onto a small road leading to the tiniest chapel I have ever seen.

I glance at him as he navigates the turn then drives the SUV around to a house behind the chapel. It, too, is small—a modest cottage that looks like it belongs in a fairy tale forest nestled among tall blowing grasses and bushes. It's a natural, wild garden through which a curving stone path leads to the front door.

Lights are on inside, and it looks inviting and cozy.

Santos parks the SUV, picks up our bag from the back, and comes to my side just as I'm slipping out.

"Wow. This is lovely," I say. A cool breeze lifts my hair from my shoulders, and I huddle into my coat.

"Come, Madelena," Santos says, enveloping my hand with his. We head up the path.

"Does it back to the water?" I ask as we near the front door because over the wind I hear the breaking of waves and smell the salty air.

"It does. The views are rugged and incredible." He smiles, and the door opens as if someone were waiting for us. A man of about fifty sees him and stops, then smiles wide and comes to wrap his arms around Santos, patting his back the way men do when they hug.

I watch Santos's shoulders relax and when he draws back, I get a good look at the man. He has a scar that bisects the right side of his face. It takes all I have not to stare at that and at the collar he's wearing. He is a priest.

"Well, I'll be," the man says, looking him up and down. "Santos Augustine. How long has it been, my friend?"

It's easy to see the affection between them.

"A few years." Santos smiles at him. "Too many."

The man studies Santos, and when he smiles, the skin around his eyes crinkles. He's kind. I know it without having to know anything else about him.

He turns to me and that smile spreads. "Welcome, my dear. Come in out of the cold." He steps out of the way to invite us into the cottage.

"I hope we're not intruding," Santos says as the man closes the door. I inhale the delicious smell of food and take in the fire crackling warm and bright in the living room's fireplace. We step into the circular room with its cozy furnishings. The light is on in the small kitchen around the corner.

"Not at all. The cottage was empty. Just needed a little tidying." He turns to me and waits expectantly.

"Madelena, this is Father Michael. Father Michael, my wife, Madelena."

"Wife?" Father Michael's eyebrows rise in surprise.

"That is happy news. I'm delighted to meet you. You must be tired after the drive. I'll get out of your way. Dinner is in the oven. Don't worry, I didn't bake it." Santos laughs at that, but it's forced. "Mary's chicken pot pie. Your favorite."

"You remembered."

"I remember how you devoured a whole one yourself once. The refrigerator is stocked, and the bed is made."

"Thank you, Father. Let me get Madelena settled and I'll come over."

Father Michael looks at me then back to Santos. "No need. Let's talk tomorrow morning. You two enjoy the peaceful night."

Santos nods and I get the feeling coming here is exactly what he needs. But the thought worries me more now than it did at the house. Something has happened, and it's not good.

After Father Michael leaves, Santos carries our duffel bag to the bedroom and shows me around.

"I hope you don't mind the simple accommodation," he says.

"It's perfect. I love it."

He smiles, pleased. "Good."

"Let me just let Odin know where I am," I say, thinking to send him a quick text.

"Ah," Santos says with a grin. "That's part of the beauty of Hells Bells. No cell service."

"What?"

"You can use the land line at the rectory. If you can

find the phone, that is. Father Michael has a habit of hiding it away. There isn't enough quiet left in the world according to him."

"There's some truth to that. Has he always been a priest?" I ask because that scar on his face tells a different story.

Santos studies me. He shakes his head. "He took vows about ten years ago. Before that, well, let's just say he has his history. But he found God."

My stomach growls and although I want to know more, I see Santos is relieved not to have to talk about it.

"You're hungry. Let's go eat. You can call Odin tomorrow." He takes my hand, and we walk down to the kitchen together. Once there, he tells me to sit down, and I watch as he takes the pie out of the oven and sets it on the mat in the middle of the small, round table with its two chairs. There is an opened bottle of wine and two glasses.

"Would you like some wine?" he asks me.

"You're not drinking, are you?"

"No. But you can, Madelena."

"I'm fine. Water is okay. Sit with me."

He does and serves me then himself. I watch him take his first bite.

"You don't strike me as a chicken pot pie lover," I say, eating my first forkful and closing my eyes as I savor the perfect texture and rich flavor.

"Mary makes the best. Father Michael used to get

me my own pie for dinner when I'd come. Best comfort food anywhere."

And he needs comfort. I can see it. "Did you used to come here a lot?"

He's quiet, face darkening. "Not a lot, but when we were up north."

"We?"

"The Commander." A shadow falls over his features. "I ran into Father Michael one night when I was out on the beach after a particularly bad event. I was drunk. Being an idiot."

"An idiot how?"

He polishes off his pie then looks at me. "Wading into the water in winter."

"Santos—"

"If he'd found me even a few minutes later, I would have died."

I reach to take his hand, hot tears filling my eyes. I lose my appetite at the sight of him like this.

"What's happened?" I ask quietly when he drops his napkin on top of his dish and pushes it away.

He shakes his head looking too sad and I get up, pulling him up with me. Without a word, I lead him up the stairs and into the bedroom, where I peel away his clothes and mine and we get into the bed. I don't put on any lights. The curtains aren't drawn, and moonlights shines in on us. We lie together listening to the wind and the waves while I hold him, and he holds me.

He's distant, his mind on something I don't know. So I take his face in my hands, feel the scruff of his overgrowing five o'clock shadow and kiss him. The kisses are soft at first but as they grow heated, as I feel him harden, I push the blanket away and climb on top of him. His grip on me changes and our kiss grows hungrier. He draws me back to look at my face for a moment, then slides his hands down over my naked body to my hips, to guide me onto himself. He looks at me as he sheathes himself in me and I sit up, straddling him, my hands on his chest as I grind myself into him.

"Fuck, Madelena. You're so perfect, you know that?" he asks, moving me along his length before winding one hand into my hair, wrapping it around his first and pulling me down onto himself. "Fucking perfect," he says, shifting our position so he's on top of me, fucking me deep and slow. We're so close, closer than any two people can be, I think, with him inside me, his weight on me, our eyes open as we watch each other, see each other in this, our most vulnerable moments. "So perfect," he mutters as his lovemaking morphs into something harder, darker.

He spreads my arms across the bed and weaves his fingers with mine and I glance at the oversized rosary hanging over the bed. His gaze follows mine and he looks up at it, too, and there's another shift in his expression, a different sort of darkening.

He mutters a curse at the thing, tears it from the wall and throws it so hard against the corner that beads come loose and bounce along the floor. He flips me onto my stomach and draws my hips up as he thrusts into me from behind, fucking me hard, pinching my clit painfully to make me cry out. I grab hold of the iron rungs of the headboard to take him as he drives into me, punishing me.

I turn back to watch him. He needs this, I think, this beastly fucking. He may have needed soft lovemaking moments ago but now, he needs to fuck. I climb up on my elbows and meet his thrusts, the old bedframe creaking so loudly beneath us I'm afraid it may break.

"Santos," I pant because I'm close.

His fingers bruise my hips and I look back to watch his face, watch him watch himself fucking me, grunting, sweat dripping down his temple onto my hip.

He's so beautiful like this, so raw. When he slides his fingers once more to my clit and squeezes, I cry out, coming hard, my body vibrating with orgasm as I watch his face, watch the effort it's taking him to hold back his release as I moan beneath him, my walls throbbing around him.

When I'm spent, Santos draws out, taking me by the hair and turning me to face him. He sits back on his heels, drawing me to him. He kisses my mouth, then pushes my face down. I know what he wants, and I open for him, taking him into my mouth, tasting myself on him as he fucks my face hard, as hard as he fucked my pussy. I pant for breath as he groans, the beast now in the place of the man. When I dig my nails into his thighs, it pushes him over the edge and I feel the first spurts of his release down my throat, his cock throbbing, too thick to breathe around. But I want it. I want him. I want this beast-man, my husband.

I swallow, greedy, until I can't, and he draws me off and brings my face to his and kisses me deeply. He draws back, catching his breath as I catch mine.

"Did I hurt you?" he asks, voice raw, eyes dark on mine.

I shake my head because I know he needed this. Needed us like this. But from the corner of my eye, I see the rosary he smashed against the far wall.

He lays me down and draws the blankets over us, sliding in behind me to hold me tight.

"Why did you bring me here?"

"Because this place is good. It heals. It forgives." He hugs me tight to him. There's more so I wait. He sighs. "And because no one can find us here."

20

SANTOS

Beads scatter across a wooden floor. Wind whips my face, icy rain pelting it. All those gathered move at a frantic pace below, coming and going, as if it's all happening in double time. Jerky, unnatural movements leave me confused as I see everything at once and too fast.

Words on a page. The same words appear, disappear, reappear over and over again as if being typed out by a ghost typist. Words I've memorized. The record of Alexia's murder. The brutal stabbing as if the killer would murder not only the mother but also the unborn child inside her womb.

Beads bounce, hundreds of them. Thousands. The sound they make is otherworldly, somehow louder than the crashing of waves. They disappear into the abyss below. Black water pounds against rocks beaten down over ages.

A man screams. A body falls.

A woman's blood-red fingernails slide along the beads of

a rosary. Lips move, murmuring prayers. A man's bloody hands count out prayers on those same beads. Or perhaps he's counting the number of those he has felled.

My mother stands perfectly still. She is young, her belly swollen. She is silent, her lips sewn crudely shut, sanguine eyes staring straight ahead into nothing.

Beside her, my brother holds her hand. He's a child one moment, a man the next. In his other hand he, too, holds a length of those beads, from the end of which slip a countless, never-ending supply of them. Bouncing on wooden planks. Disappearing with the screaming man over the abyss.

I see the connection then. The beads they each hold come from one source. Bound together. Eternal.

Darkness surrounds them all.

And I stand on the top of the world watching.

Watching.

It's as if it's all on repeat.

Until a door opens, and out walks Madelena. She's ghost-like here wearing a simple white gown of worn cotton. The wind whips the dress around her. Long hair tangles and knots like a noose circling her neck. Her feet are bare. She's naked beneath the parchment-like dress.

I scream for her to stop, to not go out there, but she doesn't hear me. I reach out and see my own hand too far to reach her. To touch her. To pull her back, away from the edge. Away from those people.

"Madelena!"

I scream and scream, my throat hoarse with the effort. And she just keeps walking toward them, entranced, the never-ending string of beads in her hand like that in my brother's. The Commander's son. My half-brother.

No one sees her though. No one turns when she passes. I breathe a sigh of relief.

But then there's someone else. Another figure enters the scene. The man who is falling. Who has fallen. His head is caved in. His body is mangled. But he walks toward her around the other side of the catwalk.

"Madelena!" I call again and again but my voice is ripped from me, wind stealing it away, smashing it against those rocks as it does the ocean. I fight against the invisible bonds holding me in place. The words detailing the stabbing of Alexia swim before my eyes, blinding me momentarily. Thiago's eyes take on that look they did before we did the worst of what we did. Before we hurt the innocents and left mangled bodies behind like the one he's walking in now.

In time, we each get what we deserve.

"Madelena!"

But they keep doing what they're doing.

The two praying.

The one staring into darkness with her bleeding lips.

My brother a child.

And then not.

And then looking up at me, a man, seeing me where I stand above the world. As Thiago reaches Madelena and Madelena reaches Thiago and the beads fall, fall, fall, and Caius tucks his hand into his pocket and cocks his head to the side the way the Commander always did and the easy smile turns into a grin that stretches from ear to ear, inhuman teeth gleaming before the sound of their screams.

Before Madelena and Thiago are gone. Both tumbling over the edge, both reaching frantic arms, eyes wide with terror as they disappear into that abyss.

I gasp for breath as my eyelids fly open. Sweat drenches me, soaks the blankets, the sheets. I stare up at the ceiling, confused. Moonlight filters in, a cloud casting shadows along the wall. A murmur beside me has me turn to find Madelena asleep beside me, her sweet face relaxed, soft. Innocent. So innocent.

My throat closes.

I slide quietly out of the bed, and when I see the rosary I smashed against the wall, I turn away from it.

The floorboards creak as I pad barefoot across the room. I put on the clothes I'd packed, a pair of jeans, a sweater, and boots. Downstairs, I take the heavy coat Father Michael left for me. It was his. He gave it to me the night he found me out in the water, wading in chest-deep. Seeking out my own death. Stalking it. Daring it.

The antique grandfather clock tolls the half-hour mark. It's four-thirty in the morning. I bundle myself in the old coat, the scent on it familiar, old, a strange comfort. I pull the door open and step out into the brisk night, closing it behind me and taking the familiar way around the house over the dune and to the beach.

Only a few clouds are in the sky tonight. From here, I can see a thousand stars. It's so fucking beautiful it almost hurts. Even the cold, the constant wind, the vast ocean are too much. I begin my walk along the miles-long beach. I need to think. To clear my head and think.

Who contacted me from Thiago's messaging app? Could it have been him warning me? Trying to clue me in? Could he have survived the fall? Why not come for revenge, then, against the man who pushed him? I am sure it was a man. Thiago is far too big, too strong for a woman to overpower him. Not to mention he is a trained fighter, an enforcer.

Unless he was caught by surprise.

If, like Madelena says, he had rescued her from falling over, he'd have been surprised by an attack before he was ready. The catwalk high on the lighthouse is the perfect place to ambush a man like him.

Why was he there? Was Camilla telling the truth about the call she overheard? Did someone arrange to meet him? About what? It had to have been something clandestine for it to take place then and there.

Madelena interrupted their meeting, but did her presence help the wrong man?

If I assume Thiago survived and lured me to that motel room to leave me those clues, why would he do that? He thought he still owed me. I know Thiago well enough to know that he always pays his debts, good or bad. Was this him repaying that debt? Making things even-Steven like he used to say?

Assuming that, did he know that Caius was the Commander's son all along?

That he and I were linked through this shared half-brother? Why tell me? What purpose does it serve?

And the beads. They're the same as the one I found on the catwalk. He might have ripped them off the wrist of the man who pushed him.

I shake my head because this is pointing me once again to Caius. Why would Caius be up there? What business would he have with Thiago?

Unless Caius did know his parentage. Unless my mother is lying. But then I remember her tears, the way she looked at me. Her fear. Her shame. He might have found out himself somehow and never told her, though. Never told anyone.

"No." I say it out loud into the wind. Not Caius. I've suspected him and been proven wrong, and that dream was just a dream—my mind fucking with me. That's all.

There was one thing, though, that is confusing. All the things I saw fit. My mother's sewn lips. The secret she was made to keep. Bea and the Commander and their eternal prayers after their horrendous acts. Caius as a boy, holding our mother's hand. Caius a man. Thiago. Madelena. The eternal length of beads connecting them. It all fits. It all belongs together.

Only one thing does not. One thing had no place in my dream.

The police report.

I stop.

A light goes on, as if on cue.

I've walked so far, I'm almost to the town center. It's the bakery light. Gustavo starts his days in the middle of the night.

In that moment, I remember something, like the light going on in the bakery triggered a light in my brain.

Alexia was left-handed. She said many of her cousins were too. A strange fact, but maybe these things run in families.

Blood ices over in my veins.

Almost everything in their kitchen was backwards, made for left-handed people. Innocuous things like the can opener, a measuring glass, scissors. I remember my frustration at trying to perform the simplest tasks and Alexia coming to my aid.

Because she and her father were both left-handed.

And, according to the police report, whoever murdered Alexia was not.

21

MADELENA

I wake up because I'm cold. I turn over on the bed, a double that is just slightly bigger than the one I slept in at college. I want to cuddle against Santos for warmth but realize why it's so cold. He's gone.

Wrapping the blanket around myself, I sit up and glance outside at the orange sky, the deep blue ocean. The hardwood floor is cold on my bare feet when I stand and walk over to the window and look out at the beautiful day dawning before me, water as far as the eye can see, but different than the cliffs of Avarice. A wild beach. Foamy peaks of waves breaking on soft sand. Green grasses high on the dunes blowing in the wind and miles and miles of nothing, of no one. Far off, the lights in the heart of the small town are coming on one by one. I stand there for a minute and watch the sun rise before I get too cold. There's a fireplace in this room, but we didn't light it. I wonder if the fireplaces are the only source of heat for the small cottage.

I dress quickly, grateful for the thick wool socks Santos told me to bring, and head downstairs.

"Santos?" I call out, but there's no answer and no lights are on. Using my new phone, I scroll to his name which is only one of two—the second being Odin—and hit the call button. But nothing happens because there's no cell service. I set the phone on the coffee table.

It's cold down here too, and I go to the fireplace, where I poke the embers of last night's fire. Beside it, the basket in which logs are kept is empty but for a few smaller twigs for kindling. I stand to look around trying to remember if I saw firewood stacked outside.

Just then there's a knock on the door.

"Santos?" I call out, thinking he locked himself out, but the door is unlocked and when I pull it open, Father Michael is standing there carrying a stack of logs in his arms.

"Good morning, Madelena. I hope I didn't wake you but wanted to bring these over first thing."

"Good morning, Father. Come in. I was awake."

He smiles but I see he heard the *I*, not *we*.

"Santos isn't here. I don't know where he is, actually. He was gone when I got up."

"Well, let me get the fire going and we'll make coffee. The car is outside, so I am going to guess he walked along the beach to Gustavo's."

"Gustavo's?"

"He's the local baker. His cinnamon rolls are sinful." He winks at the bad joke, and I can't help but smile.

"You're sure that's where he went? Isn't it too early?" I ask as he crouches down to build a fire.

Once the flame takes, he straightens, brushing off his hands. He looks at me. "If he came here, he needs the ocean. The cold. The empty space." He must see my face morph into one of concern as I remember what Santos told me about how Father Michael found him the first time. "Don't worry, Madelena. He's out walking. He will walk the length of the beach to the town, and he'll return with those cinnamon rolls I mentioned. Come, I'll make coffee."

"You're sure?" I ask.

He looks at me, then smiles. "I've known Santos for a decade now. He's stayed here more than a dozen times. I think he comes to clear his head. Process. And he walks. A lot."

"He trusts you."

"I hope so."

I follow Father Michael into the kitchen where our plates from dinner are still on the table.

"How was it?" he asks kindly, with no judgment about the mess we left.

"Delicious," I say, and I start cleaning up.

Father Michael opens a cabinet to take out a large stove-top espresso maker and, after adding ground coffee and water, he sets it on the stove and helps me clear the table.

"I'll do the dishes," I tell him when he begins to roll up his sleeves.

"Then I'll set the table for the cinnamon rolls if you promise to save me one. I have to say mass before breakfast," he adds, checking his watch.

"You're confident it's where he went?" I ask as I finish washing the few dishes we had used.

"I'm confident. He needs space, but he also needs home. And I don't think he's had much of the latter." He studies me. "I think you'll change that, Madelena. I'll see you after mass, unless you'd like to hear it too?"

"Um, I think I'll wait here for Santos. If you don't mind."

"Of course not. I'll see you later."

"Thank you, Father."

He leaves, and I look out the window over the sink as I wait for the coffee to brew. Once it does, I pour myself a mug and put on my coat and shoes. I walk out of the house and onto the dunes to the beach. It's icy cold, and I wrap my hands around the mug, looking in the direction of the town. It's got to be five or six miles to walk. Did he walk it in the dark? What was he thinking?

Finding a bench that is at least partially sheltered from the wind, I sit, and I wait for him.

22

SANTOS

Organ music from Father Michael's morning mass carries on the wind as I approach the small cottage. I stop to take it in, the sound a comfort. All the years I've been coming here, it's been the same. Even as incense clung to the stone of the walls, the wood of the pews. Even as I watched fingers counting out bead after bead as the devout prayed, being here, hearing mass here, was a comfort. One I did not deserve.

That had everything to do with Father Michael. He's a good man. He never asked any questions, not once. He simply took me in and took care of me.

The first morning, I'd crept out early in the morning, my head throbbing, sick to my stomach with the amount of alcohol I'd drunk... and the memory of what I'd tried to do. It was after that I started cutting the lines into my skin to remember the dead—to remember that they were dead because of me.

Father Michael had saved my life, but I knew in my heart it wasn't because God had intervened to save my soul. No. I lived because I didn't deserve to die. Those days, death would have been a mercy.

Suffering is for the living. So, I marked my skin with each innocent life I took.

It took three years for me to confess my sins to him. I expected him to look at me in horror, to turn me out. But all I saw in his eyes was kindness, even after he heard my confession. Knowing what I'd done, and what I was, he only looked at me with kindness. Not pity. Never that. Only gentle acceptance.

Being here now has the same feeling as then. It is a safe haven.

As I approach the entrance of the cottage, the door opens, and I see Madelena looking at me with worry. The sight of her makes me stop. She is the only person in my life whom I've brought here, who even knows the existence of this place or its meaning to me.

"Madelena."

I go to her, hug her to me, and push away the image of her face in my dream as she fell.

She resists at first, then lets herself melt into me. "You were gone."

Drawing back, I look at her. "You were worried?"

"Of course. I woke up and the bed was empty. No note, no nothing. Of course, I was worried."

I usher her inside, smell coffee, see the fire. "I'm sorry. I didn't want to wake you. I had a bad dream and needed to clear my head."

She studies me, and I remember what she told me Thiago said to her that night at the lighthouse.

In his veins is the blood of a monster.

Thiago knew about Caius. He knew they were half-brothers. I am sure of it. Thiago considered the blood in his own veins that of a monster. I'm sure he felt the same about Caius. But was he referring to Caius when he said those words to Madelena?

"Do I smell coffee?" I want to ask about that night, but I don't want to worry her more than I already have.

She nods and takes the box of pastries so I can remove my coat. She opens it, her eyes growing bigger at the sight of the freshly baked, plump cinnamon buns. When she breathes in the wafting of cinnamon, sugar, and butter, she moans.

The sight of her pleasure makes me smile. "They're best fresh," I say, leading her into the kitchen.

"Father Michael mentioned them," she says, setting the box on the table. She touches my face, then takes my hands. "You're freezing."

"Coffee will warm me up."

"Sit down, Santos." I do and watch her as she makes a fresh batch of coffee. She studies me quietly as it brews, then pours me a mug and brings it over to the table. "What was the dream?"

I see her face again as it was in the dream, and I think Thiago and I aren't even-Steven. We never will be. Because he saved her life, and I will forever be indebted to him for that.

"The lighthouse." I reach to take her hand, squeeze it. "I keep seeing you go over. You and Thiago."

"Jesus."

"It's okay. You're safe. I know that. Eat, Madelena."

She eyes the cinnamon rolls, then reaches in to take one that's sticky with buttery cinnamon-sugar. She bites it. "Oh. Wow."

I smile. "We'll have to save one for Father Michael. He has a weakness for these things. Surprised he's not big as a house considering."

"He mentioned that. He came over with firewood earlier and told me you always walk the beach when you're here and come back with cinnamon rolls."

I nod, drinking my coffee and watching her eat.

"Next time you have a bad dream, wake me up, okay?" she asks as she pops the last of it into her mouth.

"You have a little something," I start, getting up and moving toward her. I lean my face close to hers. "Cinnamon sugar." I kiss her mouth, taste the sticky sweetness of her lips. "Let's go upstairs, Madelena."

She looks up at me. I draw her to her feet and lead her up to the bedroom. I need her to not worry. To not ask questions I don't want to answer just yet.

I simply need to be close to her because like this place, she heals.

WE SPEND A FULL WEEK AT THE COTTAGE. I INTENDED ON one night but can't bring myself to leave, can't get enough of seeing Madelena as she is here. Soft, relaxed, herself. It's one week where, after leaving Caius and Odin messages to let them know we're out of town, Madelena and I walk along the beach, eat too many cinnamon rolls, and spend the nights making love in front of the fire. It's easy, simple. It's a life that can't ever be mine, not outside of this little cottage, this little forgotten town.

On the morning of the eighth day, the mood palpably different than the prior days, we pack our single duffel into the car and reluctantly say goodbye to Father Michael. I feel better than I have in a long time as I hug my old friend and savior. But I can't keep the sense of dread from creeping in as I climb into the SUV, and we begin the drive back to Avarice. Back to reality.

"You like it here?" I ask her.

"I love it here. I don't want to leave, actually."

"We'll come back. It's our secret place. No one knows about it. Hells Bells is just for us, just you and me, okay?"

She studies my face. Does she hear what I'm not saying? She nods.

As soon as we're about twenty minutes out of town and within reach of a cell tower, the barrage of text messages and emails sets my phone on fire. The lack of connectivity is one of the things that has always made

Hells Bells a haven for me, but when reality hits, it hits hard.

After glancing at a few texts from Caius asking where I am and how long I plan to be MIA, I ignore all the messages. I send a quick text to Val telling him our ETA, then tuck the phone into my pocket.

"You know, we don't have to go back," Madelena says.

I glance at her. "I think we do. Besides, I'm sure your brother will want to see you today. Happy birthday, by the way." I smile at her. She attempts a smile. "And of course there's the meeting with your uncle's lawyer."

"I'm sure we can do that another day." She turns away.

I glance at the rearview mirror. The sign welcoming visitors to Hells Bells has barely faded into the background, and already, everything feels different.

"I'm nervous." She keeps her gaze out the side window.

I squeeze her knee. "I'll be there with you. And you don't have to do anything but sign the paperwork and take the key. That's all."

She faces me and she's biting the inside of her cheek. "I want to see it."

"The house?"

She nods.

"You sure?"

"I think I should. And I know Odin wants to, too.

We had happy memories there. It's just... they're clouded over, you know?"

"You don't have to go today. I'll take you when you're ready."

"I don't know that I'll ever be ready to go into the house where he was murdered. I just have to do it."

Her words have me tightening my grip on the steering wheel. She doesn't deserve this.

Her phone dings with a text. She reads it and a small smile appears on her face. "Do you mind if I have lunch with my brother? Except for the last two years, we used to do that on our birthdays. Just the two of us."

The last two years when I've kept her locked away.

"I didn't mean..." she starts as if reading my thoughts.

"It's all right." I've had her all to myself for a week. I can let her have her lunch. "Where?"

"He made a reservation at Trattoria Maria. It's in the center of town." I check my watch. "He'll take me to the lawyer's office afterwards."

"I told you I'd take you."

"That's fine. I just want to make it easy."

"I'll drop you off at the trattoria. You'll have a soldier—"

"It's lunch in the middle of the day in the middle of town."

"He'll be subtle."

"Santos—"

"Until we figure out who was up at the lighthouse, you will not be left unguarded. That's my condition,

Madelena. If you want to have lunch with your brother, you will be accompanied by a soldier."

"Fine." She folds her arms across her chest, tension between us, the ease of the last week vanished.

I squeeze her knee. "I won't take a chance with you."

She exhales. "You're going overboard."

"Humor me."

"Fine."

We ride in silence, each of us lost in our own thoughts. When we get to the trattoria, a soldier is already waiting there. I'd prefer Val, but I need him for something else. I park the SUV and walk around to Madelena's side. She's already out by the time I reach her.

"I'll walk you in." I set my hand at her lower back, and we head toward the restaurant's glass door. It's located in a strip mall. I wouldn't look at it twice, but as soon as we're inside, I realize why it's so busy. The food smells delicious.

"Maria's grandmother opened this place before I was born," Madelena says. "It doesn't look like much on the outside, but the food is the best."

"I can smell that." I look around at the dozen tables, which are all full. I spot Odin at the back. When he sees me, he scowls, but gets to his feet.

I turn Madelena toward me and kiss her cheek. "Remember, Hells Bells is our secret."

"We have so many," she tells me as Odin approaches.

"Happy birthday," Odin tells his sister, kissing her on the cheek. "Table is set for two," he says, holding onto one of Madelena's hands.

"Don't worry, I'm leaving."

Madelena rolls her eyes. "I'm starving."

A woman watches us from behind the cash register. Madelena waves.

"Maria?" I ask Madelena.

She nods. "Want me to introduce you?"

"Nope. I'll introduce myself."

"Santos—"

"Go, have your lunch. You have a little more than an hour before you have to be at the law office."

"Come on, Maddy," Odin says. He leads her to their table. Once she's settled, I approach Maria, who is measuring me up.

"So, you're the Augustine they're all talking about," she says.

"That's probably my brother," I say, extending a hand. "Santos. Pleased to meet you."

"Maria." She shakes it. "I've known those kids since they were little." We both glance at Odin and Madelena. "And as long as the trattoria has been open, we've never had a soldier stationed outside." She gives me a disapproving look.

"First time for everything." I take my wallet out and set two hundred-dollar bills on the counter. "If this doesn't cover their bill, he'll take care of the rest," I say, gesturing toward the soldier.

She pushes the bills back. "Birthday lunches are on

me. And anyway, how much do you think lunch costs? I don't extort money from my patrons. I'm not the mafia."

"Touché. Think of it as a generous tip then." I leave the money on the counter and walk toward my wife. I kiss her on the top of her head, memorizing the floral scent of her shampoo, and tell her to have a good lunch, then leave. I'm barely out the door when my phone rings. I take it out of my pocket to find it's Val.

"What is it?" I ask, climbing into the car.

"You have company. Bea Avery."

"At the house?" I ask, surprised.

"You want me to get rid of her?"

"No. I'm about ten minutes away. Put her in my office but stay with her."

"Will do."

I head home, seeing the ever-present shadow of the looming lighthouse. Hating it. I could tear it down, make a modern structure out of it to function as a lighthouse. I decide to look into it.

When I get home, two soldiers I don't know stand outside of their SUV at my front door. I need to gate off the property. I hand the keys off to one of my men and head inside, straight to my office. I greet Val, excusing him as Bea Avery turns her head to watch me approach. She doesn't get up.

Val closes the door, and I cross the room to take my seat behind the desk. Tables have turned. I wonder what she wants.

I think about what my mother told me, too. What

Bea did to her. That and the fact that she knows Caius is the Commander's son.

"What an unpleasant surprise," I say to open the conversation.

"You've been in contact with him."

"Excuse me?"

She reaches into her purse, takes out a sheet of paper that looks like it's been crumpled in her bag for days and slams it onto my desk. "You and my son have been in contact."

I glance at the sheet of paper, making out a part of my text conversation with Thiago—although conversation is a big word here.

"What game are you two playing?" she asks.

"No game. And I wouldn't say we've been in contact. I got an address. That's it. If Thiago wants to disappear, that's his prerogative." I have to keep in mind that she doesn't know about Thiago's presence at the lighthouse.

She gets to her feet, sets her hands on the edge of the desk, and leans toward me. She's a small woman. I never really noticed that. I know not to underestimate her, though. Bea Avery is dangerous.

"Thiago took something that doesn't belong to him."

"And what's that?"

She glares. "That's none of your business."

"Now I'm confused. If it's not my business, why are you here?" My question, asked casually, irritates her. That fact makes me smile.

"He's been in touch with you. I know that from his phone records. Where is he?"

"I have no idea, and as far as I'm concerned, I hope he stays gone because it seems like that's what he wants."

"Well, we all want things, don't we, Santos? But we all have a duty." She sits back down, studies me. "Obligations to our family. Thiago owes me."

"What does he owe you, exactly?" That seems to surprise her.

"He's my son. He owes me his loyalty."

"And his life?"

She grins.

"I think he's more than paid, don't you? You let the Commander make an enforcer out of him. You know what he's done. You know what that cost him."

"Enlighten me."

"His soul."

"That's dramatic, isn't it?"

"It fits."

"Have you lost your soul too, then?"

I grit my teeth, force myself to file her words away for another time. But she sees the impact they have on me, and her grin widens.

"You'll both burn in hell for what you did all those years."

"And you think your prayers will save you? We'll all burn together, Bea." I stand and lean toward her over my desk. "I know what you did," I say in a low voice.

"What I did?"

"My mother came to you for help. I know what you did to her."

Her eyes grow wide, eyebrows disappearing into her hairline. Then she surprises me by laughing out loud.

"What I did to her? What did she tell you exactly? Let me guess, a lie." I am caught off guard, and she sees it and continues. "You think she came to me for help? Is that what she told you? Let me tell you how it really went, Santos." She sits back in her seat, cocks her head to the side. "She came to me for money. Money to keep her mouth shut about who fathered her bastard. She didn't come to me for help. She came to blackmail me. She thought if Alistair found out, he'd set me aside and marry her. She was a stupid girl then, a stupid woman now. What I did was explain reality to her."

"And what was your version of reality?"

"He'd take the bastard and get rid of her, and you know it." I do. It's how the Commander operated. He'd feel he owned Caius. "And what do you think he'd have done with your brother? Do you want me to spell it out?"

"Get out, Bea."

"He'd make another Thiago out of him. So, I did help her, just not in the way she wanted. I helped her go. But not without leaving my mark on her. So every time she looked in the mirror, which the vain woman does often, I am sure, she'd remember me. Your mother is nothing. She was always nothing. A whore.

A liar who would sell her own son to save her neck. Who *did* sell her own son."

"She did what she did to *save* her son."

She opens her mouth, closes it and grins wide, her eyes gleaming. "Ask her to tell you the whole story sometime, Santos. Because she does have *two* sons."

I'm at a loss for words and she knows it. Satisfied with her advantage over me, she stands.

"Find Thiago, and I'll tell you what your mother won't—although you may not want to hear it. Truth is often a bitter pill to swallow, isn't it?"

She walks toward the door, and I walk after her, capturing her arm and spinning her to face me.

"What the hell are you talking about?"

"Get your hand off me."

"What are you talking about?"

"Is that Italian place any good?" she asks casually. Her words turn the blood in my veins to ice. I tighten my grip, but she only grins wider. "It's so hard when the innocents are hurt because of us, isn't it?"

"Val!" He opens the door in an instant, and I toss her at him. "Get her off my property!" I order, not looking back but stalking out the front door and back into my car. I call Madelena's cell phone as I peel off the driveway and drive like a bat out of hell back to the strip mall.

23

MADELENA

I am thanking the waiter who has just set my panna cotta down when the glass door of the restaurant slams against the wall so hard, it cracks. I jump, along with everyone else in the place. Odin mutters a curse under his breath and two big guys, Maria's brothers, come out from the kitchen. One of them reaches under the counter to grab what a quick glance at the black shiny metal tells me is a gun before Maria puts a hand out to stop him.

"You've got to be fucking kidding me," Odin says, standing as Santos steps into the restaurant, forehead creased in worry or rage, or both, and only when his eyes land on me does he exhale. He takes in the room of panicked patrons, several of which are hurrying to get their coats and bags and leave. Four soldiers follow Santos in, and I see more outside. They look so completely out of place in the strip mall as they fan out, peering into every shop, every cafe.

Santos makes way for those slipping out, then looks at Maria and her brothers—one of whom still has the pistol in his hand, while the other is coming around the counter with a baseball bat in his.

I stand, my napkin slipping to the floor, as Santos stalks toward me.

"What the hell is going on?" I ask as he takes my arm and hands me off to one of his men.

"Take her to the car," he tells him, not bothering to say a word to me. I resist, and as I'm marched out, I see Maria and her brothers getting in Santos's face.

"What's going on?" I call as I'm marched out by one of his goons, who plants me in the backseat of the SUV closest to the trattoria and locks the door. He fucking locks the door! I can see from here the conversation they're having and when Santos comes nose-to-nose with one of the brothers, I bang on the window to get his attention, but he doesn't hear me. Or if he does, he doesn't turn. Odin looks toward the SUV, but no one moves. More minutes pass, and I watch as conversation continues until, eventually, Santos takes his wallet out and hands a wad of cash over to Maria. He says something to the remaining patrons in the restaurant. He and Odin have words before Odin picks up my purse, which Santos snatches from him, and they walk out.

"What the hell?" I scream at Santos when he opens the SUV door.

"When I fucking give you a phone, you fucking answer!" He rummages in my purse for the phone, drops the bag to the ground when he finds it and holds it out to me. "Do you fucking understand?"

"I understand that you're insane! You knew where I was. You had a soldier at the door!" I snatch the phone from him and look at the screen, seeing the dozen or so missed calls.

One of his soldiers comes toward him, talking into his earpiece like he's the fucking FBI. "It's clear. If they were here, they're gone," the soldier says.

Santos nods, jaw tightly clenched as he scans the lot.

"What's going on?" I ask, glancing at Odin, who is looking a little pale.

Santos looks at me. "Nothing. It's fine."

"Nothing? It's fine? You don't just break the fucking door of the restaurant, scare the patrons half to death and drag me out before I've even finished and then get to tell me it's nothing!"

"What? You want dessert?"

"No! Fuck you! You owe me answers, Santos!"

"I'll pay for the door. I covered all the meals." He closes the door, and my mouth falls open that he just did that mid-conversation, but then he steps into the SUV from the other side. He checks his watch. "Move," he tells the driver then turns to me. "Why didn't you answer my calls?"

"I didn't hear them. My phone was in my bag on silent."

"Why was it silenced?"

"Because... I don't know! I didn't even realize it was.

It's not like I have a slew of friends calling me all day. What's going on?"

He pushes a hand into his hair. The movement pushes his jacket back, and I see the butt of his gun.

"What the hell is going on, Santos?"

"You're not going anywhere without Val from now on. Val and two more men. And I will know where you are at all times, and you will not silence your phone. You understand?" he asks, taking my phone and flipping the switch so it's no longer silenced.

"What happened?" I ask, worried now as the parking lot and all those soldiers and Odin disappear into the distance.

Santos sighs. "Bea Avery knew where you were."

"What? She's having me followed?"

He draws me to him, kisses my forehead then looks at my face, eyes searching mine. "Don't worry. I won't let them hurt you. I swear it on my life."

"I'm not afraid of them," I say but I'm not sure it's true. If someone was following me, I was clueless. There's only one reason she'd have me followed. I'm an easy target—and if they want to get to Santos, I'm also the perfect target.

I'm being naïve to think I'm safe. I know the world the Avery and the Augustine families come from. He removed me from it over the last two years, and our seven days in Hells Bells have made me forget. But I can't lose sight of what these people are capable of. If I needed a brutal reminder of that, then I got one at the lighthouse.

"Don't worry, Madelena. Let's get you to the lawyer's office," he says absently as his phone rings. I see it's Val before he answers. "Yeah."

Val speaks but I can't hear what he says. I watch Santos's face though, as his jaw tightens, and his eyes narrow infinitesimally.

"When did that happen?" he asks. Val answers but I can't hear it. "Look into that for me. I want all the details." He glances at me, then turns away. They talk about increasing security at the house, and he disconnects as we pull into the parking lot of the building that houses Uncle Jax's attorney's offices.

"What is it?" I ask.

He shakes his head, rubbing the spot between his eyebrows like he's getting a headache. "Let's get this done," Santos says, getting out of the car without answering. Odin pulls into the lot as I'm slipping out, Santos's hand firm around my arm. Soldiers flank us as Santos leads me inside without waiting for Odin.

As soon as we enter, a receptionist looks up from her large desk.

"My wife has an appointment with Mr. Jamison," Santos says before I can speak.

The woman smiles. "Ms. De León."

"Mrs. Augustine," Santos corrects.

"Relax," I tell Santos.

He turns to me and opens his mouth, but she clears her throat, and he forces a tight smile in her direction. I'd say her gaze becomes a little more panicked when she sees that smile. She apologizes for her mistake.

"I'll let Mr. Jamison know."

Odin enters just then and comes to stand at my side only once the soldier gets the okay from Santos to allow him.

"What are you doing?" I whisper to Santos. "Tell them to move away from me. And let go of my arm. I'm your wife, remember? Not your prisoner."

He grits his teeth, but before he can do anything, the office door opens and a man I assume is Mr. Jamison steps out into the reception area and walks toward us. He takes in the collected men and only momentarily shows concern. I wonder if he's used to this sort of thing.

"Mrs. Augustine," he says, clearly having been forewarned by the receptionist. "It's wonderful to meet you." He shakes my hand.

"It's nice to meet you, Mr. Jamison. Um, this is my husband, Santos Augustine."

"Mr. Augustine," he says with a smile and a handshake. "Odin." He nods to Odin with whom he does not shake hands because of the number of soldiers between them. "I'm afraid only the De Léon siblings will be able to be present. It was a requirement from your uncle," he says that last part to me and Odin.

"Probably for Dad," I tell Santos. "It's fine. You can wait for me."

"I don't like this," Santos says.

"Don't be ridiculous. I'll be right there." I point to the office.

"Check the room," Santos tells two soldiers who walk past Mr. Jamison and do just that.

Mr. Jamison's eyebrows rise but he doesn't comment.

Once Santos's men give him the all-clear, Mr. Jamison clears his throat and gestures to the office.

"Are you going to charge in all Rambo style?" I ask Santos when he loosens his grip on me.

He just gestures to the office with a jerk of his head. I roll my eyes and walk into the office followed by Odin and Mr. Jamison. Before Mr. Jamison closes the door, I see Santos settle himself in the middle of the large leather sofa in the waiting room, and from the window, I see the heads of two of his men.

"What was that?" Odin asks.

I shrug as Mr. Jamison settles into his seat and opens a folder. "Something with the Avery family. I guess they're having me followed."

Odin's forehead furrows. He opens his mouth to ask something, but Mr. Jamison clears his throat, and we both turn to him.

24

SANTOS

I wait impatiently to take my wife home, irritated at not being in the attorney's office with her, but also needing this time to get my thoughts together. Today is turning into a shit show, as if I will pay for the last seven days of peace with just this one.

Bea Avery knowing where Madelena was shouldn't come as a surprise to me. Find your enemy's weakness. Exploit that weakness. It's your way in. I learned that even before I met the Commander. But my reaction to her comment? That was just stupidity on my part. The way I peeled out of there confirmed to her that Madelena is my weakness.

I made her a target.

As I sit staring at that closed door, I go through our conversation again. I didn't expect her to come clean about my mother. But what she said, and her satisfied expression? It's bothering me. She got under my skin today, and she knows it.

I get to my feet and push a hand into my hair, pacing. My phone dings with an email. It's the police report. I'd told Val to get me in touch with Detective Hayes, the agent who'd worked on Alexia's case. I have the paper version of the coroner's report at the house. I want to talk to Hayes about the stab wounds and the fact that according to the coroner, they were made by a right-handed person. But it turns out I can't talk to Hayes. No one can, because he died in a hiking accident weeks after he closed Alexia's case. Got too close to the edge of a cliff apparently.

What if I was wrong about Alexia's father? What if it hadn't been him who killed her? Then who? Who would murder her so violently, so cruelly, then pose her the way they did? Alexia had no enemies. She was kind, friendly and warm, and there was rage in the killer's hand.

My phone dings with a message.

> Caius: Back from the dead?
>
> Me: Don't be an ass.
>
> Caius: What the hell's going on, Santos? We used to talk, remember?

I rub my throbbing temple.

> Caius: Drinks to celebrate wifey's birthday?
>
> Me: Wifey?

> Caius: Typo. Fat thumbs. Drink?

> Me: Tomorrow. It's been a long day.

Caius sends two thumbs up emojis and follows it up with the middle finger. It makes me smile because that's him.

> Me: Meet you at the club, brother.

> Caius: Augustine's remember? Dad will turn over in his grave if he hears you call it the club.

The office door opens then, so I type out a quick response telling him the time, then tuck my phone into my pocket.

Madelena shakes Jamison's hand and thanks him. She's holding a folder and looks a little paler than when she went in, but when she meets my eyes, she musters up her anger. It's good. Anger makes you strong. I need her strong right now.

I go to her, stand a few inches from her, then turn to Jamison. "All done here?"

He nods.

I look to Madelena. "Home or your uncle's house?"

"Home."

"We can go over together when you're ready," Odin tells her.

"I don't think so," I tell them both.

Jamison clears his throat and excuses himself. "What do you mean, you don't think so?" Madelena asks me.

"I'll take you myself. I already told you I would." I set my hand at her lower back and nudge her forward.

"I want to go with my brother," she says, not budging.

"He can be there. That's fine. But I'll be there too. Let's go." I shift my grip to her arm to march her out, wanting her safely inside the house.

"What's your problem? Why are you being like this?" She tries to pull free, but I lift her into the backseat of the SUV. Odin closes his hand over my arm, and I turn to him, surprised.

"Don't hurt her."

"I'm not hurting her." I face him, blocking Madelena's exit with my body. "I'm trying to get her home where I can ensure her safety. Go."

He steps toward me like he's looking for a fight, which would be idiotic on his part, but I think I'll engage. Why the fuck not?

"I and only I will decide how I keep my wife safe. Now go before I beat your ass."

"Don't touch him!" Madelena says from behind me, hands on my shoulders.

"Walk away, Odin," I tell him.

"Go, Odin. I'll call you," she says.

Odin glances at his sister.

"You heard her," I say.

"Odin, please," Madelena says to which he reluctantly responds, giving me one final glare before turning and walking away. "Fucking bully," she mutters once I climb into the SUV.

I close my hand over her thigh, squeeze. "Like I told him, and I've told you enough times, you should know it by now: I'll do whatever I need to do to keep you safe." One of my men closes my door and we're off. Madelena folds her arms across her chest and keeps her gaze out the window.

I'll wait until we're home to talk to her. Besides, my mind is busy trying to connect all the goddamned dots. But once we're in the house, Madelena walks up the stairs without looking back. I follow her into our bedroom and close the door.

"You okay?" I ask her, watching her slip off her shoes and draw the blankets back. I think she's going to ignore me, but she drops the blanket, shakes her head, and stalks across the room to stand nose-to-nose with me.

"I want the Santos back from yesterday. From the days before. I don't like being here in Avarice with you. You're different when you're here. You turn into a fucking bully, and I've dealt with enough of those in my life that I don't need another one! I won't have it!"

She spins on her heel to walk away but I capture her arm and stop her. She sets her hands against my chest to keep distance between us.

"You asked me what my problem was, so I'll tell you what it is. I'm a husband trying to protect his wife. If you think that's bullying, so be it. You're mine, Madelena. I brought you into my world, a world you don't know. And when it comes to your safety, I will make the decisions because I am the one out of the two of us equipped to do so."

"Whether I like it or not?"

"Whether you like it or not."

"See that's the thing. You did bring me into your world. You forced me into it. Why couldn't you just leave me alone? Just let me live my life without you?"

Her words hit their mark. They wound, but they also infuriate. "You want a life without me?" I tug her closer. "Is that how shallow your words are? Because I didn't think love worked that way."

"Let me go."

"Am I wrong? Does telling someone you love them mean nothing to you? Are those words just lip service? Empty and meaningless? Tell me. I'm fucking dying to know."

"I'm tired, Santos."

"Yeah, I think you are. But we're in this together now, Little Kitty. You're mine, and whether you like it or not, I'm yours."

"Whether I like it or not. Again."

"Correct."

"Go to hell, Santos."

She tries to pull free, but I tug her to me. "When I make a promise, Madelena, it means something. I thought you knew that. Or did you forget?"

I walk her backward to the bed, spin her around and hold both of her wrists in one of my hands at her back. I tug them down, forcing her shoulders back.

When I bring my mouth to her ear, she turns her face toward me, her breathing shallow. Being this close does to her exactly what it does to me, and the wild beating of the pulse at her neck tells me this moment is no exception.

"Do you need a reminder?" I ask in a low whisper.

She shudders.

I slide my hand along her inner thigh, up under her skirt and into her panties. From behind, my fingers tickle the cleft of her ass, tips of my longest fingers closing over her clit, my thumb rubbing her asshole.

Her breath trembles.

"You're wet." I press my cock against her back as I play with her. "I know the marriage vow was forced, but the words 'I love you' were not. Don't tell me you already forgot having said them." I push my thumb into her asshole, circle four fingers over her swollen clit, and listen to her moan with pleasure.

I smile.

"You're mine, Madelena." I bend her over the bed, release her wrists, and draw my hand out of her panties.

She makes a sound of protest as I push her skirt up and her panties down.

"Don't worry, sweetheart. I'm going to show you what it means to be mine."

I undo my belt, my slacks, freeing my cock and push into her in one hard thrust that makes her grunt. "Mine." I draw back, slide one finger into her tight ass, watching myself fuck her as she fists handfuls of the blankets.

I take her hard and deep, and it's not to make her come. She doesn't deserve to come. It's to make sure she knows who she belongs to and that words carry weight with me.

"You and I belong to each other now. For better or for worse. Until death do us part. And I mean every word of that."

"Santos," she starts, arching her back.

"You want to come?" I ask before closing my teeth over the curve of her neck.

She nods hard.

"Do you deserve to come?"

She looks back at me. "Please," she mutters, arching into my cock, my finger, her muscles tight around both. I curse myself because I can't fucking resist her. When I slide my free hand to her clit, she cries out, her knees buckling. Her body squeezes around me, throbbing, forcing my release as I drape myself over her and empty into her tight heat.

We're both panting when I pull out to flip her onto her back. I search her face, kiss her, watching her eyes as she looks into mine.

"I can't be without you anymore. You know that, don't you?" I ask.

She kisses me, then lets her head fall back as her mouth opens on a pant. I kiss her exposed throat, take her lower lip into my mouth and bite just hard enough to make her look at me again.

"Tell me you know that."

"I do. I know." She smiles, eyelids heavy.

I smile too. Everything I said is true, is right. She belongs to me as much as I belong to her. And I will destroy anyone who tries to hurt her—who tries to take her from me.

25

MADELENA

The next few weeks pass quietly. It's strange, and I'm afraid to settle into the peace or to let my guard down, but things are good between Santos and me. We've seen his family a few times, but I get the feeling Santos is avoiding them as much as I always have. He won't talk about why, but I know something has come up with Alexia's murder that he doesn't like. I heard him discussing it with Val one night. But that's not all. There's something else that's weighing on him, and it has to do with Caius.

Santos sits watching me at the dining room table as I polish off the last bite of my second slice of lasagna, leftovers from the night before. He shakes his head, checks his watch and turns to me.

"Where do you put it?" he asks with a smile.

"Are you saying I eat a lot?" I ask, picking up my glass of water and drinking it before sitting back and rubbing my stomach.

"You can put it away for being so small."

I flip him off.

He winks, then gets up and comes to me. Cupping the back of my head, he plants a kiss on my forehead. "We should go if you want to meet Odin in time. Unless you'd like another slice, of course."

"Ha-ha." I push back from the table. We're meeting Odin at Uncle Jax's house. It will be the first time I set foot inside since his death. The day is bright and sunny and although still cool, I swear I smell the promise of spring. It's my favorite time of year, especially after winters in Avarice, which seem unending. Spring is hopeful. It's a fresh start.

Val and another soldier accompany us in the SUV, and two others follow in a separate vehicle. Santos is always armed and always seems to be scanning the area, wherever we are and no matter how many men are with us. Since the day Bea Avery let him know she had someone following me, nothing has happened, and the few times we have been at Augustine's, no members of the Avery family have been present.

I weigh the key to Uncle Jax's house in the palm of my hand. Well, it's not Uncle Jax's anymore. It's my house now.

"Ready?" Santos asks as we turn onto what feels like a miles-long driveway.

"Yep," I say, although I'm not sure I will ever be ready. But Uncle Jax left me the house to be sure I was looked after, and I am grateful for that. For him.

Odin is leaning against his car when we reach the

front entrance. I climb out of the SUV when we park, and he comes to me.

"Hey Maddy," he says with a hug. He glances at the empty house. He is as anxious as I am. I can see it on his face, hear it in his voice.

"Are we late?"

"Nah. I just got here early."

Santos greets him with a nod, and Odin does the same. Since the day at Mr. Jamison's office, the two of them only talk in grunts at best. I like that Odin stands up to Santos, though. Santos is easily twice as big as my brother, but Odin isn't cowed, and I think Santos respects that.

I roll my eyes at them anyway and head up to the door, the key heavy in my clammy hand as I slide it into the lock. I feel nauseous. Anxious. It's strange being here. I take a deep breath in and turn the key, and the instant I open the door, the alarm starts its warning beep. I take one of the sheets of paper Mr. Jamison gave me and punch in the code to silence it.

After a breath, I turn and take in the sprawling ranch style house that was a haven to me for years. It spans a generous portion of an acre of land with a wall of windows at the back. I remember how the outdoor pool would glisten in the summer. You could see it from every angle of the open floor plan, but it's been drained now. I assume and hope the indoor pool, the one he drowned in, has also been drained. That's one room I'm not sure I'll be able to go into.

"It smells the same," Odin says beside me. He's taking it all in, just like I am.

I nod because he's right even though the house has mostly been closed up for years. Mr. Jamison had arranged for its upkeep and monthly cleaning, but no one has lived here since Uncle Jax's death. I'd always wondered why Dad didn't sell it. I'd never realized he couldn't.

Odin and I walk together through the house. After a quick look around, Santos remains in the living room, but he sends two men with us as we stroll through memories. Everything is exactly the same. The photos on the walls. The record collection he cherished, along with the various record players themselves. He would only use them on special occasions, but it was one of his passions. He was a collector.

"I'm going to the library," I tell Odin. It was my favorite place. He nods, caught up in his own memories, and I walk down the hall toward the library. Just beyond it are the bedrooms. I won't go there just yet, though.

This is nothing like the Augustines' library. The house itself is more of a 70s style, but I always loved the library mostly because every book that was in it had been hand selected by Uncle Jax or Mom. Each one was read and loved, and I must have spent hours in here and read half the library.

I push the curtains open. Sunlight makes diamond specks out of dust motes floating in the air. On the side table by Uncle Jax's favorite chair is a thriller I recognize that makes me stop, makes me miss him again. He was reading it before he died. He was halfway through, and I remember how he'd told me just a few nights before his death he thought he had the mystery figured out but wasn't sure.

Picking it up, I check the page. I wonder if he'd guessed right. I memorize the page number and close the book to take it home with me. I'll read it tonight.

At the back of the library is a hidden door that is the entrance to Jax's office. I only know it because I spent so much time here growing up and caught him going in or coming out once or twice. He was always very private about his home office, uncharacteristically so. Rarely have I been inside it. When I was little, he made a game of it and called it his secret hiding place I couldn't tell anyone about.

Behind a small panel made to look like the spines of books is the electronic lock for the door. From the same sheet of paper the house alarm code was on, I punch in the one to unlock the door. I hear a buzz, then a click, and the secret door pops open.

"What's that?" Santos asks, making me jump and apologizing when he sees he has startled me. "Okay?"

"I'm fine. Just lost in thoughts I guess."

"What is that?" He looks beyond me into the dark room.

"It's Uncle Jax's home office," I say.

He nods and when I enter he follows me in. I flip the overhead light on because this room has no windows. I always found that strange, but Uncle Jax said it helped him to stay focused. There is an oversized desk. It's neither an antique nor is it pretty, just functional. Along the shelves on the walls are some books about business, but mostly it's boxes. One of them sits open on top of Jax's desk. I realize there's nowhere to sit except the big chair behind the behemoth.

Santos is busy looking at a photograph. I take the chair and sit down. His computer had been state of the art six years ago, but now it looks obsolete. On top of the desk are a few file folders, and I peer inside them to find they're work documents.

Santos looks into the box on the desk and flips through a few of the folders. I watch as he reads one, his forehead furrowing. He flips to another page.

"What is it?"

"Financials from eight years ago." He puts it away and glances at another one but loses interest quickly. "I guess he didn't have company in here."

"No, never. We weren't even allowed in. I'm pretty sure he kept its existence a secret."

He walks around the desk and notices the locks on the drawers. "Any idea what's in there?"

"We'll find out." I unlock one of the two drawers. They're deep and contain hanging folders.

Santos comes closer, leans over to have a look at the tabs. He shifts his gaze to me, and I know why. The folders are marked with names. Some I recognize, most I don't.

But there's one that catches my eye. That has me

feeling that nausea again. I glance up at Santos, then back to it. This folder has my father's name on the tab.

"You sure you want to look at these files, Madelena?" Santos asks.

My eyes are locked on that folder. I don't answer Santos. Instead, I reach to pull it out. But before I can, he sets his hand over mine.

"Your uncle is dead and gone. He won't be able to explain what you find in there, and it may be upsetting."

"I need to do this."

"Do you want me to look through it first?"

"I'm not sure you should be looking through anything at all," Odin says to Santos from the doorway. "Our uncle was a very private man."

"I mean no harm. Madelena knows that."

Odin ignores him. "What is it?" he asks me.

I put the folder on the desk, so Odin sees the tab too. Santos's phone rings and he excuses himself, leaving Odin and I alone.

"We don't know what's in here, Maddy," he says, glancing at the door where we can hear Santos answer the call. "You and I should look at it first before anyone else sees."

"You can trust him. I do." I realize as I say it that it's true.

Odin studies me but doesn't say anything. Instead, he flips the folder open, and we read. I see Odin's face pale in my peripheral vision and feel the blood drain from my own. I think about what Santos just said. Even as I turn the page over, my hand trembling, the temperature in the room seems to drop. Because I understand what the folders contain. What Santos once told me about Uncle Jax, about what he'd done, is all right here, in more detail than Santos had shared, than I'd wanted him to share, with full-color photos to back it up.

"Odin," I mutter.

I finish reading before Odin does and put my hand to my forehead to feel the sheen of sweat there.

Odin's eyes are wide as he closes the folder. "Jesus," he says, wrapping a hand around the back of his neck. "Jesus Christ." He looks at me.

"This is it. The thing that connects everything. It's why it all happened."

"Revenge. It's all because of what our father did."

I get to my feet, holding on to the edge of the desk to steady myself.

"Are you okay, Maddy?"

"I'm going to be sick," I say and run from the room into the small, attached bathroom, just making it to the toilet before I throw up.

26

SANTOS

"What do you mean, she just left there?" I ask Val.

"You asked me to have them followed, remember?" Val asks me.

I do remember giving the order to have Caius and my mother both followed. I'd done it after finding the familiar stone on the catwalk when I'd suspected my brother of being up there. I'd never called them off. It had slipped my mind.

"Yeah, I remember," I sigh. "Tell me again."

"Your mother just left Dr. Fairweather's office. I thought you should know, considering."

"You're sure?"

"I'm sure. Could he be your mother's doctor?"

"I don't know." Will this be another coincidence? "Where is she now?"

"Looks like she's headed home."

"Let me know when she's there. And station

someone at the doctor's office. Keep an eye on his movements until I say otherwise." I disconnect and walk back into Jax's office to find Madelena gone and Odin standing at the door of the bathroom. "What is it?" I rush to the bathroom, shoving him out of the way just as Madelena reaches up from her kneeling position on the floor to flush the toilet. She sits back, wiping her mouth with the back of her hand and looking deathly pale. "What happened?" I crouch down to help her up.

She pushes me away once she's at the sink and bends to rinse her mouth then washes her hands and splashes water on her face.

"Madelena?"

"I just need a minute." She glances at Odin, who is standing behind me. He walks back into the office.

Beads of sweat dot her forehead, the skin around her eyes pink. Whatever she saw in that folder has upset her.

"Can we go?" she asks.

I nod, wrap an arm around her waist and when I walk into the office, I see Odin tucking a folder back into the drawer. I can guess which one. He looks up.

"You okay?" he asks her.

"I'm going to go home, actually. I don't feel good."

"I want to stay a while. Look through a few more things."

"Are you sure?" she asks.

"Yeah. I'll lock up when I'm done."

She nods. "All the keys and codes are in there." She

points to the envelope. "I'll call you later." She turns to me, and I walk her out of that office. "Have two men stay here with her brother," I tell one of the soldiers. I lead Madelena to the SUV and help her in. She's silent on the drive to the house, her forehead lined with worry. When we get there, we go upstairs to the bedroom, where she draws the covers back and sits on the edge of the bed.

"Do you want me to call a doctor?"

"No. I'll be fine. I just... It was a lot."

I study her. "What was it exactly?"

It takes her a minute to look at me and even longer to speak. "The blackmail... What he had on Dad."

I raise my eyebrows. "He had a physical file with details?"

"I understand why your father was obsessed with mine now. My uncle knew, too. He had a report. And... photographs."

"Shit." I didn't realize there were photographs. But fuck, he kept physical files?

This isn't how she should have found out. Her father is a monster, yes. So was mine, in a different way.

So am I, for the things I've done.

Her uncle, like my father, was a collector of information. I've said it before, and I'll say it again. No man can hold so much power and have his hands remain perfectly clean. It's impossible.

The Augustine family has lived in Avarice for a while, but we're not founding families like the De León or Donovan families—and certainly not in the same class. We only grew our wealth to where it is now with my father at the helm. Before that, the Augustines served the De Léons of this world.

My aunt had the misfortune of catching Marnix De Léon's eye—Marnix De Léon, and his friends. They, much like the Commander, don't take kindly to the word no, and back then, there wasn't a whole lot a lowly Augustine could do against a legion of De Léons.

But we Augustines have long memories, and we are a patient lot. We wait. We keep watch. Because in time, everyone trips up. Each of those men have been dealt with, but at the helm of that ship was Marnix De Léon. He took a little longer to stumble, but stumble he did. Now, because of that, because of him, we own their world—a world that does not belong to us, one that we took from them. Just like they took what did not belong to them from my father's sister.

But saying that everything we've done was to avenge my aunt is a generous way to look at things. It casts us in a noble light. Almost. I'm not sure an Augustine can ever be truly noble.

I sometimes wonder what my father's plan was. Was it to wipe out Avarice altogether? To erase the elite of the town? What it's become is something else. Intentions and motivations get confused over time, morph into obsession. And obsession is a whole other animal.

What is my plan, my goal? Now that my father is gone and Marnix De Léon has been punished, those men have been punished, what do I want? What happens after the vengeance?

I study Madelena, take in her dark, somber beauty, her fragility. I am not obsessed with Avarice or its people. I don't care about their existence or their destruction. My obsession is wholly different.

"You shouldn't have found out those details," I tell her.

"I wish you'd told me."

"No, you don't. There are some things better left alone."

She looks up at me. "You were right about him."

"It doesn't make a difference, Madelena. Your time with him, your memories of him, they're separate things. They're clean."

"How is that?"

I go to her, take her hands. "Jax Donovan, at least in the short time I knew him, wasn't a wicked man. He was ruthless when it came to his enemies. Anyone in his position would have to be. And he protected those he loved fiercely, as best as he could."

She pulls her hands out of mine and rubs her face, her eyes, oblivious or uncaring about the smeared liner.

"Lie down, sweetheart."

She does, and I lean down to kiss her forehead, her mouth. She touches my cheek, prolonging our kiss. When I draw back, I brush a strand of dark hair from her face and look at her.

Her uncle kept her safe. He protected her from the

darkness of his world, kept her separate from it. Have I done half as much?

I take her hand, turn it over to look at the scar on her palm.

The mark I put there.

I trace it.

She turns her hand around to hold mine, and I meet her eyes.

As Avarice and the destruction of it and its people were the obsession of my father, so is Madelena my obsession. There is a weight deep in my gut at the thought of her, the sight of her. I will ensure she survives this, survives my family. Me.

But even so, her innocence is gone, stolen by monsters. I will keep her safe now, but the damage done before me I cannot erase. In a way, it was her destiny for the simple fact that she was born to Marnix De Léon. I am a part of that destiny, our combined fates sealed. For better or worse. Until death do us part.

"I want to be alone for a little bit," she says. I open my mouth to protest but she puts a finger to my lips. "I'm tired."

Reluctantly, I nod and she closes her eyes. I watch a tear slide down over her temple and it takes all I have to turn and walk out of the bedroom and not climb into that bed to hold her, to wipe away her tears and battle her demons.

As I'm on my way down the stairs, my phone buzzes with a message. I pause to read it. It's Val telling me my mother is home. I glance up the stairs to our bedroom door. Can man beat destiny?

Shaking my head, I continue down the stairs and go out the front door, taking no men with me. I drive to Augustine's. It's one of those drives where you're not quite sure how you got there once you arrive but my mood shifts, darkening upon arrival. I have a bad feeling about what's coming.

I climb out, hand the keys to a valet and head into the building, onto the private elevator that will lead to the top floor. A soldier is stationed at the door to the apartment where Caius and my mother are living. He nods, knocks on the door and, without waiting for a reply, he opens it and steps aside.

I walk in to find the living room empty.

"Mom?" I call out, walking toward her bedroom.

"Santos? Is that you?" she asks from the study. I walk in to find her sitting behind the desk. "What are you doing here?"

I close the door and look at her. I can't read my mother. I've never been able to read her, apart from that day she confessed about Caius—the moment when I saw her fear, her shame.

I know what you did, and this is your punishment.

The sentence read aloud by the executor of Dad's will repeats in my head except that I hear my father say the words this time. Did he know about Caius? He wouldn't punish Mom for what the Commander did to her when she was no more than a girl, though. My father was fair.

But if he learned the truth himself, if he thought she'd lied to him... that he would punish. He couldn't tolerate lies. Betrayals. He had no mercy for liars and traitors.

I shake my head to clear the thoughts and focus my gaze on her, on now.

"What were you doing at Dr. Fairweather's office?" I ask outright.

If she's surprised that I know, it doesn't show on her face. But there is a moment of silence before she leans back in her chair and tilts her head.

"Phase two," she says flatly.

It takes me a minute. I guess I expect her to deny her presence there. Or, no, she wouldn't do that. She's too smart for that. I expect her to tell me Fairweather is her doctor and ask me what business it is of mine— because that's what I want this to be. A coincidence. Not a malicious act committed against me or my wife by my mother. Not a betrayal.

"How long have you been having me followed?" she asks.

"Elaborate on phase two," I say, not bothering to answer her question.

"Lawrence, Dr. Cummings," she clarifies. "He knows Fairweather. It's a small town."

"And?"

"They were having a drink and Fairweather apparently mentioned the house to him. Said he was looking forward to seeing the renovations your father made."

The door opens behind me, but I don't turn. My mom's gaze moves momentarily over my shoulder.

"What's this?" Caius asks.

"Continue," I tell my mother.

"I was just asking your brother how long he's been having me followed," she tells Caius, who moves to stand against the wall so he's in my line of vision.

"Mother," I press.

"Like I said, it's a small town. So, when Fairweather mentioned his upcoming visit and the purpose of it, well, Lawrence was confused. He had assumed he was your wife's doctor, not this Fairweather. But apparently you didn't trust him."

I glance to Caius who has his arms folded over his chest, feet crossed at the ankles, watching us. The bracelet on his wrist catches my eye before I turn back to our mother.

"What happened to phase two, Santos?" she asks.

"What happened to patient-doctor confidentiality, Mother?"

She snorts, stands to walk over to the side table containing various bottles of vodka and whiskey on a silver tray. She pours herself a drink and turns to face me.

"You know that bullshit doesn't apply to us."

I stop, just hearing something she said. "Cummings saw Fairweather before Fairweather came to the house?"

She studies me for a very long minute. "What happened to phase two? Because a birth control shot was certainly not going to get your wife pregnant, was it?"

"Was?"

She blinks, drinks the rest of the vodka in her glass and stands taller when she faces me again. "*Was.* How is your wife feeling these days? Any happy news for us? You two did have that second honeymoon, another secret you kept, so tell us, does the happy couple have news of an impending birth?"

Was.

My stomach drops out as I process the word. Its meaning.

Cummings knew what I'd talked to Fairweather about. He knew and interceded.

I stand, my stomach tight, my hands fists at my sides. "What did you do, Mother?"

She swallows, turns to pour herself a second vodka and drinks it before facing me gain. I creep toward her. "What did you do?"

"I made sure we stayed on track for phase two, that's what."

My hand is around her throat before I can register the movement. I'm so angry, I don't think. I can't. I can barely breathe. Her eyes go wide, and her glass drops to the floor, but in an instant, Caius is pulling me off. Or trying to. He's yelling at me to let her go, but his voice is a far-away echo because *fuck! Fuck! Fuck! Fuck!*

Madelena's appetite of late. The few mornings she's not felt well, although those bursts passed so quickly neither of us gave it any thought. Today, throwing up like she was, was it because of what she'd learned? Or was it because my mother had interfered? Because the birth control shot wasn't one at all.

"What have you done?"

Caius tears me away from her and shoves me across the room.

"Mom. Get out," Caius tells her.

"I won't—" she starts, but he cuts her off.

"Get out!" he orders her, gripping me by the collar as I stalk toward her.

"I told you… Fuck! I told you I would do this in my time. Mine. Not yours. Not my brother's. Mine. How dare you? How dare you?"

"How dare I?" she asks. She's half-in, half-out of the door. It's taking all Caius has to hold me back. If he releases me, I'm not sure what I'll do. "How dare *you* choose the spawn of the man who raped your father's sister, who passed her around to his friends to be raped by each and every one of them, over your own family?" she spits, eyes ablaze, ugly now. Hateful. Vengeful.

"Brother, calm down," Caius tries. "Mom. Get the hell out of here!"

"You choose her again, now. Over us!" my mother hisses.

"Get out!" Caius roars, and she runs just as I get free of my brother. He's closer to the door though and slams it shut, blocking my path.

"Get out of my way. Get the fuck out of my way!" I order.

"What are you going to do? Kill your own mother?" he asks.

I take another step before his words penetrate my skull. Then stop. I push my hands into my hair, pulling at it, because what the fuck am I going to do?

Madelena's breasts have felt fuller. We were joking about how much she can eat just this afternoon. God. I'm a fucking idiot. Is she pregnant? Is Madelena pregnant?

I spin and wrap my hand around my brother's throat. I hold him against the door. "Did you know?"

"No. Fuck, no." He pulls me off. We battle as I try to get my hands around his throat, and he fights to keep me off.

"Are you fucking sure?" I ask.

"Don't you already know? You think I haven't noticed I'm being followed too?"

I turn my head to shake it, but my gaze catches on something. During our struggle, the sleeve of his sweater got pushed up, and I can see the bracelet, see the clasp that keeps it closed.

I stop as soon as I do, confused.

Caius's resistance vanishes and I glance at him, then back down. I take hold of his arm, push the sweater away and hold my arm against his. I compare the bracelets. The clasps are different.

The clasps are fucking different.

"I'm going to go after Mom. You go somewhere and cool the fuck off," Caius says, but I don't let go of his arm.

"It's different," I say.

He raises his eyebrows, looking irritated and confused at once. "What's different?"

"This isn't the bracelet I gave you."

He looks down at it, then back at me. "Are we back to that?"

"Was it you? Were you up there on the catwalk? Did you push Thiago?"

He snorts, shakes his head, the look in his eyes that of a man betrayed. "I had it repaired after the climb a few years ago. I broke it. Fucking searched for an hour for all the beads. I didn't think about what kind of clasp the jeweler was putting on it. Didn't think it mattered. Had I known you'd accuse me of murder, I'd have paid more attention. Asked for a fucking receipt." He shoves me away. "You know what, fuck you. Fuck you, Santos. Mom's right. You've forgotten what side you're on. Why we're doing this. You got lost in that girl years ago, you know that? Before you even bedded her, you were under her spell. I knew it from day one. I knew it from the way you looked at her. Another Alexia, a second chance. You're a fucking idiot, Brother. Get the fuck out of here, and if you fucking touch a hair on our mother's head, I swear, I will make your wife pay. Like for like."

I slam my hands against his chest and shove him against the wall. "You go near her, never mind touching her—you go near her, and I'll fucking tear you limb from limb. You hear me? I'll fucking kill you,

Caius. Mark my words. I will kill you. Stay away from my wife. Stay away from us. This is over."

I shove him out of the way and stalk out of that apartment, that building. As dark clouds swallow up the bright blue of this once-promising day, I walk, and I walk because I've failed Madelena... and I've lost my family.

27

SANTOS

I drive myself in a rage-filled fog to Fairweather's office. Val meets me there, and we head in along with one more soldier. The receptionist looks up from her place behind a desk that spans almost the length of the wall, alarm registering immediately in her eyes. Two women seated in the waiting area glance at us from their magazines.

"Can I help you?" the receptionist asks, looking from me to Val and back.

"Fairweather. Where is he?"

"Um, he's with a patient. Do you..." I think she's going to ask me if I have an appointment but since it's obvious I don't have a vagina, why would I? Fairweather is a gynecologist.

I raise my eyebrows and she clears her throat.

"Where is he?"

"Room 1." She points down a hall, where I can see four doors. Two are numbered, one has Fairweather's name on it and the other, the only one without a door, looks to be a nurse's station. "But he's with a patient. You can't go in."

"You're going to need to cancel his other appointments," I tell her after a glance at the waiting women. "Probably for the week. I'll wait in his office. Is there another exit?" I ask as the women who were seated quietly get to their feet and head toward the door without having to be asked.

"Through there." She points.

I gesture to the soldier to go to that exit. "Pack up. Day's over," I tell the woman.

Val hovers in the waiting area as the receptionist gets ready to leave. I walk into the doctor's office and have a look around. It's my second time here. I met with him regarding Madelena's birth control. It's a nice office with decent furnishings, clean and orderly. He does well for himself and lives with his wife in a McMansion but doesn't serve the elite of the town. It's why I'd chosen him, thinking it was my safest bet for privacy.

I take off my jacket and walk behind Fairweather's desk to read the diplomas hanging there. He'd graduated with honors from a prestigious university. Good for him.

Draping my jacket over the back of a chair, I go to the window to take in the parking lot as I roll up my shirt sleeves.

Movement in the hallway alerts me that the good doctor is finished with his exam. I hear a woman's voice, a door closing, then someone stumbling. A moment later, the office door opens, and Val gives Fairweather a shove inside. Val follows him in, closes the door and stands with his arms folded across his chest at the exit.

Fairweather pales when he sees me and sends a panicked glance behind himself, then faces me again.

"Mr. Augustine. I didn't expect to see you." He tries for a faltering smile.

"No, I guess you didn't. Lucky you, two Augustines in one day. My mother was here earlier."

"Oh. Yes. She's, uh, a new patient."

"Is she?"

He swallows, holds onto the back of one of the chairs set in front of his desk.

"What did you inject my wife with?"

He opens his mouth, stutters. I go to him, grab him by the back of his head, and push him into a seat. I tug on his hair to pull his head back, so he looks up at me.

"Dr. Fairweather, what did you give my wife?"

"Nothing that would hurt her. I swear."

I smile, then let him go. "Stand up."

"I swear. It was nothing that would hurt her. I swear!"

"Hard of hearing, this one," I say to Val who comes over, grabs Fairweather by the shoulders and pulls him up to his feet. He's about my height, not quite my build and soft in the middle, but that's not my problem. I draw my arm back and punch him in the gut. He wheezes, doubles over, stumbling backward and knocking the chair on its side.

"Sit," I tell him as Val rights his chair.

He tries, I'll give him that. I nod to Val who, with one hand on his shoulder, plants him back in the chair.

"What. Did. You. Give. My. Wife?"

"A... fer... fertility injection."

My world goes sideways. My brain literally slams up against my skull and makes the world fucking tilt on its axis.

"Up," I tell him, somehow managing to sound calm.

He shakes his head, holding his hands up in surrender but again, Val assists him, and I land a second hit to his gut. I call out his name and he looks up at me and when he does, I punch him. His head snaps back and again, he stumbles backward. This time, he falls on top of the chair, getting his legs tangled with it.

"Up."

He stutters something as Val hauls him up, rights the chair, and sits him down.

"On whose order? Cummings or my mother?"

He opens his mouth, pushing a tooth out into the palm of his hand. He looks horrified, and I don't mention that I haven't gotten started yet. This one won't get a line carved into my skin when I'm done with him. This one is guilty as hell.

I lean down, fist his hair, and tug his head backward. He whimpers, holds his hands up, tears streaming down his face.

"Please," he begs.

"Cummings or my mother?" Because if Cummings ordered it, he's a dead man.

He shakes his head. Well, he tries to. He blubbers and Val, ever helpful, walks over to the small, glass front refrigerator and brings him a bottle of water, even opening it for him. I let go of his hair and he drinks a sip, spilling some down his chin and shirt front.

I lean against his desk and watch the son of a bitch. "I'll ask once more, then I'll get down to business. Cummings or my mother?"

"Your mother. Cummings... He... I told him I was going to see the house. I've always loved that house." He begins weeping, and it's fucking pathetic. "Mrs. Augustine, she said... she said..." He shakes his head.

"How much did you get paid?"

At that, he stops his sobbing and looks up at me, real worry making him look older.

I raise my eyebrows. "I hate repeating myself."

"Ten thousand dollars."

I whistle. "Let me ask you something. Do you need that money? Because if I look around, you seem to be doing all right. Your house is nice enough. Is it the wife? Does she like expensive things?"

He just sobs like a pathetic coward.

"You don't have kids. A sick sibling maybe? Older parents? Nothing I found when I looked into who you were. So why did you need that money?"

"I just... I'm sorry, Mr. Augustine. I'm sorry."

"Tell me why you needed that money."

"I... I..."

"You want me to tell you? Would that be easier? All right. It's the same fucking thing everyone in this aptly named godforsaken town is obsessed with. You're no different. That was my fault. I should have gone out of Avarice."

"Please, I—"

I cut him off and continue, "Greed, Dr. Fairweather. Greed. That's why you took the money, and you did something that will irrevocably change a young woman's life." I gesture to Val, who stands him up one more time. "A young woman I happen to care about. And so, now, you pay. And I'm going to extract every single cent of that ten grand and then some, you mother fucking bastard."

28

MADELENA

It's late when Santos finally gets home. I go to him as he and Val walk in. Val gives me a nod and disappears. Santos's forehead is creased with worry, his eyes dark. But when I see the splatters of red on his shirt, I stop.

"Santos?"

He closes the space between us. I take his hands, ignore the brown paper bag he's holding and look at his swollen, red knuckles, the blood on his cuffs.

"What happened? Where were you?"

"Come, Madelena." He shifts a hand to my lower back in an effort to guide me toward the stairs.

"Why are you bloody?"

"Upstairs. Let's go."

I study his eyes, the green dark like a forest in shadows. I let him lead me upstairs. Once we're in the bedroom and the door is closed, he takes my hands and looks at me with something I don't see often in him. Something like remorse.

"What is it? Whose blood is that?"

"Fairweather."

"Dr. Fairweather? Why?"

He takes a deep breath in, sighs his exhale, and takes what's inside the bag out.

I stare at it. Close my eyes. Open them. Because that can't be what I think it is. I look up at him. "Santos?"

"Take it," he says.

"No." I move backward a step.

He follows me. "Take it, Madelena. We need to know for sure."

I shake my head. "It's not possible. He gave me a birth control shot. There's no way."

But as I scan the specks of deep red and the splatter on his jaw, too, I think maybe there is a way. Maybe.

"No," I say, the word sounding like a plea.

"Apparently he's friends with Dr. Cummings, who is with my mother."

"With your mother?"

"Dating. I guess that's what you call it. I don't fucking know."

"I don't understand."

"He told Cummings he was going to come over here. He was excited to see the house. Cummings relayed the information to my mother, and she paid Fairweather a visit. What he gave you wasn't birth control."

"What?" I stumble over the words I'm hearing as my brain highlights all the signs pointing to what I don't want to know. To see. The nausea, light but consistent. The swollen breasts, their increased sensitivity. My appetite. But I shake my head again in denial. "He gave me the shot. You were here. You saw him do it."

"It was a fertility injection."

"Wh..." My throat is too dry to finish.

"Take the test, Madelena. Then we'll know for sure."

"Then what? What if I'm... What if I'm pregnant? Oh, God." I drop to the edge of the bed.

Santos comes to sit beside me. He takes one of my hands in both of his. "Then we'll deal with it."

"Deal how?"

"Just take the test. Please. Maybe it's negative."

It won't be. I know it as surely as I know my name. But I take the package from him, and he stands as I cross the room to the bathroom. I go in and close the door because I want to do this alone. I have to.

The instructions are simple: pee on the stick. One line means I'm not pregnant. Two means I am. A happy woman is pictured looking at her test. They don't show the result she's seeing though. I peel the first of two tests out of its package and sit on the toilet. I'm shaking as I pee, my heart pounding when I hold the test in the flow. When I'm finished, I set it on top of the box, and I don't look at it as I wash my hands. I don't look as I dry them. Instead, I perch at the edge of the tub and think.

We'll deal with it, he said. I pull my sweater sleeves down into my palms and bite on a fingernail.

Deal with it.

I'm not supposed to get pregnant. I've always made sure I never would, no matter what happened. Not that I was sexually active, but I wasn't taking any chances. How will I *deal with it* if it's two lines?

I get up, walk out of the bathroom and past Santos who hasn't moved. I don't look at the test. He walks into the bathroom and returns a moment later. He comes to where I'm standing at the window looking out over the backyard. It's a huge property with a swimming pool that is covered over, dead leaves weighing down the tarp. Can't have a pool without a gate around it with a toddler running around, I think, still nibbling on that fingernail. And farther back, the wooded area. How big is it? How much acreage? A child could get lost. This house is too dangerous for a child. This whole world is.

"We'll do what you want," Santos says, pulling me to him.

I don't look at him, and I don't need to ask him the result. I just bury my face in his chest and let him hold me. I don't even cry. I can't.

"I don't understand why your mother would want this," I say into his chest. "You have me. You have control of my father's company. You practically own Avarice." I draw back. "A child makes no difference, not in any way. I don't understand why she would do this."

He holds my face, wipes his thumbs over my cheeks. I guess I was crying after all. He pulls me to him again and rests his chin on top of my head. "I don't know, Madelena. But you don't need to worry about that. We'll take care of it. If you want that."

I turn my head, so my ear is to his chest. His heart is beating fast. I listen to the thud of it. He's so strong. Strong enough for us both. For all three of us. The image of the other baby he lost comes to mind, the blurry sonogram image. I look up at him and he looks down at me.

"Would you have kept Alexia's baby? I mean, you were so young, both of you. Would you have kept it?"

He nods without hesitation and looks as if he's almost confused by the question. As if he or they hadn't considered the alternative at all.

I pull back and study his face. "Does it do something for you if I'm pregnant? Something I don't know?"

"What do you mean?"

"Do you have something to gain if I'm pregnant?"

"Of course not," he says, pulling back. "I didn't want this for you. I wouldn't have done this. Not like this."

"Is Dr. Fairweather alive?"

He nods once.

"That's his blood."

Another nod.

"How did you find out?" I ask, looking at those stains. He beat Fairweather. He didn't want this. I have to trust that. Trust him.

"I was having my mother followed."

"What?"

"She paid Fairweather a visit, and when I confronted her, she told me what she'd done. That's how I found out, Madelena. So, no, I didn't know, and I didn't plan this for you. So if that's where your head is going, stop now. Understand?" His voice hardens at the end of his speech.

I nod.

"What did I tell you?" he asks, taking me in his arms again, one hand in my hair to draw my head backward just a little. It's not painful, but he is making a point. "You're mine and I'm yours. Say it."

"You're mine and I'm yours," I repeat.

"Do you trust me?"

"I'm pregnant, Santos." To say the words out loud makes this more real somehow.

"Do you trust me?"

I nod. I have to.

"Tell me what you want."

I turn away, take a deep breath in. This isn't a decision I ever wanted to make. In fact, it's exactly why I never wanted to be in this position. I push the heels of my hands into my eyes to stave off stupid, useless tears.

I don't want to hurt my baby, but I'm afraid. I am afraid I will hurt her, just like my mother almost hurt me. Because what if I am like her? What if I'm sick too?

"Come here, sweetheart." He pulls me to him, ignoring my struggles to be free, and holds me so tight all I can do is hold him back, cling to him. Let myself surrender to him. It's a little weight off, at least, that surrender. To have him hold me.

29

SANTOS

I don't see my brother or my mother over the next two weeks. My mother isn't at the apartment, according to Val. It's just Caius there. But I know she'll be back by tomorrow night. She needs to be. She's hosting a special event at Augustine's. She cares too much for appearances to miss it.

I watch Madelena closely. She's quiet, but I'm glad to see her eat at least a little. The nausea that comes on in the mornings is more marked now, or maybe we're more aware of it, although it doesn't seem to trouble her once she eats something. I haven't asked her what she wants, and she hasn't said, but we have an appointment tomorrow to find out how far along she is. I'll learn then what our options are and how long she has to decide.

Today, however, I am headed to Mansfield, Connecticut to see the kid who gave a statement to police regarding Hayes's death. That statement was buried in the file I was able to get my hands on, courtesy of Rick. I've left Val at the house. He's the only one I trust fully to watch over Madelena and have considered sending her up to Hells Bells where no one knows where she is. Because my enemies can get to her. Bea Avery showed me that. And my mother—is she my enemy? Or is she acting for the good of the family as far as she sees it? But why this? Why the pregnancy? It doesn't add value. I'm missing something.

Two soldiers follow in a separate car. I needed to be on my own to think during the three-hour long drive up here. I double check the address I have for Mitch Forest. He's the man who happened to be hiking near where Hayes was the day he was killed. Mitch, who is twenty-five now, would have been around fifteen at the time. He currently lives with his mother in a ranch-style house that looks like it needs updating. He works the early shift at the local grocery store. I've timed my arrival and as I pull up to the curb in front of his house, I see Mitch's old model Jeep turning onto the driveway.

I give him a minute to park. When he looks at the two black SUVs on the street, I climb out. The men in the other vehicle know to stay put inside so as not to scare Mitch.

The driveway is long and leads down a gradual decline toward the unremarkable house. I see a curtain move inside as Mitch walks to the mailbox to grab the mail, never taking his eyes off me as he does. It's a bright, cool day and he's not wearing sunglasses. He squints in the sunshine to see me.

"Mitch?" I ask, extending my hand. "I'm Santos Augustine. Good to meet you."

He looks at it, at my suit and dark glasses, then back at the SUVs before nodding and wiping his hand on his pants before shaking mine. He's in his store uniform.

"I don't think I know you."

"I was a friend of Detective Hayes."

He's quick to recognize the name and his nervous gaze bounces back to the SUVs.

"How did you find me?"

"It wasn't too hard."

He swallows, and I'm pretty sure he can make out the outline of the men inside the second parked vehicle.

"Don't worry about them. Can we go inside? I'd like to ask you a few questions."

"You're a detective?" he asks, but he doesn't think so.

"No." I consider my answer for a minute and decide to go with the truth. "Hayes was investigating the death of someone close to me when he had his accident." I push my hands into my pockets. "It's cold out here. Can we go in?"

"My mom's inside."

I put a hand on his shoulder. "I just have a couple of questions about what you told the police you saw. That's all. Just a few minutes, Mitch. I came a long way to talk to you."

He nods because I am pretty sure he knows I'm not going away. I follow him to the front door, which he opens. He calls out to his mom to tell her he's home. I walk in after him and close the door, taking in the old house with its yellowed lace curtains covering the windows, the furniture looking like it's been here for decades.

"Mitch," an older woman says, coming out of the small kitchen. Her gaze is squarely on me. "Who's this?"

"Santos Augustine, Ms. Forest," I say, walking toward her and extending a hand.

She looks me over from head to toe and doesn't shake my hand. Instead, she glances over her shoulder at her son.

"It's okay, Mom. Mr. Augustine was friends with that man who died."

"Was he?" she asks, gaze back on me. "He had a lot of well-dressed friends, that man."

I'm about to ask what she means when she walks around me. "Five minutes," she tells Mitch.

He nods and I can see he's anxious. "It's okay, Mom, promise."

She gives me one more look before she disappears down a hallway.

I turn to Mitch. "What did she mean about friends?"

He shakes his head and points to the living room, and I follow him in. He sits on the edge of the couch, and I take the armchair. Mitch leans his elbows on his knees and puts his head in his hands. He tries not to look at me directly.

"After that man... Some guys dressed like you came by saying they wanted to make sure I was okay. The trauma and all. They came a couple of times."

"Oh? Do you know who they were?"

Mitch shakes his head. "No, but they didn't seem very nice." I wait. "I'd told the police I saw the man before he went over."

"You mean before he fell?"

He glances at the corridor where his mom disappeared. "He didn't fall."

"What happened?"

"I'm a hiker, and we used to live up there. Still would if it was up to me. I know the area really well. I was hiking along a lesser known path toward the cliff point where he'd been and when I heard them, something told me to stop. Being a hiker on your own, you listen to your instincts, you know?"

"Mhm, go on."

"He wasn't alone like they said in the news. There were two other men there. Came out of nowhere when that guy was looking out over the view. Just taking it in. He saw them and he was scared. He dropped his phone, he was so startled, and was looking around like he might bolt."

"You saw this?"

"Yeah." He bites on the edge of his thumbnail, looking off into the distance but I can see the fear in his eyes.

"What happened next?"

"It went really fast. One of them said something. The other one laughed, and I thought they knew each other but..." He shakes his head. "They grabbed him and the poor guy barely had a chance to scream before they threw him over." He stands, pushes his hands into his hair, and paces the room before returning. He doesn't sit down and is bouncing with anxiety.

"Go on, Mitch."

"I waited. I was in a wooded area, so they didn't see me and... They threw his phone over next after smashing it under their boots." He draws a shaky breath in. "I didn't know what to do. I was fifteen. And I was fucking scared. I walked to the edge to see if I could see him or hear him. It was full dark though, and I didn't want to stick around. There was no sound anyway. There's no way someone could have survived a fall there, I knew that much. I came back home later when I was sure no one would see me. Mom was beside herself. Cops were here. That's when I told them what I'd seen. The next day some other men came back and told me they were friends of Mr. Hayes too and that I couldn't talk to anyone. But I'm pretty sure they weren't his friends. Then a few months after that, the same men came to make sure I hadn't told anyone anything." He looks me over. "They were dressed like you. That's who Mom meant. They made some comments about fires in the area and houses going up in smoke, and they were just fucking thugs, you know?"

"Is that why you moved?"

He glances again at where his mom disappeared to and nods. "Mom and Dad got divorced so I moved here with my mom. They sold the house. Dad's in Utah."

"And you changed your name to your mother's maiden name?"

He nods. "I thought maybe... if those guys tried to find me it wouldn't be as easy."

"Would you recognize any of those men who came by? Or who pushed Hayes? Can you describe any of them?"

He shakes his head. "All I know is if I came across them on a dark street I'd cross to the other side. That's the kind of people they were."

"All right. Here." I hand him a card with my number on it, just that, no name. "If anyone else comes by to see you, you call me."

"You think they'll come back?"

"I don't think so. I was just curious." I look around, take my wallet out and leave several hundred-dollar bills on the coffee table. "Thanks, Mitch. I'll see myself out."

"They murdered him," he says when I reach the door. "I was too scared to go back to the cops, but they killed that man. And they laughed afterwards like it was funny, one of them whistling and then going *splat* like it was a fucking cartoon."

I look back at the kid, see how haunted his eyes look, and I see the countless kids who witnessed similar things over the five years I was the Commander's enforcer.

"Call me if you need anything, okay? Anything at all."

He nods.

I walk out.

30

MADELENA

Santos and I have an appointment in the morning with a gynecologist out of town. After what happened with Fairweather, he's not taking any chances. We drive together along with two soldiers and Val to the office of Dr. Amelia Moore.

I like Dr. Moore right away. She seems warm and is younger than both Fairweather and Cummings. The fact that she's a woman helps too.

Santos does most of the talking. I'm still processing everything to be honest. He wants to find out how far along I am and how much time I have to decide on what path we're taking. He means termination, although neither of us are saying the word.

After getting those details out of the way, Dr. Moore examines me, explains she'll be doing a transvaginal ultrasound because the baby is likely too small to see otherwise.

Santos sits on a chair as I lay on the table and stare

up at the ceiling, my mind not quite processing that this is happening. That I'm here in this office, on this table. That I'm pregnant.

The probe is uncomfortable and Dr. Moore senses it.

"It's cold, I know, honey," she says lightly. "There we go." She turns the monitor toward us. I don't look at it yet, but Santos watches intently. I just listen to the strange echo-like sound. She describes things to Santos, who asks questions while I keep staring up at the ceiling.

Then something happens that has me bite the inside of my cheek as I listen.

The echoing sound changes. Dr. Moore says something, but I don't hear what it is. I'm hearing something else.

A heartbeat.

I feel a tear slide down my temple, and Santos takes my hand, squeezes it.

"Their hearts beat fast, like they're running a race," Dr. Moore is saying. "Everything looks good with your baby."

Our baby.

"It's too early to tell the sex just yet, if you wanted to know that, but I'd say you're almost seven weeks along. I'll print a few pictures for you," she says, removing the probe. "Come on into my office once you're dressed, Madelena."

"Thanks," I say, and wait until they both leave to sit up and look at the screen. At the little blob frozen there that definitely doesn't look human just yet. I touch my stomach. It's a little rounder than usual but probably more bloating than anything else. It's too early for me to be showing.

I am certain of one thing as I get up and get dressed again. I know I won't terminate this pregnancy. I can't do that. I don't know why, and I have no judgment for any woman who chooses that path, but I know I can't.

Before leaving that room, I splash a little water onto my face then straighten and steel my spine. I look the same, although I'm wearing less makeup. I haven't had the energy. And maybe I'm a little paler. But the same mostly. I close my hand over my stomach and look down.

"Poor you," I tell her. She's a her for some reason. Then I walk out of the examination room and into Dr. Moore's office, where Santos is looking at each of the pictures the doctor has printed. He is in awe. I watch him for a minute, see how lines appear around his eyes as he smiles and asks questions, pointing at things on the small speck that is our baby. He'll make a good dad, I think. Good enough to make up for me as a mom.

That night Santos's mother is hosting a dinner at Augustine's. There's a part of me that wants to crawl into bed and hide from that woman, but there's another part, the stronger, rebellious one, that wants to show her she hasn't won.

Santos has told me it's up to me if I join him or not, but he will be there. He doesn't seem happy about it, though.

We haven't talked about the ultrasound, but I find him watching me anxiously at times. I should tell him I don't want to end the pregnancy. I know he wants to keep the baby, too, and I also know if I decided to terminate, he would support me. There's something keeping me from talking about it though, and it's not to punish him or anything like that. I just can't seem to open my mouth about it yet.

"You're going to come tonight?" Santos asks when he walks into the bedroom to find me getting dressed.

"Yep," I say, looking at myself in profile in the full-length mirror. "I can't hide forever." I face him. "Besides, I don't want her to think she holds any power over me. She doesn't."

Santos is watchful. "Are you sure?" he asks after a minute. "It's early yet. If you need time to process, you have it. As much as you need."

I take a deep breath in and exhale it out. "I'm fine."

"All right. I'm glad you'll be there. And we can come home whenever you're ready."

"Thanks."

Santos slips his arm around me seemingly even more careful with me now than he's always been—and he has always been careful. From the first moment we met, when he asked for forgiveness before doing what he had to do, he's always taken care with me.

I lean into him. We drive together to the event with Val and another soldier following in a second vehicle.

The event itself is a charity for children in war-torn countries, which Mrs. Augustine apparently feels passionately about. I don't believe it. Not for a second. The only thing that woman has any feelings for is herself, and maybe Caius. Santos? I'm not so sure.

I'm glad the ballroom is full of people though, and when Santos discreetly hands me a flute of sparkling water, I take it and stand at his side as he makes conversation with all those waiting to talk to him. He's a fixture now, an important man to the people of Avarice. I know he's making his way toward his mother, though, who is holding court in the far corner. I can see she's anticipating his arrival, too. I wonder if she's anxious about it. If she's afraid of him.

The Avery family is also here, and strangely, I find I don't much care. Not about them. Not about Mrs. Augustine. Not any of it. Because that's one thing this unplanned pregnancy has done, and I don't think it was Evelyn Augustine's intention. It's shifted my priorities. It's brought me back to myself in a way.

"Excuse me," I say. Santos pauses mid-sentence and looks at me, eyebrows raised. I nod to tell him I'm okay, and he lets me slip away. I feel his eyes on my back as I cross the room even as I hear him pick up his conversation.

I walk to the wall of windows at the back. The night

is clear and the water calm. The beacon light scans the horizon warning any ships that may be in the nearby waters not to come too close. Those cliffs mean business. I know.

I sip from my glass as I take in the lighthouse, making myself look at it, see it. Maybe it's the circumstances that have changed or this new weight of a brand-new life that will depend solely on me for the next seven plus months. For the years to come. But as I stare at it, it's just a lighthouse. A building with a shitty past. A shitty present. But it can't hurt me. It, like Evelyn Augustine, has no power over me.

"Should you be drinking that?" comes a soft voice from so close behind me that I feel breath on my skin. The hairs on the back of my neck stand on end, and I turn to find Ana standing just a few inches from me. She has cut her hair at a sharp angle and has a new, thick fringe of bangs that come to the tops of her eyebrows almost like someone took a ruler to get them so precise. It's freshly dyed blue-black and flat-ironed so straight I swear I can smell how she's fried it.

"You like it?" she asks, brushing her bangs down with her index finger.

"You look great," I say, turning away.

She grabs my shoulder and gives me a stupid smile. She raises her eyebrows at my drink. "Isn't that bad for the baby?" she whispers loudly.

"What are you talking about?" I ask, because how the fuck does she know?

"Don't worry, I'll keep your secret," she says,

curling her fingers around my hand. She comes to stand shoulder to shoulder with me and looks out toward the lighthouse.

"I heard you and Caius broke up." I pull my fingers away with effort.

She shrugs a shoulder. "He's come over since. Don't worry about us. We'll sort it out. He can't resist me. Or my bed. You know men," she says with a wink, then gestures to the looming structure of the lighthouse. "You must worry you'll be like your mom." She smiles that cruel little smile of hers. "It must be on your mind that fear that you'll hurt the little bundle?"

I can't quite form a response out of sheer shock that anyone would say something like that.

"I mean," she starts, shrugging her shoulders. "It runs in families, right? Mental illness?"

I watch her, not believing what I'm hearing.

"Don't worry. Caius and I can adopt it. Take it off your hands. Keep it safe." I don't miss how she refers to the baby as an it. "I mean, I know Caius will want to have our own, but he'll need this one. Sad fact." She makes a mock sad face. "I'll treat it as if it were my own, don't worry."

Now that, that makes me angry. I pull out of arm's reach because I can't be near her for another second. "Jesus. What is wrong with you?"

"What the fuck are you doing?" Caius says, grabbing Ana roughly by the arm and jerking her away.

Ana looks surprised, then cocks her head and

smiles that stupid, fake smile. "I was just talking to my friend. You're hurting me, Caius."

He twists his hand around her arm and walks her away from me, backing her against a wall. He gets right in her face, and I see a side of Caius I don't see often. Because when he's being an asshole to me, which is often, he's controlled. Almost enjoying himself. Now, though, he's violent. Furious. And I can see what it's taking him to master himself.

"Do not fucking go near her. Do you fucking hear me, you crazy bitch?" he hisses the words, and Ana looks shocked and then terrified. I take a step toward them to stop him but a cold hand wraps around my wrist. I turn to find Camilla Avery at my side.

This must be my lucky night.

"He's very protective of you for a brother-in-law. You'd almost think he's your husband."

"Oh my God. Get off me!"

Her grip tightens. She smiles and holds up the book she borrowed from my room. "I have your book! It wasn't as good as I hoped but you know how these things go. I did promise to return it. Here."

She holds it out to me just as Caius returns, minus Ana. "For fuck's sake." He gets in Camilla's face, and she backs up, right into Liam. "What is this, Grand Central Station for freaks?"

I look at him, see how he doesn't look like he usually does either. The stubble on his jaw is not as neat, his hair is messier than normal, and I smell alcohol on his breath.

"No need to be rude, Caius," Camilla tells him. "I was just returning a book." She turns back to me. "Page seventy-seven is where it gets interesting. Byeeee!" She exaggerates the word, waves, turns and walks off, and my mind is boggled.

"Fucking freak," Caius mutters. He looks me over. "You okay?"

"I'm fine. I don't need you to rescue me." I look down at the book that looks like it's been through a war. "And don't be a jerk to Ana. She's just..." I shake my head because I don't really know what she is.

"She's a cunt to you. You don't need to defend her."

"And you're my friend suddenly?"

"Suddenly? You're telling me we weren't always friends?"

"I thought you two broke up anyway."

"Fucking has nothing to do with anything."

"You're something else, Caius." I exhale, exasperated, and turn away to look out the windows again. I wish he'd leave me alone. Wish they'd all leave me alone.

"I heard... You feel okay?" he asks in a tone that's quieter and way less cocky than his usual.

"I'm fine. As if you'd care if I wasn't. Thanks for telling Ana, by the way," I tell him.

"If it makes any difference, if I'd known my mother was going to interfere like that, I'd have stopped her."

"Yeah, it doesn't make any difference, Caius. Excuse me."

I make to walk away, but he stops me. "I mean it, Madelena. I can understand it's not what you want."

"You don't know me, and we are not friends. Excuse me." I walk away, setting my glass down on a tray and finding Val standing against the wall when I can't find Santos. "Can you take me home?"

He searches the room, nods once. "Just a minute." He takes his phone out, texts something. I assume he's telling Santos or asking permission or whatever. I don't really care. I just want to go. A moment later, he has a response. "All right," he says, and gestures for me to go ahead.

I glance back once more because I guess I hoped Santos would come but I don't see him, so I walk out alone with Val at my back and another soldier waiting for me at the front entrance, so used to them now that I barely notice.

31

SANTOS

"Your wife looks good," my mother says when I reach her. Her gaze is on Madelena, who is on her way out with Val. I wonder what is going on in her head. "Pregnancy becomes her."

I shift my gaze to my mom, take her elbow, and lead her to a quiet corner.

"This isn't the time, Santos." She smiles at someone over my shoulder and tries to walk past me. I don't let her go.

"It's the perfect time."

She looks down at where I'm holding her then back up at me. "You're more like the Commander every day, you know that?"

"What the hell does that mean?"

"It means you already left bruises on my neck. Are you going to give me fresh ones on my arm?" I loosen my hold on her, noticing the shadows hidden by makeup on her neck.

I meet her hard eyes. I don't apologize. "Help me understand something, Mother." I need to talk to her to try to make sense of why she'd do this, what there is to gain. Because I'm missing a piece of the puzzle.

"What don't you understand, Santos? What part of your father's plan have you forgotten?"

"Yeah, that's the thing. We've accomplished what we set out to do. We own Avarice. Look at the people around you. They'll take any crumb from your table just so long as you toss one in their direction. Marnix De Léon? We have him. We have control of the company. It's all ours. Everything is ours."

She raises her chin a little, smiling victoriously as her eyes turn to slits to study those crumb-seekers who make up the room of guests.

"What I don't understand though, is the pregnancy. It doesn't add any value."

"You don't value a child?"

I snort. "You're not doing this to become a grandmother. I know you, Mom. What is it? What am I missing?"

"If your little wife decided to divorce you, what happens then?"

"What?"

"With a child, she's locked in. We have her. We have the De Léon name."

"We no longer need it. That's my point."

"And what about your father's sister and what those men did to her?"

"You're talking about revenge for my aunt? For a

woman you have no connection to. A woman who died before I was born."

"She's your blood."

"That's the point. She's not your blood. I can understand Dad wanting to take it further. But I can't wrap my brain around why you would. It doesn't fit."

She studies me, and it's almost like this is news to her, like she hasn't thought about this part. It tells me something. This isn't her motivation. It's something else.

"Don't you want a child after what happened to Alexia? To your baby?" she asks.

I stop. Blink. Because I'm not expecting this. This is too far, even for her. But I'm caught off guard, and she misreads my silence.

"Don't you?" she pushes. "Maybe you should be thanking me."

But then I realize something. "How did you know about that?" The only person I'd told about the pregnancy was Caius.

She shakes her head, then looks down into her nearly empty glass. "Caius told me after everything. He asked me not to tell you that I knew."

"Caius told you?"

"He was worried about you. We all were. The way you found her, the word *whore* spelled out on her stomach, she didn't deserve that. And for you to have seen her like that, seen what her father did to her, knowing she was pregnant with your child." She shakes her head. "I could better understand the violence that followed."

My brain rattles inside my skull at this very vivid forced memory.

"Caius blamed himself for not being there with you. And then not protecting you against the Commander. He acted like a coward, at least in his own mind. We all love you very much, Santos. I think sometimes you forget that."

"I don't forget it," I say the words and I'm looking at her, but I almost can't see her. I'm seeing other things. Remembering other things.

"Your brother isn't doing well since the night you fought. He's drinking. A lot. And he's back in that Ana's bed. She's no good for him."

I scan the room for him but don't see him.

"He didn't have anything to do with Fairweather," she says. "That was my plan. Only mine. Don't punish him for what I did."

I push my hand into my hair just as Cummings walks up to my mother with a couple in tow.

"Evelyn, there you are. I want to introduce you to..."

I walk away, walk out of that ballroom, and come across one of my soldiers. "Where is my brother?"

"Went outside about twenty minutes ago, sir."

"Outside? Which way?"

"Said he was going to take in the views."

"Shit." I walk out the way Caius went because I'm pretty sure of the views he means.

Wind howls like it always does out here. It sounds like banshees screaming. I banish the thought, force aside the feeling of foreboding their warning carries as I glance up at the looming structure of the lighthouse. I can't see it separate of its history. First Madelena's mother, then Thiago. Madelena almost dying out there once when she was five and once just weeks ago.

I stop for a minute and look out over the black night, the blacker waters. Waves punish the cliffs, and I wonder how many centuries it will take for the salt to break down the rock. For the sea to swallow the town of Avarice up along with its residents and its history.

Madelena is right. I am different here. I don't like myself here.

In the distance closer to the lighthouse, I see movement. A figure. I recognize my brother and follow the winding edge of the cliff toward him. Drops of salty water splash my face at intervals. Lost in his own thoughts, Caius only notices me when I'm a few feet from him. It seems to take him a minute to recognize me. When he does, he turns back toward the sea without a smile.

"Calm tonight," he says. "If this is calm." He brings the bottle of whiskey to his lips and drinks.

I shove my hands into my pockets and stand beside him to look out at the horizon. Nothing but blackness for miles and miles.

"I'm sorry about the other day," I say. From my periphery I see him turn to look at me, eyebrows high.

"Are you now?" He studies me.

"Don't be an asshole. I'm apologizing."

He drinks from the bottle.

"You didn't know she did what she did?" I ask.

"Mom?"

I nod.

"What do you think?"

I reach for the bottle, and he hands it to me. I notice how much is in there and wonder if he drank the third that's missing, then drink a swallow before giving it back. It feels good, the burn. There are days I miss that burn. The oblivion enough of it brings.

"So, I'm going to be an uncle," he says.

"It's up to Madelena."

"What do you mean?"

"What do you think I mean?"

He considers me. "She's not going to get rid of it, if that's what you're thinking."

"How do you know that?"

"I know. She's tougher than you think. You treat her like she's going to fucking break any second. She won't."

"You have all the insights tonight."

He takes the bottle back and holds it up. "Whiskey will do that," he says and drinks. We fall into silence as he watches the sea and I watch him. "Do you think you're a monster, Santos?"

His question is odd, and he shifts his gaze to me to wait for an answer that takes too long to formulate.

"I know I deserve to burn in hell for the things I have done when my time comes."

"Who is responsible? You for the acts you committed? The Commander for ordering them?"

"Just had this conversation with my wife."

"So, you know the answer?"

"I'm responsible for my choices. I know that. I accept it. We are all responsible for the choices we make. Why are you asking this?"

He drinks. "Being complicit even if you're not the one committing the crime also makes you a monster, you agree?"

"What are you getting at?"

He shakes his head. "Do you think monsters are born or made? Think it's in our DNA?"

"What's going on, Caius?"

He exhales on a chuckle, a private joke, drinks three glugs of whiskey, then turns to me. "What if I told you it was in mine?" His face is serious. I watch him and wait. "What would you say?"

"I'd say you're drunk." I reach for the bottle, but he holds it away, then stumbles backward. "Christ!" I catch his arm to pull him away from the edge.

"I know you know, Santos."

"Give me the bottle, Caius."

He shakes his head, walking away from me. I go to him, grab it from him, and throw it over the cliff's edge. We both turn to watch it go but don't hear it crash over the sound of the waves.

"Well, that's a waste of good whiskey."

"I'm taking you inside. You're fucking drunk, and

you shouldn't be out here." I put my hands on his shoulders, but he stops me.

"Did you hear what I said?"

"I hear you're drunk. Let's go."

"I know you know," he says more forcefully as I try to walk him toward the building. "I know you know I'm his son."

I stop. Close my eyes. My chest feels tight. My gut, too. And I can't look at my brother.

"I'm his son. Alistair Avery's blood runs in my veins. Look at me," he says when I shake my head. "Fucking look at me."

I do.

"You see it? The resemblance?"

"No, I don't. Don't be a fucking idiot."

"It's in the eyes. In the abyss in the eyes." He points to his eyes. I don't know if he's aware that his hand is in the shape of a gun pointed to the brain.

"There's no fucking abyss in your eyes. Shut the fuck up. You're drunk. Let's go."

"I know she told you. And she also told you I was unaware of the fact."

Again, I stop.

"Always protecting her baby boy. Oh, I mean me. Not you. She'll do anything for me, huh? Any-fucking-thing. It's fucked up."

"How long have you known?"

He shakes his head, looks up into the sky like he's doing math. "What am I, thirty-two? Let's say a while."

"Did you know when everything happened? When he took me?"

He nods a heavy nod.

"It doesn't matter, Caius. You're still my brother."

He laughs, pats my arm, shakes his head. "Santos. You don't know the half of it." His words send a chill through me.

"Then tell me."

He studies me for a long, long time, then laughs again. "You remember when you told me what Camilla said? That little bitch, I fucking share blood with her. Can you believe it? And she tried to make you think she and I... Jesus. Fucking freak of nature, that one."

"Do they know? Camilla and Liam? Thiago?"

"Thiago has always known."

This comes as a surprise to me, one that wounds because Thiago and I were close—like brothers ourselves. But I look at my other brother and think maybe this is the way of things. Brothers keep secrets too, as do mothers and fathers.

"Camilla and Liam, I don't know. Don't care," he says. He takes a deep breath in. "I'm going in. I'm fucking tired and ready for this night to be over." He moves away, but stops, comes back to me and puts his hands on my shoulders. "I'm going to tell you something, Brother. For you and her. For history. Because it goes on a loop, doesn't it?"

"What?"

"You don't want what happened to Alexia to repeat."

"What the fuck, Caius?" I shove him.

"And favors never come for free. They, too, are on a loop. The world goes around and around. And love is a mother fucker. It becomes hate when you're not paying attention."

"Caius, what the fuck is going on?"

"Get her out of here. Get your wife out of here. Take her somewhere none of us can find her and hide her away. It's the only way to save her."

Then, without waiting for me, he marches back toward the building. I follow him, keeping a few steps back and we don't say goodbye when he gets on the elevator to go upstairs. I watch him get on, see the look in his eyes like that of a condemned man as the doors slide closed.

He has known all these years that he was the Commander's son. He's known. What that must have done to him… And what the hell was that warning? Because it felt like exactly that: a warning.

I feel it in the very depths of myself.

I walk out of that building, my steps hurried as I move toward the SUV, soldiers on my heels. I need to get to her. I need to get her out of Avarice. He's right. I should never have brought Madelena back here.

32

MADELENA

I'm just getting ready for bed when Santos comes into the bedroom. His hair is windblown and his hands when he comes to take mine are ice-cold. He searches my face, eyes wild.

"What is it?" I ask. "Has something happened?"

"You're okay?"

"I'm fine. I just wanted to go and Val—"

"I know." He keeps nodding like his mind is on something else.

"Santos?" It takes him a minute to focus his eyes on me. I put one of his hands over my stomach. "I want to keep the baby. Okay?" He swallows a lump and only half-smiles. I expected more. "Don't you want to? I thought—"

"I want to. I want to, believe me, I want to. But there's something... I need to get you out of here now."

"What?"

"I'll pack a few things and send more later. But I need to get you out of Avarice."

He walks away from me into the closet and returns with the same duffel bag we'd taken to Hells Bells. He starts to pack things, underwear, nighties, random things that don't make sense. I follow him around the room.

"Santos, what's going on?"

"I'll come as soon as I can." He walks into the bathroom and returns a moment later with a bag of toiletries. He picks up the bottle of vitamins Dr. Moore gave me. He looks at it, nods. "I'll get this refilled."

"Santos. Stop." I go to him, take his face in my hands. "What's going on?"

He looks at me, but he's distracted. I can see it in his eyes. But a moment later, it's like he gets something, and whatever it is has him stumbling back two steps before he drops to the edge of the bed.

"What is it?" I ask.

He looks up at me, forehead furrowed, not seeing me even though he's looking right at me.

"Santos?"

"Val!" He bolts to his feet, opens the door, and calls again to Val. A few minutes later, I can hear Val's heavy steps charging up the stairs. He gets to our room just as Santos zips up the duffel and takes me by the arm.

"Sir?" Val asks.

He hands Val the bag. "Get two men. Men you trust." Val's eyes grow concerned. "We're going to Hells Bells. You'll stay with her. Understand?"

"What?" I ask.

"We have to go, Madelena. Now." He walks me out of the room and down the stairs, Val on our heels.

"Why? What's going on?"

Val goes out the front door. Santos finally stops and looks at me. "I think Caius was trying to warn me tonight. I think..." He shakes his head. "I don't know. I don't fucking know. But I need you safe. I'm going to take you myself. Val will stay with you. We can trust Father Michael and Val. You understand?"

"No, I don't. And I don't want to go—"

"You have to."

"I don't want to stay there without you." He pulls me to him, hugs me so tight, tighter than he's ever held me.

"I love you, sweetheart. And I'll keep my promise to you. I will keep you safe. No matter what." He draws back as Val comes back up the stairs after getting the SUV and additional soldiers sorted.

"Ready," Val says as a second SUV pulls up behind the one already there.

Santos nods, hurries me into the back of one of the SUVs. He closes my door and opens the driver's side one. "Sit in the back with her," he instructs Val, then climbs into the driver's seat.

"What's going on?" I ask again as Val is seated beside me.

Santos doesn't answer me, though. His jaw is set tight, eyes dark, his gaze locked on the road ahead as he puts the car into drive and takes off. I'm jolted backward, and Val clamps an arm across me as he straps me in.

For the entire drive to Hells Bells, Santos doesn't speak. Not to us, at least. When he does say anything, he's talking to himself and he's angry. He slams a fist against the steering wheel and goes twenty miles over the speed limit for the entire drive. I'm surprised we aren't pulled over for speeding.

When we get to the small cottage, the feel is completely different than the other night. There is no calm, no quiet. The lights are on, and Father Michael rushes out to meet us. Even he is worried.

"Father," Santos says, taking my hand, holding on to me tight. "I'm so sorry to get you up so late."

Father Michael shakes off his concern as he takes in the crew. Santos grabs my duffel while Val gives the two soldiers instructions, which must include checking the perimeter.

"Are we in danger?" I ask Santos when Father Michael turns to lead the way in.

Santos looks at me. "You'll be safe here."

I pull back when he urges me toward the front entrance. "Tell me what's going on. What's happened."

"No time," he says, and we walk into the cottage. Santos releases me, hands the duffel to Val who takes it upstairs. Where will the three of them even sleep? There's only the one bedroom.

Father Michael's face is concerned as Santos leads him outside. I try to follow but Val blocks my way so all I can do is watch from the front door. I don't hear them speak but can see them as Santos opens the trunk. He says something, but Father Michael shakes his head and takes a step backward. Santos follows him, puts a hand on his elbow and it looks like he's pleading with him. A moment later, Father Michael looks up at Santos and holds out his hand to accept whatever it is Santos hands him. I don't see it at first, but then Father Michael looks toward the house, to me. He nods and turns away and I realize what it is as he begins his walk back to his own house.

"Was that a gun?" I ask Santos who returns to me. Val steps out of the way, and Santos walks me into the cottage.

"I'll be back for you as soon as I can." He takes my arms, rubs them, and looks at me so sadly, I fall silent. "I love you, Madelena. You know that, right?"

I nod, tears filling my eyes. "Stay with me." His forehead furrows and I swear there's more gray in his beard tonight than there was days ago. "What is it? What's happened?"

He gets that same look he got earlier, like he's realizing something, processing something. I wonder if there's a whole second conversation going on in his head.

He opens his mouth, closes it again and shakes his head. "I'm sorry."

Before I can make heads or tails of what just happened, before I can ask him what he's sorry for, he hands me off to Val and walks away. I take a step to go after him, but Val has his orders because his grip is like a vise around my arm.

"Santos?"

He turns back when he gets to the door, but whatever is on his mind is heavy. Then he's gone. Just like that, and without another word, he's gone.

33

SANTOS

My mind is a blur of facts and faces, my head full of words spoken by the dead and the living alike.

Thiago's warning to Madelena when the third person appeared on the catwalk. *The blood of a monster runs in his veins.* He'd know better than anyone. He shared that blood, too. Same as Caius.

Caius telling me he had his bracelet repaired after he broke it climbing. I remember that climbing event. It was years ago. But he'd backed out after getting there. I remember picking him up from some bar, where he'd spent the afternoon. Caius is afraid of heights. He's always been afraid of heights.

So how was he on the catwalk?

Camilla telling me Thiago was meeting someone at the lighthouse. Thiago knew all along that Caius was the Commander's son. Did he threaten to expose him? Did Caius feel like it was a possibility? But who would care? Me? What did he think I'd do with the information?

No. There's more. I'm missing vital pieces.

My father's final words to us. *I know what you did, and this is your punishment.*

Did he know my mother lied to him about who fathered Caius? That's a hell of a punishment to cut Caius out when Caius himself wasn't guilty of anything. He was simply born of what equated to rape.

Rape.

Bea Avery's version of history varies from my mother's. But they both tell one part exactly the same way. The Commander did not know of Caius's existence. If he did, he would've demanded to take him. Hell, he wouldn't have bothered to demand. He'd just have taken.

But he took me. What a coincidence that he found me, that my crime so perfectly fitted his needs.

"Damn it!" I slam my fist into the steering wheel.

It's late by the time I get home from Hells Bells. I switch off the engine but instruct the soldier at the door to leave the keys in the ignition. I don't think I'll be here long. I'm not sure why I came anyway. I know what I'm looking for will only confirm what I already know. I have the police report from Alexia's murder memorized.

Besides, I know what I did when I found her, and only I know.

I push both hands into my hair and pull when I get

to the study door. Because what will this mean? What does it mean?

I enter the study and close the door. I'm not really here to look at the report even though it's what I busy myself doing, opening the safe, taking it out, setting it on the desk. I am trying to wrap my brain around the fact that I've been betrayed.

The folder sits closed on my desk. I get up, walk into the living room and reach over the bar to get the bottle of whiskey. It's Caius's. I drink a very long swallow, carry it back into the study and sit behind my desk again. I look up at my father's portrait and I swear his eyes are different. I swear he's looking at me asking me the same questions I'm asking myself.

What the fuck am I going to do?

Because the police report doesn't contain the detail that my mother knew. Caius couldn't have known it. I never told it to him. I never told anyone. Because it was too shameful, too wrong. Too much a betrayal of Alexia.

As I open the folder and re-read the report I know by heart, I feel a twisting inside my gut and my chest. I wonder if this is what Dad felt when he found out about Caius, assuming that's what triggered the changing of the will.

A right-handed person killed Alexia.

I killed her father because I was insane with rage and fury and convinced it was him. There was no one else it could've been. Caius had even told me to go get Alexia, to not leave her there with her father because of what he'd do to her if he were to find out. It was all laid out for me. All I had to do was play my part—and I did, exactly as the script was written.

But after finding her and before I went after her father, I closed her legs, and I wiped away the word W-H-O-R-E the killer had written in her blood across her stomach. I wiped it away because she wasn't that, and I wouldn't have anyone think she was.

How did my mother know? Did Caius tell her that, too, just as he told her Alexia was pregnant? Did he tell her that after killing her and writing out that word to taunt me? To push me so far, I couldn't come back from it?

But why?

Why?

The coincidence of the Commander choosing me of all people—me to take to make his enforcer. Me, who he couldn't have known, except that now I know he and I were connected long before I was even born.

With a roar, I stand and hurl the decanter across the room. It crashes, leaving brown liquid streaking down the wall. I stalk out of the room and call for two soldiers to follow me out into the SUV. I drive to Augustine's, and when I reach it, I don't care that most of the building's lights are out. The only ones still on are a random window on the third floor and the dimmed lights of the front lobby.

I get out of the car and slam the door. It echoes in the darkness, even the crashing of waves distant and muffled by the bulk of the building between me and the cliffs. I barely feel the cold as I walk toward the front door.

The glass doors slide open, and I hear Caius's warning to get Madelena out. Away from here. Is that remorse?

The old man working the night shift looks up in surprise when he sees me. It takes him a moment to recognize me.

"Mr. Augustine, a pleasure—"

I am on the elevator and the doors are closing before he finishes. On the top floor, the soldier assigned to stand guard startles awake. He's quick to get on his feet.

"Sir. Sorry, I..."

"Get out of my way."

He nods, steps aside before I've reached the door. It's unlocked and I push it open. The apartment is silent and dark, a lone lamp on in the corner.

"Stay here," I tell the soldiers and stalk toward Caius's bedroom.

"Caius!" I call out, flipping light switches on as I go. He took my old room, which is at the end of the corridor. I push it open and turn on the light. I'm surprised when I hear a woman's startled gasp.

There, sitting up on the bed is a naked Ana covering her tits. But she's alone. "Where is my brother?" I demand.

She shakes her head, clearly terrified.

The beacon light catches my eye, and I watch it scan the horizon from the floor-to-ceiling windows.

Clothes are scattered over the back of a chair, the foot of the bed. There's a half-full bottle of whiskey on the nightstand.

"Caius?" I stalk toward the bathroom but it's quiet. When I open the door, it's dark and empty. "Where the fuck is he?"

"What the hell is going on?" a man asks, and I turn to find Lawrence Cummings standing at the door in a T-shirt and boxers. He's holding a pistol at his side.

"What are you doing here?" I ask him, not afraid of him or his stupid little gun, which I'm pretty sure he doesn't know how to use.

"Santos?" My mother comes running behind him. She's tying her robe. "How..."

Cummings looks like he might piss his pants and backs up into the hallway.

"What's going on?" my mother asks me.

"Where is my brother?" I ask, and when I pass her to get into the hallway, she presses her back flat to the wall.

"Do you know what time it is?" she asks, mustering up her courage to follow me to the study.

"Caius? Where the fuck are you?" I push the study door open so hard it slams against the wall and rattles. But I find it, too, dark and empty. There are two more bedrooms down the other corridor. "See if my brother is in one of the rooms," I tell one of the soldiers.

"What's going on?" my mother demands.

I turn to her, and she shrinks back a little. Good. I stalk toward her. "How did you know?"

"How did I know what?"

"Do you want me to call the police, Evelyn?" Cummings asks.

I turn to him, not even having time to tell him off before my mom snaps at him, "Go to bed. Don't be an idiot!"

"Your brother isn't here," the soldier tells me.

I turn to my mother, turn on her. "How did you know what the killer had written on her stomach?"

Her mouth opens. Closes. She swallows. "I don't know what you're talking about. You're scaring me, Santos. You sound like your father. His temper— "

"W-H-O-R-E." I spell it out, cutting her off. "How did you know? Because I cleaned that off her before the cops got there. No one knew. No one but me and the killer." Not even Alexia. She was, thankfully, dead by then. My mom's eyes fill with tears, and I feel that twisting in my chest. "Her killer was right-handed. Her father couldn't fucking blow his nose with his right hand." There's a long, heavy pause and fuck, is this happening? Is this really fucking happening? "Mom?" I ask, hearing the break in my voice.

She shakes her head, wipes a tear.

"Your brother—"

I slam my fist into the wall just an inch from her head. She screams, jumps, and I pull my hand back. It throbs and there's a fist-size hole in the wall.

"Where is he?"

Her lower lip trembles. A thing I've never seen before.

"Where the fuck is he?"

"I don't know. He'd been talking about that lighthouse. I went to bed. Oh, God, do you think..." she trails off, running past me toward Caius's room and straight to the windows. "He was drunk. He was—"

"Was it him?" I ask her.

She turns to me. "Go after him. Please. Go after him. Santos, whatever you think, it's not true. Just go after him, bring him back. Please!"

I look past her shoulder to the hulking lighthouse. Did he go out there? For what reason? I know what state he was in when I left him. If he's up there... shit! I spin on my heel and charge through the apartment to the front door. "Keep her here. She doesn't go anywhere. You're with me!" I tell one of the soldiers, and I'm halfway down the hall when someone screams for me to stop.

I do and turn to find Ana with the blanket wrapped around her, my mother on her heels.

"He's not at the lighthouse. He said he'd be back tomorrow."

I stalk toward her. "Where did he go?"

"Some strange place. I'd never heard of it." She shakes her head, trying to remember, and a sick feeling overwhelms the one of betrayal like a weight in my gut, a fist around my heart.

"Where?" I ask, my voice foreign.

She looks up at me. "Hells Bells."

34

MADELENA

I try to sleep. There's nothing else I can do. I can't even call Santos to talk to him. None of our cell phones work and it's the middle of the night. I won't disturb Father Michael now... not after what he's had to do already.

The only problem is after tossing and turning for over an hour, I'm still wide awake. I switch on the light on the bedside table and get up. When I set my feet on the hardwood floor, I'm grateful for the thick socks Santos had packed, surprised he'd even thought of it in his mad dash. I get out of the bed and go to the window. It looks different than the last time I was here; only a partial moon shines over the water tonight. I wrap my arms around myself as I take in the view, realizing how completely alone we are out here.

After putting on a sweater over my T-shirt, one of Santos's, I make my way downstairs quietly, not sure if I'll run into Val or the other soldiers. They were taking shifts, and at least one of them was going to sleep on the sofa, so half-way down I peer over to see if he's there. He is. It's not Val, but one of the others I don't know. He's huddled beneath the thick blanket, asleep. The fire is down to its dying embers.

I glance out of the window looking over the back of the property and see the other soldier. He's facing away from me, and he must be freezing. But then I notice the puff of smoke. He's just out there having his cigarette. Feeling slightly less guilty, I make my way to the kitchen and open the cupboards until I find tea bags and mugs. I pour water into the kettle and switch on the gas stove, wincing at the sound the old stove makes because it's loud. But the man on the couch doesn't stir, and as I wait for the water to heat up, I look out the window over the sink and take in the stark beauty of the place. I can imagine a younger Santos here. I can see it as the sanctuary it was to him. To be isolated in nature, and to be forgiven and accepted by the man who takes you in. I think he needed that more than anything else those years.

Santos. My concern returns as the kettle steams. I switch off the gas and pour the boiling water into my cup. What happened tonight that he needed to get me out of Avarice the way he did? What is he dealing with that I don't even think Val knows about? Because Val is possibly his closest confidante. I think so, at least. I wonder where Caius falls. They're close but there's something between them, a jealousy, an accusation? Something I can't quite put a word to. I wonder if whatever it is that sent him into that frenzy has to do with Caius.

Once the tea is ready, I throw away the teabag and make my way back up to the bedroom because I don't know where else to go. I stoke the fire and lay another log on it. Before climbing back into the bed, I notice something in the duffel bag. It's the book Camilla returned to me. Santos must have packed it by accident in his rush.

I pick it out now and get back into the bed. After propping the pillows, I set the book on my lap, and my mind conjures up Camilla's image. She's strange. Beautiful and wicked but also just a little off. But I guess being the Commander's daughter will do that to you.

I turn the book over and wonder what she did to it. Drop it in water then trample it? At least it's not one I loved. I read it years ago, and I have to agree with Camilla that it wasn't as good as I'd hoped, but there isn't anything else to read. So, I open it and immediately stop. Because I see what she's done. Why the book looks so warped and actually feels heavier than it should. It's a hardback but still.

She's printed out a photo on plain paper, crudely cut it out and taped it into the book. She's basically used my book as a photo album. What the hell?

I look at the first photo. It's a house—well, a mansion—and I can see palm trees in the garden. Miami? Maybe their house in Miami. Santos said that's where the Commander lived, right? In front, too small to see their faces, is a woman and a very young child at her side. He's holding her hand. He's maybe two. It's too blurred and small for me to make out who it is, and Camilla didn't provide a caption. Well, I guess she did in the highlights of certain words and letters. I set the book aside and get out of bed to cross to the small writing table against the far wall. From inside the single drawer, I take out a pencil and a pad of paper, which I carry back to the bed.

Settling on the bed, I write out the letters she highlighted in order.

Miami. Home. Mom and T.

The T must be Thiago.

I have no idea what she was doing or what her intention was, but I flip to the next page. This one is of three cats, but there are no highlights. Just a collection of hearts drawn around the cats forming a heart themselves. It's something a child would do. I turn the page.

Some of them have random pictures but they do seem to follow some timeline because soon I see one labeled *twins*. In this one Thiago is older, maybe seven or so. He's standing at his mother's side, again, and she's holding both babies, one in each arm. He looks miserable, and I wonder if he ever smiled growing up.

I set the book aside for a minute because I recall that night on the catwalk. Recall his face as he was pushed. I hear his scream. He didn't deserve what happened to him, but I am holding on to hope that he's alive, that he somehow survived.

After a few more of these pages, I try to recall the part she said she liked. Page seventy something. As soon as I get to the one she referenced, I know it, and it makes my heartbeat pick up because there is Santos. He must be eighteen, and he's miserable. He's thinner than he is now, less muscular, and I can see the shadows under his eyes even in this grainy, poor-quality print. His shoulders are slumped, and his appearance overall is unkempt, but he is looking at the camera. It's just that the look in his eyes is vacant, like the man is absent even though he's standing right there. Beside him is a young Camilla. She's holding onto one of Santos's hands and beside her is her twin, Liam. Thiago stands on the other side of Santos. The only person smiling is Camilla.

I write out the highlighter letters. *Santos the day he came into our little family.*

It's hard to look at the next few pages but the years progress quickly. Santos grows older, his expression fiercer. He loses the face of the mourning boy and becomes the man to be reckoned with—a man I'd cross to the other side of the street to avoid, especially when he and Thiago are pictured together.

There's one caption beneath a photo of the two together that spells out *besties*. In this one, horns have been drawn coming out of Thiago's head and a sticker of a pistol has been added to Santos's hand. It's weird, and she's weird, and this book makes me feel icky in a way. Is she trying to send some message or just being an asshole? I'm going to go with the latter.

I flip to one more page before I close it. This one is a clear image. A photograph. And I can feel the evil coming off the man pictured. I know without a doubt, without having to read the highlighted letters, that this is her father. This is the Commander.

The devil who stole Santos's soul.

I close the book and get up to throw it into the fire because it's disgusting. The fire hisses when I drop the book in as it displaces the log that's still a little damp. The book lands on its spine and falls open to that page with the Commander smiling a wide, evil smile.

Something has me snatching the photo out just as the rest of the book catches fire. I don't know what it is, but as I kneel on the floor and study it, it's familiar in a way. He's familiar. Is it Thiago I'm remembering? No, Thiago doesn't look like him. He looks like his mother. It's not his face exactly. It's something else, something I can't quite put my finger on.

A loud thud comes from downstairs, and I startle, my gaze snapping to the door. Someone mutters a curse and I wonder if it's the second soldier or even Val. It's pretty dark down there and cramped with furniture. I guess one of them walked into something.

Footsteps begin to come up the stairs, and I get to my feet, picking up that photo and setting it on the nightstand. I pull my sweater closer and count the footsteps. Thirteen to get to the second floor. A soft knock comes. Assuming it's Val coming to check on me, I am about to walk over to open it, but he opens it from the outside. It squeaks on its hinges as the top of his head comes into view.

Except that's not Val's head. It's not either of the soldiers either. Neither of them has blond hair.

A chill creeps along my spine making the hair on the back of my neck stand on end. When he peers all the way around and our eyes meet, I realize what was familiar about the photo of the Commander. No, that's not right. It's not then. It's when he walks inside and shoves one hand into his pocket and cocks his head in the opposite direction. It's exactly how the Commander is standing in that photo. Otherwise, there's no physical similarity. Until he smiles and that dimple forms on his cheek.

I glance at the photo and see it then, clear as day. How has Santos not noticed it? I blink and shift my gaze from the photo to Caius and feel the blood drain from my face, feel my mouth drop open and my throat go dry as I stare in shock at what's been right before my eyes all along.

"Hope I didn't wake you," Caius says in a fake attempt to be quiet. "They're out cold downstairs. Some guards, huh?"

"Wh... What are you doing here?" I ask, stepping in front of the nightstand and turning the photo upside down behind me.

He comes into the room, looks around it, nods. "Cute, I guess. Not my style, but cute. Didn't think it was my brother's style either but goes to show you never really know anyone."

He's drunk. I can hear it in his voice, see it in his movements. He turns to me, and I see how bloodshot his eyes are when he steps closer. It is almost morning. He hasn't slept. Like me.

"You know what I wish, Madelena?" he asks, coming toward me. I have nowhere to go. I'm trapped by the bed and nightstand, and to flee I'd have to leap across the bed.

"What?" I ask, standing where I am, trying to appear normal.

"I wish," he starts, coming close enough to push a finger into my belly. "I wish you'd never gotten pregnant. That's what."

I find myself pushing his hand away and setting mine over my stomach to protect the tiny being inside. Santos's baby. My baby.

"Did Santos send you to bring me back?" I ask, knowing he didn't—knowing the fact that Caius is here and Santos is not is a very, very bad thing.

He smiles at me, shifts his gaze over my shoulder and reaches around me to pick up that photograph. He holds it between us, looks at it. I watch his face, his expression, and I see how it darkens. When he meets my eyes again, I swallow hard.

"Where did you get this?"

"Your sister."

One corner of his mouth lifts, and my blood turns to ice.

He studies me, looking more than anything else, sad. Miserable even. He shakes his head. "No, he didn't," he says, and I'm momentarily confused. "Santos didn't send me," he clarifies, setting the photo down, ignoring the comment about his sister altogether. "Where are your clothes?" he asks, looking around. He finds the duffel bag without me having to point it out and goes to take out some clothes, jeans, another sweater, although when he sees I'm wearing a sweater, he shoves it back into the bag and returns to me.

"Put these on. It's fucking freezing here. Worse than Suicide Rock," he says, holding the jeans out to me.

I take the jeans. "There are soldiers downstairs." I don't tell him how many.

"Like I said, out cold. Let's go. Sun's coming up."

"Where?"

"A walk. On the beach. We'll get some fresh air. Watch the new day begin. It's good for the baby," he adds.

"We should call Santos," I start, licking my lips, my throat dry.

"Sure," he says, producing his phone. "Except no cell service. What kind of town has no cell service?"

I'm about to suggest going to the rectory, but then I think about Father Michael. I'd be putting him in danger if we did that. If Caius even took me there to make the call, that is. I can't risk his life because Caius is here to do damage. Tonight he'll prove just how dangerous he is.

"Give me a minute. I'll get changed and be right out," I tell him.

He smiles, sits on the bed. "Just slip them on here."

"It'll just—"

"I said do it here."

I pull on the jeans. Once they're on, he stands and takes my hand. When I try to slip free, he tightens his grip.

"Don't make this harder than it needs to be."

We walk down the stairs where the lights are on. I gasp when I see what's in the living room. The thud I heard, I realize, wasn't someone walking into furniture. It was a body. Val's.

"Oh my God."

He's leaning against the wall like he's sitting there except that his head has flopped forward. In his stomach is a hole through which he bled out. His hands are cupped around a knife on his lap. He must have pulled it out. Not that it mattered much.

"Fucking goon." Caius shakes his head.

And the other man, the one on the couch. He hasn't moved. Well, that's not true. He's been moved and I see now the stain of the dark red that has spread like a circle on the floral print couch.

"What did you do?" I cover my mouth.

"Don't get sick on me now, Mama. Besides, it's nothing compared to what my brother has done, and you've happily crawled into his bed. Come, Madelena." Caius tugs me toward him. "Put on your boots."

"Caius. Oh God..."

He pushes me down onto the bench and hands me a boot. I take it, and he gestures for me to put it on. I do. He hands me the other one. I notice the gun tucked into the back of his pants, seeing the handle of it around his side. I shift my gaze to the two dead soldiers, then up to his to find him watching me. He didn't need a gun to do what he did to those two, trained, armed men. He certainly doesn't need one to do the same to me.

"Caius? What's happening?"

He looks at the coats hanging there and grabs mine. I notice he's not wearing one. He's in a button-down shirt and slacks. The shirt is black, and now I see the dark stains on it. Blood of the men he killed.

"What's happening?" He hauls me to my feet and puts the coat on me. I slip my arms in and he zips me up, standing so close I have to crane my neck to look up at him. He's as big as Santos, as powerfully built. Not to mention the gun. Not to mention his determination.

"What do you want, Caius?" I ask, wondering where the third soldier is. If he's seeing this—if he's watching us and biding his time.

"What do I want? This has nothing to do with what I want, just to be clear. It's what needs to be. I don't want to hurt you. I won't enjoy it. I really won't."

"You don't have to hurt me."

"That's the thing, I do. It's either you or Santos—"

He's interrupted then by a car pulling up outside, doors opening and closing.

I open my mouth to scream but he has his gun in his hand and it's pointing to my belly before I can even take a full breath in.

"I'll kill you right here. I'll kill your fucking baby right here. Right fucking now!"

I put my hands over my stomach and shake my head.

"Be fucking quiet, you hear me? I have nothing to lose."

I nod violently as a flashlight shines against the window. The drapes are drawn though, so there's not much they can see. A knock comes on the door, and Caius looks from me to it then back.

"Ask who it is," he tells me, and before they knock a second time, he cocks the pistol he's holding to my stomach.

"Who is it?" I ask as calmly as I can.

"Police, ma'am. We were called about a disturbance."

I look at Caius who only has to narrow his eyes for me to respond to the officers. "No. It's fine. Just... It's fine."

Quiet on the other side. "If you'll open the door, ma'am."

"Tell them to wait," Caius whispers to me.

"Just a minute," I say, and watch as Caius attaches what I guess is a silencer to his gun. Before I can say another word, he shoves me backward so hard, I crash against the wall, my head bouncing off it. As I watch, he opens the door. Before the officers can even blink, he fires off two shots.

I scream, trying to scramble to my feet.

Caius peers out, then tucks his pistol back into his pants. As I'm straightening, he takes hold of me again.

I stare, paralyzed with horror, at the two dead men.

"Where was I? Now that you're pregnant, the next part comes into play. Phase two, as my mother says." He looks off for a moment, shakes his head. I can see his exhaustion when he turns back to me. "Come on. Let's go."

"What do you mean? What's phase two?" I ask, digging my heels in when he tries to haul me out.

"Do you love him?" he asks.

I don't answer but stare up at him, trying not to see the bodies on the ground. Movement in the tall grass has me glance over his shoulder.

Caius leans in my face when I don't answer. "Do you love my brother?"

"Yes."

"That's the thing. I do too. And I know what I have to do is going to hurt him, but it's better than the alternative."

"What do you think you have to do?"

He doesn't answer but he shakes his head infinitesimally.

"You don't have to hurt me," I tell him.

"But the alternative is to hurt him. And you wouldn't want that, would you?"

"I don't understand. Why do you have to hurt either of us? He loves you."

"And like I said, I love him. And that's why I'm

choosing you. Because if there's no baby, he doesn't have to die."

"What?"

He grins a grin that is not smug, not happy. Not remotely. He looks the opposite actually. Like he's in so much pain.

"The will. The exact words Brutus Augustine chose. Only an Augustine by blood can inherit. That's not me, sweetheart," he says and squeezes his eyes shut.

"Because you're the Commander's son," I say.

"How did you figure it out? I'm curious. I mean, thank goodness I don't share any physical similarities."

"Caius, please—"

"*How?*" he barks, making me jump.

"It's the way you stand sometimes."

"Ah."

"Does Santos know?"

"He does now. But it doesn't matter anymore. Oh, by the way, Uncle Jax? That was me. I sent you the photo too. Early wedding gift. Not nice, I know."

"You? You k-killed my uncle."

"Leverage. Anywho," he says, casually playing with the word. "Back to the matter at hand. The fact stands that I can't inherit a fucking penny. He cut me out. My mother too. If it weren't for Santos's generosity, we'd be out on the street."

"Then why would you do what you're doing?"

"Do you have any idea about the scale of the Augustine fortune?"

I shake my head. "I don't care."

"Yeah, you do. Money makes the world go around. And you can say you don't care all you like, but you'd care if it impacted your day-to-day life. Since you don't know, though, let me tell you. My brother, mother, and I couldn't spend it in a thousand lifetimes. But the old man set it up the way he did to protect his son. His only son. And his son's descendants, of course. And to punish my mother." He shifts his gaze to my stomach. "You can imagine how that's gone over with her."

When he tugs me out of that cottage, I know this is it. I know what he's going to do once I'm on that beach. I open my mouth to scream, but he's fast and in an instant, he pulls me to himself and clasps a hand over my mouth.

"Shut up. Just shut the fuck up. You don't want me to hurt that poor vicar or whatever the fuck he is do you? I took the time to put the silencer on for his sake. Don't make me regret it."

I try to shake my head but he's holding me too hard, and I can't.

"If I see him, I'll kill him, Madelena, and it'll be on you. So, are you going to shut up or not?"

I try to nod.

"Fucking answer me."

I make a sound and nod harder.

"Good." He moves his hand from my mouth but wraps it over my arm in a death grip. "Let's go to the beach."

He pulls me forward and we walk around the

house. I look out for the soldier. He must be here. He has to be. But Caius leans toward me.

"Looking for the third man?" he asks. "Don't bother. He can't help you."

"Did you hurt him, too?" I ask, trying to pry his hand off me now that we're around the back of the cottage.

"Santos trusted them more than he did me." He just keeps jerking me forward up toward the dune that will lead to the beach.

"I can see why," I yell over the wind, falling when he gives me a shove at the top of the dune. I scramble to my feet, stumble, but he has me before I'm even upright.

He grips my jaw, fingers digging painfully into my face. "You don't get to say that. You get to shut the fuck up and die, and if you're good, I won't make it hurt any more than it needs to. For my brother's sake. Move."

He hurls me forward, so I stumble and slide down halfway before I'm able to get up.

"What are you going to tell him? How are you going to explain it?" Running is impossible in this soft sand, and he's just faster than me and stronger than me. But I keep trying. I have to.

"What am I going to tell him?" he asks, his big hand landing between my shoulder blades and pushing me hard. I fall to my hands and knees, winded. He leans over me, grabs a handful of hair, and hauls me back to my up. He doesn't let go of my hair as he walks me to the water.

"Caius. Please!" I scream, my voice lost over the sound of the waves as I wrap one hand around his forearm, trying to stay upright as he marches me forward.

"People drown all the time, Madelena."

He pushes me to my knees in the icy water and I scream. He kneels too, and I don't know how he's not feeling the cold. He brings my face to his, but I can barely see him through the spray of water.

"Besides, you're sick, aren't you? Like Mom. Maybe you walked into the water yourself. Willingly."

"I wouldn't do that. He knows—"

He pushes my head down roughly. Wet sand gets in my nose, my eyes, but it's when the water rushes me that true panic has me windmilling my arms trying to pull him off me, trying to get my head above the water.

Then I'm up again. He's pulling me out. I cough up saltwater and sand. I claw him, try to leave some mark. Something. Anything. Because I'm not going to survive this. I know. And Santos can't think I killed his baby. He can't.

"Maybe," he says, pulling me to my feet, dragging me deeper into the water so we're waist deep. "Maybe you drowned her now because you didn't want to wimp out like Mommy did."

"I wouldn't. I wouldn't!" But I'm under again, water bubbling around me, choking me. He pushes me down, and I see his dark form above me before a wave throws him off balance and he loses his grip on me. I gasp for air, swallow water, loudly choke it up as I try to run for the beach.

I won't make it though. I know that.

He's on his feet again, and he grabs hold of me. This time, his face is set when I see him for the last time. His mouth is hard. His rage makes his blue eyes blaze even in this darkness.

As water bubbles around me, I stop fighting. Because there's no air left and there's no time. Even as I feel myself slip away, even as my arms stop their grasping and my legs float on the salty bed of water, he keeps me down. Keeps me under.

And I keep thinking about my baby. About Santos. Until I'm gone.

35

SANTOS

I can't be too late. I can't be too late.

I keep trying Father Michael's land line. I keep calling and calling, but he must have it unplugged. Police from the next town over went out to the cottage. At least there's that. I drive like a mad man to Hells Bells.

The sun is breaking the horizon when I turn onto the street where the chapel is quiet, the windows of Father Michael's rooms still dark. I can see from here, though, that the lights in the cottage are on. When I pull up, I see the police cruiser.

For a moment, I'm relieved.

I park and open the door of the SUV. It's quiet. Keeping my eyes on the window with its drawn curtains, I reach across to the glove compartment and take out my gun before stepping out of the vehicle. The first light of morning shines across the driveway. I make no sound as I walk toward the too-still house, weapon at my side. It's when I get around the cruiser that I see it. There, on the ground, are the police officers. I don't need to check either of their pulses. I know how dead looks, and they're dead.

Something sharp spears my insides as I get closer and take in the bullet holes. One was shot in the middle of the forehead. The other man in the heart. The one who took the bullet to the brain wouldn't have seen it coming.

The door of the cottage is open, and I move toward it, readying my weapon, my heart pounding out of my chest.

The sight that greets me makes me stop dead.

"No. Fucking no!" I rush to Val, who is slumped against the wall, the knife that killed him in his hands. He stopped bleeding a while ago. A man lies dead on the sofa. I don't know where the third soldier is. "Madelena!" I yell as I fly up the stairs. But the house is too quiet. She's not here. I know it before I get into the bedroom. Before I see the dying fire, the unmade bed.

I don't waste time here. I run down the stairs and out the front door. There's no car. Did he take her somewhere? But then I hear something, a faint sound on the wind. It's coming from the beach.

Pistol at my side, I move quickly around the side of the house and toward the path that will lead to the beach. The wind is always fiercest in the mornings here. It dies down once the sun has fully risen. It whips my hair and face, blowing sand into my eyes as I round the cottage. There I see the third soldier lying face down, half hidden by the tall grass. Like the cops, I don't need to check to see if he's still alive. I see the bullet hole in the back of his head.

Madelena.

I can't be too late. Please don't let me be too late. Not for me, but for her. For her and for the baby.

A vision of Alexia's dead body dances before my eyes as I hurry toward the beach, climbing the sand dune. At the top, I stop to take in the beach as sunlight turns the cloudy sky orange and the sea a deep blue. And there I see him.

Caius.

He's in the water, waist deep. He looks almost disoriented. And he's alone.

My chest tightens, a fist twisting my heart, wringing it out.

"Caius!" I scream, running toward him, the soft sand making it so much harder, making me so much slower. "Caius!" I yell again because no, he's not alone. I see that when he sees me. When he looks over and watches me run toward him. He's not alone. She's there, too. She's floating face down beside him.

No.

No.

"Get away from her!"

He looks dazed as I drop my pistol on the sand and rush into the water.

"Brother," he starts, a wave propelling him forward. "It's too late."

I lose my footing, right myself, and that same wave

carries Madelena's body closer. I catch hold of her ankle, pull her to me. But Caius tugs me away.

"It's too late. Let her go!"

I try to shove him away, but he has a grip on my shirt, so I punch him hard and send him toppling into the water. I turn Madelena over and gather her up. Her clothes weigh her down. Her head hangs off my arm, and her eyes remain closed, face pale.

"Madelena?" I talk to her as I carry her out of the water, but her arms hang limp at her sides, her body heavy with the sea-soaked clothes. "Open your eyes, sweetheart. Open your eyes for me."

"I tried to stop her," Caius says as I drag myself out of the water. "I was too late."

I don't look at him. I don't waste any time. I lay her on the sand, and someone calls my name. I look up to find Father Michael rushing toward us.

"Move away!" he calls out, stripping off his big coat and laying it over her legs. He drops to his knees beside her and listens for breath, listens for her heart then starts compressions.

I watch, too stunned to act. All I can do is watch her pale face, her unresponsive body.

"Maddy," I say, knowing she hates anyone but Odin calling her that, as if I could enrage her to open her eyes. To tell me off.

"Breathe for her," Father Michael tells me after a count. "Pinch her nose, tilt her head back and breathe for her."

I do as he says. I know how this works. I touch my

lips to her cold ones and close her nose and breathe into her mouth until he tells me to stop and takes over with compressions again, leaning his full weight into her. She's so small. So fragile.

"She's pregnant," I tell him.

He doesn't miss a beat as he nods, continues his count.

"Breathe," he says. I do. I don't know how long but all I know is I can't stop.

"I can't lose you. I can't," I tell her when he starts compressions again, her lips too cold, too blue. "Don't let her die," I tell Father Michael who is oblivious to all but her. But his count. His work. "Please, God, don't let her die."

And then a miracle occurs.

I watch her face, her beautiful face, bleached white.

Sunlight beams down on her, and when Father Michael next presses into her chest, when I hear the sick cracking sound of ribs as he forces her heart to beat, she coughs.

We both stop and look at her face and watch her turn her head and throw up water.

"Madelena! Jesus. Madelena." I cradle her head, pull it onto my lap, turning her onto her side as she vomits up more water mixed with sand. She gasps for breaths between coughs, and it's the sweetest sound. God. It's the sweetest fucking sound. Because she's alive. She's alive.

"Santos?" she says weakly as I lift her, hug her to me, pushing wet hair from her face to kiss her forehead, her cheeks, her mouth, her hands. But then I watch the horror come over her as her gaze moves over my shoulder.

I stiffen.

"Santos," Father Michael says, following Madelena's line of vision.

I stand, lift her in my arms and once Father Michael is on his feet, I hand her over to him.

"Get her inside. Get her warm."

"Santos," he starts, taking her from me because he has no choice. "Don't do anything rash."

Rash. There will be nothing rash in what I will do.

"Get her inside. Now."

I glance once more to my drowned Madelena before turning my back on them to face my brother.

36

SANTOS

"You would contaminate this place," I say.

"That's a little dramatic, don't you think?" Caius asks, not quite steady on his feet.

"It was you. It was you all along."

I pick up my pistol from the sand, tuck it into the waistband of my pants and stalk toward my brother. He stands his ground. He looks as drowned as Madelena. I'm sure I look much the same.

"I had no choice, when it came down to it," he says, a pathetic defense. I swing at him, catch him in the jaw. He spins, stumbles, rights himself. "It was her or you. And I wasn't going to lose you. Not again."

I hit him again, on the other side of his face this time. I'm right-handed, but my left-hook is just as powerful as my right. Shoutout to the Commander's training.

"You had a choice. You always have a fucking

choice." I punch him again. Blood splatters the sand wall at his back.

"Not really, no." He touches his face, fingers coming away red.

"What the fuck do you mean you won't lose me again?" I ask. "You never lost me, you asshole." I repeat the right-hook. This time, he falls on his ass and I take hold of his shirt to get him back up because we're not done yet. We're only just getting started. "You know what, it doesn't matter. Just tell me one thing. Just one fucking thing. Why Alexia? What did she do to you to deserve what you did?"

"Oh." He shakes his head. "Alexia wasn't me."

I stop, not expecting that. But then I shake my head. "You're lying." I draw my arm back and ram it into his gut.

He grunts, doubles over. "I'm not, brother," he manages after a minute, spitting blood when he straightens to face me again. He's not fighting me. He's taking the beating. It's not like him.

"Don't call me that. We are no longer brothers."

"I'm not lying. Not about Alexia." I watch him and I realize he's not lying. I know his tell. It's consistent. But no, I'm wrong. I have to be wrong.

"Then who? Who would want to hurt her? She did nothing to anyone!"

"You really don't want to know, Santos."

I shove him backward against the dune. "Yeah, I really do. I really want to know before I squeeze the last breath out of you."

"That's the thing. I don't care if I die."

"I don't give a fuck what you care about. Tell. Me. Who."

He looks away for a long moment, emotions warring in his eyes. On his face. When he faces me again, he looks a decade older.

"Our mother."

I stop dead. "What?" I hear myself ask as my arm drops to my side.

"See, told you that you wouldn't want to know." Caius slides down onto the sand. "He came for me. It was me he wanted," Caius says, and I see the effort it's taking him to keep his eyes on mine. "When the Commander found out about me, he came to take me. Our mother made a deal with him. She traded you for me."

His words are like a punch to the gut I don't understand.

"I told you that you didn't want to know."

"I don't believe you."

"Yeah, you do. You know I have no reason to lie about this. Not anymore."

"Tell me. Tell me all of it." My throat is tight. I'm sick to my stomach.

"You're a fucking masochist. How many times do you want me to repeat it? She sold you to save me."

"All. Of. It." I demand.

"All of it?" He asks. I nod. "Okay. All of it." He takes a minute. "She made an agreement with that bastard, and she needed an event. Something to get you and

Brutus into a position where you'd have to make a deal."

"Our mother is not a murderer."

"No?"

No. She's not. Is she? My chest tightens, betrayal twisting my heart. "Why Alexia?"

"Well, I was supposed to do the deed, but got squeamish. Believe it or not, murder makes me nauseous."

I snort.

He tries for a cocky smile but just turns a little green. "So, she did it knowing you'd think it was Alexia's father. She positioned her the way she did. Wrote what she wrote on her stomach."

I watch and listen... and I can't fucking breathe.

"Voila!" He makes a grand arm gesture. "The Commander had his enforcer."

I stare at him, trying to make sense of this. "Our father found out," I say. "That's why the change in the will. That's why that cryptic letter."

"Your father. Not ours. But yes. That's why. Thia go?" He holds up his wrist where the bracelet sits. "New bracelet. That fucker knew it all. He was going to blackmail us. We were to meet at the lighthouse, but then your wife showed up."

"You could have hurt her then. Killed her. You didn't. Why hurt her now?"

He shrugs his shoulders. "It was her or you, and like I said, I wasn't going to lose you again." He must see the confusion on my face. "Mom's phase two wasn't what you thought. At least you didn't know the whole of it. You needed to get her pregnant. Then we'd get you out of the way. I'd marry Madelena, adopt the kid with Augustine blood in his veins." He raises his eyebrows to make sure I'm following. "Exactly to the letter as Brutus Augustine's will states. She hated him by the end. Did you know that?"

I process this. I did in a way. I didn't understand why but their relationship over the last few years of his life had deteriorated to the point they had separate bedrooms and rarely were in the same room together.

But my own mother? "She wouldn't do this."

His face goes dead serious, and I see something in his eyes that I've never seen before. Not in his. Resignation. He's given up.

"You don't know her, Santos. You don't know anything about her. Now," he staggers to his feet, starts to root around in his pocket, and pulls out a pocketknife. He flips it open, and I watch him and prepare for an attack.

Except it doesn't come.

Instead, he turns the knife around and holds it out for me to take it. I look from it to him, and I understand.

He expects me to kill him, and he wants to die.

"And you don't know me either, brother," he says.

I look at that knife again and take it. I step toward him. He draws a deep breath in and waits for the attack.

But I close the switchblade and tuck it into my pocket. I take hold of my gun instead.

"Turn around," I tell him.

He looks at the gun, then at me, and he knows I'm not going to kill him. I won't give him the gift of death.

"Turn around, *brother*."

He swallows. I watch his throat work. He nods once. Does he know what I will do? He must. He's seen me do it before. That whole murder makes him nauseous bullshit? It's exactly that. Bullshit. And torture never bothered him.

He turns slowly. He hangs his head.

I aim the gun at the back of his right knee. And I shoot.

37

MADELENA

A gunshot pierces the heavy stillness of the chapel. Father Michael hears it too. I see his head snap to the stained-glass window. I'm sitting on the front pew, wrapped in a heavy duvet. He is lighting all the candles on the altar. When we got here, he left me in the chapel, locked the door, and disappeared for a few minutes to bring me dry clothes. I'm not sure whose they are, but they're about three sizes too big. I don't care though. They're dry.

I try to get to my feet. I need to get to Santos, but my ribs ache.

"He could be hurt," I say. "We have to help him."

He shakes his head, keeps hold of my hands as he crouches down before me. I'm shaking, and although it's not cold in here, I don't know that I'll ever feel warm again.

I can still hear the echo of water, hear my scream

beneath the surface. Feel my terror as Caius held me down, as he drowned me.

"Santos can take care of himself, Madelena.'"

"Caius..."

He shakes his head. "Shh. Your baby is under stress already."

Did the baby even survive? I don't feel anything. But I've never felt anything.

An eternity later, someone tries the locked door. I watch Father Michael hurry down the aisle toward it as I hear Santos's voice.

"It's me. Father Michael. Let me in," he calls out, rattling the doors.

Relief has fresh tears running down my face, and I stand and let the duvet fall from my shoulders as the door is unlocked and Santos enters the chapel. He stops for a moment, just a moment, and looks at me and then he's at my side, taking me in his arms, sitting with me on his lap and cradling me. I cling to him, kiss his cheek, then bury my face in his neck.

"I trusted him," Santos says against my ear.

"Is he... Did you?" I look up at him, see the splatter of blood on his shirt.

He looks at me, then gets to his feet with me in his arms. "We need to get you to a doctor." He and Father Michael exchange a look, and Santos carries me out of the chapel. He sets me down on the passenger side of the SUV and turns to Father Michael.

"I'll send some people, but we need to get the cruiser moved," Santos says.

"I'll take care of it," Father Michael says, surprising me—making me wonder again about his past.

"Val was a friend," Santos says.

"I know." The priest takes hold of Santos's shoulders, then takes something out of his pocket and pushes it into Santos's hands.

"I don't want that," Santos says.

Father Michael closes his hands over whatever it is. "You witnessed a miracle today." He glances at me. "You know that."

Santos is quiet.

"Go. Take care of your wife."

Santos nods. They man-hug, and a moment later, he closes my door and climbs into the driver's seat as he tucks the thing Father Michael gave him into his pocket.

It's a rosary.

38

SANTOS

I send soldiers to Augustine's to secure the apartment and make sure my mother stays put until I get there.

When we get to the parking lot of the small building that houses Dr. Moore's practice, three SUVs are parked in the lot, each with two soldiers inside. As we pull in, they climb out of their vehicles and wait.

Dr. Moore opens the door and anxiously looks around at the men. She canceled her first few appointments in order to see us when I called and explained it was an emergency.

I know she knows who I am, what I do. So, when she sees the state we're both in by the time we get to her office, she doesn't ask any questions but leads us into the same examining room as last time.

"I'm all right. I'm fine," Madelena insists as the doctor and I help her out of her clothes, and she examines her. I see the bruises all over her body, and I know the pain of cracked ribs. "The baby though."

Dr. Moore doesn't look convinced she is fine. "I'm an OB-GYN. You need to take your wife to a proper doctor to be looked at," she tells me.

"I will. The baby."

Dr. Moore nods. My phone rings as I watch her arrange the stirrups and ready the probe.

"Yes?" I answer, turning my back to the women.

"Sir, she's gone. I have Cummings here and the girl. Ana."

"Gone?"

"Soldier said she left soon after you did."

"Santos?" Madelena asks.

"Keep them there. I'll come soon." I disconnect the call and turn to my wife. This time, as I take her hand, she holds onto mine, and she too, looks at the monitor along with me. My heart is racing and I'm sure she can see the anxiety on my face.

"Here we go," Dr. Moore says and inserts the probe. I hold my breath. I think Madelena is holding hers too. But in an instant, that racing heartbeat fills the room. Madelena's exhale matches my own. When I dip my head into her neck, she wraps a hand around it and holds me to herself because the weight of this, and the relief, they're almost unbearable. And I'm so fucking grateful.

"She's okay," Madelena tells me. "She's okay." She's comforting me for a change.

"She?" Dr. Moore says, trying to lighten the mood.

I raise my head and my eyebrows. Madelena turns to Dr. Moore and shrugs. "It's just a feeling."

The doctor smiles too. "Well, you can find out in a few more weeks if you want that." She puts the probe away and removes her gloves.

Madelena touches my face and I force a smile, but she sees the effort it takes me. Because this isn't over.

"Do you need a referral for a good doctor nearby?" Dr. Moore asks.

"Yes, actually," I say, standing. Because I don't trust anyone in Avarice.

"I'll get you a card." She looks at both of us, smiles, then leaves.

Madelena turns to me. "Caius?"

"Caius will never come near you again."

I know she wants to ask what this means, but I help her up, help her get dressed in the awful clothes Father Michael provided.

"Let's go home. I'll have the doctor come to see you there."

She nods and, after taking the card from Dr. Moore, we walk out into the lot. Madelena takes in the collection of soldiers. I sent twice the number and a cleaner to Hells Bells. Having dead cops involved is going to complicate things, but between my connections and Father Michael's, we'll figure it out.

The fact that Val is gone hits me as I help her into the SUV, but I set the thought aside for now. It's not yet time to mourn the dead. It will come, but not yet.

"What happened? What was that call?" Madelena

asks as I climb into the driver's side, and we head home.

"Nothing."

"It's not nothing."

I keep my eyes on the road and feel hers burn into me. She has questions, but I'm not ready to answer them just yet.

"Santos." She touches my hand and I turn to her. "I almost died today. We almost lost the baby. Maybe I almost lost you. Please talk to me. No secrets."

I grit my teeth, but she's right. "My mother. This all started with her years ago. More than a decade ago."

"Your mother?"

"And my brother. To a different extent. But guilty is guilty."

"What was the call?"

"She's gone."

"Gone?"

I nod, draw a deep breath in and exhale it out. "I'll go to Augustine's later. Figure it out." We stop at a traffic light, and I turn to her, touch her cheek. "Let me take care of you first." I shake my head, pull her to me, and kiss her forehead. "I thought I lost you."

"You didn't." A tear rolls down her cheek. "I'm here. We're both here."

I nod.

"Your brother. Are you going to be okay?"

"I have to be. I love you, sweetheart. I love you so much. You know that, right?" She smiles, looks at me with such warmth it's almost hard to look at her. "I don't deserve you."

"I love you, too, Santos. And I'm here with you. We're not alone anymore. Neither of us."

The car behind us honks their horn.

Madelena looks back then flips him off, which makes me laugh. Caius was right about her. She's tough as nails.

When we get home, I run a hot bath for her as the cook prepares a warm meal. I bathe her, shower myself, and help her eat a little bit before the doctor arrives. I stay in the room as he examines her. She will heal but it will take time and she's exhausted by the time he leaves. I lay her down in the bed and climb in beside her.

"You're going, aren't you? When I fall asleep," she says as I hold her to me.

I'm fully clothed, so it's pretty obvious, I guess. "I'll be here when you wake up, and I've stationed two men at the door, more throughout the house and outside. You'll be safe."

"I know. I just don't want you to go."

"I have to."

"I know that too." Her eyelids close. "I can sleep for days."

I kiss her forehead and don't even get a chance to reply before she's out.

CUMMINGS IS SWEATING, HE'S SO FUCKING ANXIOUS. Ana, on the other hand, stands calmly by the windows, her arms folded across her chest, eyes narrowed as she studies me. She's framed by sunlight in the floor-to-ceiling window of the living room. I wonder about her. She reminds me a little of Camilla.

"So she didn't tell you where she was going?" I ask Cummings again.

"She didn't even tell me she was going. I woke up and she was gone. That's all. Can I go? I'm behind on my appointments."

"Sure," I tell him because I don't think he knows anything. I think Mom used him.

He stands, adjusts his jacket.

I walk closer to him. "If you hear from her, I'd love to know. You understand me?"

He clears his throat, face flushing with nerves. "Of course."

"Good. I'd hate to be on opposite sides, Dr. Cummings."

"Understood."

I gesture to the soldier standing nearby to let him out and turn to Ana.

She cocks her head, lets her gaze move over me. One corner of her mouth lifts suggestively. She doesn't think I'm remotely attracted to her, does she?

"Sit," I tell her, pointing to the couch.

"Your brother likes to give orders too. It must run in the family." She sits, and I just watch her, confused.

"I thought you and Caius broke up."

She shrugs a shoulder. "It was temporary."

"Was it?"

She puts her thumbnail into her mouth, and I see how young she is. She's Madelena's age but a very different person.

"He won't be back. He will never return to Avarice. You understand that, don't you?"

"Why not?"

I ignore her question. I know she was just a pawn, someone Caius and my mother both used. "You should go home, Ana. Forget about him. And forget about my wife. I don't want you upsetting her."

"Because she's pregnant."

I neither confirm nor negate.

"Is he dead?" she asks.

"No, he's not dead. But if he shows his face here, he will be. There is one thing, though. If my mother or Caius have contact with you, you will let me know. Just like Dr. Cummings. Do you understand?"

"Why?"

"That doesn't matter. What matters is that you understand me. Do you?"

She nods.

"Good. Do you need a ride home?"

She shakes her head. "I need to get my things," she says, standing and taking a step toward Caius's bedroom.

I put out an arm to stop her. "I'll have them sent to you. My men will see you out. I don't want to see you back here for the foreseeable future, clear?"

"Is that what Madelena wants?"

"It's what I want. Are we clear, Ana?"

"Yes."

"Good. Go."

The soldier escorts her out, and I turn and walk down the empty corridor toward the study. I've already looked through it. There's nothing here. No note, no letter. Just nothing. Caius's bedroom, too, came up empty.

It's not Caius I'm worried about. He won't return. There's nothing for him here except enemies. My mother is a different story. I sit behind the desk, see the empty glass with lipstick staining it. She is a different woman than I thought, and I will catch up with her. She and I do have one thing in common. We both have long memories, and I won't soon forget what she did.

For now, though, I take one last look around and get up to go home to my wife.

39

SANTOS

Three Months Later

It takes three long months to locate my mother. In that time, I hear nothing of my brother. He has disappeared, as I expected him to. He can lick his wounds and do whatever the fuck he needs to do as long as it doesn't involve him coming near my wife, my family.

Val should be with me as I exit the SUV outside the nondescript house along the outskirts of a forgettable town in the middle of Florida. I look around, thinking how unlike my mother this is.

Not that this is where I found her. No. She was in Monaco living a life she had become accustomed to with my father. She'd only arrived here, escorted, two nights ago.

The sky is overcast, clouds heavy and the heat uncomfortable. I stand in a fading sunset that may be pretty anywhere but here and listen to the constant cadence of what sounds like a thousand cicadas. Ahead of me stands the house my mother grew up in. The house itself is buried by an overgrowth of trees, bushes and weeds. Once upon a time, it may have been nestled within the foliage but now, it's just old and very tired.

It's surrounded by three acres, most of which is unusable wetland, and I have the feeling of wanting to be away, be gone, before I've even set foot inside. I can imagine my mother's despair growing up here. Feeling stuck here.

I never knew anything about my grandparents from my mother's side. They were dead, and my mother hadn't had a great relationship with them when they were alive. She'd supported them is all I knew, or all I'd been told. I'm not sure much of anything I know about my mother is true, though.

Bringing her back here, to this house, is cruel punishment, but it's better than she deserves. This is my mercy, although I doubt she'll see it as such. My father had bought the house the year he married my mother. I hadn't realized the significance of it when we'd been going over his holdings after his passing. I don't know if my mother even knew he'd done that because the soldiers who escorted her back told me of her surprise when she realized where she was being taken.

A second car pulls up onto the driveway alongside mine. The driver steps out, nods his greeting, and reaches into the backseat to lift out a black bag. I walk toward the front door, and he follows. The two men stationed at the door greet me and open it to let me in. The man follows, takes in the space, the woman seated on the old sofa in the middle of the dusty, abandoned room and melts back against the shadows to await his orders.

I take in the old house, smell the old smell. Workers will begin their work on the interior soon, although it won't be anything like my mother has become accustomed to. They've already started on the exterior. It's uninhabitable as-is.

My mother's eyes are locked on mine when I turn my gaze to hers. As usual, she's unreadable.

I approach her, lifting a chair from around the old dining table, placing it a few feet from her and taking a seat.

Her wary gaze moves over my shoulder to the man with the bag before settling on me, and it's like she's a stranger, like I don't know this woman at all.

"Mother. I've had a hell of a time tracking you down."

She casts a disdainful glance at the two men behind her. "I don't appreciate being kidnapped and brought here against my will by my own son."

I exhale, finding it hard to keep my hands from clenching, my mouth from spouting accusation upon accusation.

"I don't much care what you appreciate. I know what you *did*, and this is *your* punishment." My father's words, repeated in my own voice; my heart, twisting inside my chest. "It was you all along. You who started everything."

She has the grace to lower her lashes for an instant. But maybe I'm giving her too much credit. Maybe it's just the moment she needs to gather her defenses, prepare her denial.

But to her credit, when she opens her mouth, it's not to deny. "I had no choice, Santos. It was you or Caius."

"That in itself is a choice."

"So you'd rather I'd have let him take Caius?"

"Do you hear yourself? How do you justify the selling of one son over another?"

Her gaze falters momentarily, only momentarily. "You had your father. Who has Caius had apart from me?"

"I'm your son too," I say, the words coming out more broken than angry because I feel the weight of her betrayal so acutely, it's like salt in an open wound.

She folds her arms across her chest and leans back in her seat. "What do you want from me? An apology? All right. I'm sorry I had to make an impossible choice. But look at you now. Look how far you've come."

I open my mouth, but I'm dumbstruck for words. "Do you feel any remorse at all for any of it?" I finally ask.

"Why should I? I saved one son. I could only save one son."

"Alexia. Our child. It was you."

Her jaw clenches. I see a bead of sweat at her hairline, but when she speaks there's a hint of distaste to her words, at least the first part. "Your brother couldn't stomach the thought. I had to step in. I saved him from the Commander. Would you have wanted it to be him and not you?"

"Don't you dare turn this around."

"He didn't deserve what you did to him."

"He drowned my wife. He deserved worse. Dad found out. That's why he cut you and Caius off."

"He found out that Caius was the Commander's son and that I'd made an agreement with him to trade you."

"Tell me why Alexia. Why not just send me to him if you were so desperate to save Caius?"

"You think your father would have allowed you, his beloved heir, his blood-born son, to go? I couldn't leave him with a choice. Alexia was collateral damage."

"Alexia was a human being! As was our child! And the way..." It takes me a minute to continue, to find the words. "The way you laid her out for me to find. Why?"

"I needed you angry. I knew you'd think it was her father. I knew you'd blame yourself and you'd go after him, and I knew it was the only way to save one of you."

"Don't pretend for one fucking second you thought to save me, that it even occurred to you that you'd be sending me, your other son I might remind you, to that monster."

She opens her mouth, closes it again, and for the

first time, she looks chastened. Not repentant though. She has spent too many years justifying her crime to herself.

I stand up. "We're finished here. I can't stand to look at you for another minute."

She glances back at the man with the bag who steps out of the shadows. I replace the chair at the dining table, which is only a few steps away because the house is so small.

"What do you mean, we're finished?" she asks, gaze on that man as she makes to stand. One of the soldiers at her back lays his big hand on her shoulder, keeping her seated.

"I mean you and I are finished. But your punishment has just begun." This brings me no joy. Not that I expected it to. No, it feels like it did when I hurt the innocents, even knowing she is as far from innocent as anyone can be. Hell, she is the catalyst of it all.

"And what is that, son?" she asks, teeth tight together as she tries to appear angry and not frightened.

"You'll live here, in the house you were so desperate to escape."

"It's uninhabitable—"

"Repairs have begun. You will have the bare minimum. You will be under constant guard. You will be alone."

"Prison."

"And no one will know where you are."

At that she swallows. "You can't do this. You won't."

"I can. I am."

"How long?"

"For the rest of your life. I thought that was self-explanatory."

"Santos, I..."

"I'm not finished." I nod to the man with the bag. He sets it on the coffee table, sending dust motes into the air. He unzips it, and I know it takes all she has not to peer into it because a black duffel is never a good sign, is it?

I wait until she meets my eyes again to speak.

"You're a conniving, slithering thing. A snake. Although a snake is only acting on the instinct to survive. A snake is not evil," I say, feeling sick for the words. "You've hurt so many, taken too much. Even Caius, you've damaged beyond repair."

"I—"

I shake my head and she quiets. "But you are my mother still. And I am merciful, still, in spite of the Commander." I turn to the man. "I want her knocked out during the procedure. Make sure there are antibiotics. I don't want infection. But no painkillers. Understood?"

"Yes, sir."

"Santos!" My mother is on her feet, the hand on her shoulder the only thing holding her back.

I turn to her.

"What are you going to do?"

"You'll wear the tongue of a serpent. For all the lies you've told, for all the damage you've done."

She blanches but waits. I'm not finished and she knows it.

"And you will lose the hand that began this."

"Wh... What?"

I step toward her but find I don't want to be too close. "But you will live. Not like so many others who are long dead."

Her face loses the last of its color.

"That is my mercy. It's more than you deserve."

"Please—"

"It's what I learned all those years. An eye for an eye, a tooth for a tooth. But like I said, you are my mother, and perhaps in that warped mind of yours, you thought you were doing the right thing. I'm going to try really hard to believe that."

"Santos, you can't."

I can't look at her for another minute because the longer I do, the filthier I feel.

"Goodbye, Mother."

"No! Wait!"

But I don't. I turn my back on my mother as she calls for me, panicked, and walk out of that house. I want to run, to get away from her. From it. I want to burn my clothes and scrub my skin and forget this day. I decide to do just that, even as her scream pierces my ear long after I've closed the door, long after I'm miles away. Long after I leave the disease that is my mother behind forever.

I vow that no matter what, I will not let my sons

and daughters ever know the blood that taints us all, that dirties us, uglies us.

I swear to keep them innocent, to keep them good.

Like Madelena is innocent, is good.

And I return home to her. To my salvation.

EPILOGUE
MADELENA

It's a warm day, and I'm sitting outside on one of the patio chairs sipping lemonade from a tall glass and watching the workmen fill the swimming pool. Odin is sitting in the chair beside mine, sunglasses in place, watching one man in particular. Santos is on a business trip, although the word business is used quite loosely, I'm learning, with him. I wonder if he found his mother.

I tilt my sunglasses up and look at my brother. "I thought you were in a relationship," I say to him.

Odin came out a few weeks ago when our father decided it was time he settled down. Odin agreed wholeheartedly and announced he'd be settling down with Rick—not exactly what our father meant, but it doesn't matter. He'll get over it. Besides, the worst he can do is cut Odin out of his life and his will. The former doesn't matter, and the latter won't happen. If he cuts Odin out, who will he leave the De Léon fortune to? Not me. And certainly not a charity. He's too greedy for that.

Besides, when I mentioned what Uncle Jax had kept, he tucked tail like the coward he is. We hardly see him.

Odin glances at me. "I thought *you* were married."

I push my sunglasses back down.

Odin has grown stronger over the last few months. Less fearful of our father. I think Santos is to thank for that but not because he voluntarily helped him. More because he forced Odin to become the man he is now.

"I see you looking too, by the way. You're not fooling anyone with those huge glasses."

I sip the last of my lemonade and grin, putting a hand to my very round belly to feel the baby do a little flip.

"I will never get used to seeing that," Odin says, looking a little creeped out.

"Never get used to seeing what?" Santos asks. I look up at him. He's freshly showered, hair still wet. I guess he showered before coming out to see us.

"When did you get back?"

"Just twenty minutes ago. Wanted to get the grime off."

Grime. I don't push.

He leans over my chair to kiss me on the lips and raises his eyebrows at the movement beneath the thin material of my dress.

I watch my husband, who has a little more gray in his hair these days. Whose eyes, although used to laughter now, still carry inside them the shadow of the past. But with me, it's almost as though he clings to the light, as if he will have the light no matter what.

"I'm out, sis," Odin says and gets up. "You coming by tomorrow?"

I lift my glasses up and look at him. "Yeah. I'll be there." Odin and Rick moved into Uncle Jax's house a few weeks ago, and they've just started renovating. I transferred the title to his name and handed over the keys and couldn't be happier about it. It didn't feel right to sell the place, but I'd never live in it. Besides, I love this house. I realize it's not Avarice that changes Santos. It's his family, and them being gone makes all the difference.

"See you." He shakes hands with Santos. The two are on slightly friendlier terms these days.

Once he's gone, Santos sits on the chair beside mine facing me.

"So. Entertaining yourself while I'm away?" he asks, nodding toward one of the men.

"He's too young for me. I prefer them old," I tell him, getting up to sit on his lap. "Like you."

"Old, huh?" He kisses me, and the baby does a somersault.

"Whoa," I say.

"She's active," he adds. I was right. She is a girl.

"Did you find what you were looking for?" I ask, unable not to although unwilling to let go of the ease of the moment.

He told me what he did to Caius on that beach.

Told me he left him alive. I'm glad for that because I don't want him to have his brother's blood on his hands. Caius deserved to be punished, without a doubt, but he was manipulated too, and, in a way, the brothers do love each other.

Santos considers my question for a very long minute. "I found what I needed to find," he says, cryptic. Something in his eyes tells me not to push for more.

Evelyn Augustine disappeared the night Caius ambushed me in Hells Bells. No one has heard from her in three months, although Santos did notice the chunk of money that vanished with her. She'd been stealing from the Augustine inheritance for years—for a decade, probably preparing for when she'd be found out. I don't know the punishment he has planned for her, and as much as I don't want Caius's blood on his hands, I also don't want his mother's on them.

Santos smiles, the light returning to his eyes. He glances at the workers and stands, wrapping his arms around me and cupping my ass. "Mrs. Augustine, you seem distracted."

"Do I, Mr. Augustine? You've been busy. I'm just passing the time..."

He's taken on the management of Augustine & Donovan Media and removed Dad from the business altogether. He's also employed Odin in a management position. Although Santos will never be able to erase his past, he is creating a different future. A legitimate one.

The Avery family is sticking around. It's an annoyance, but not much more. After everything that's happened, I don't feel threatened by them. They're powerless to hurt us, just like Ana. Just like Caius. Just like his mother.

"Just passing the time, huh?" He lifts me up in his arms making me yelp. "Let me help with that."

"I'm too heavy," I protest as he carries me into the house and up the stairs.

"Hardly." When we reach our bedroom, he stands me up and makes quick work of undressing me, taking a long moment to look at me, to take in my ever-growing belly. The look in his eyes when he does it, it's so beautiful and tender that I reach out to touch his cheek.

"Are you all right?" I ask him.

He shifts his gaze to mine, eyes a little sad. "I'm perfect when I'm with you, my love."

My love.

That's new. But I don't have time to dwell when he bends his head to kiss my mouth, my neck, my breasts. He lays me down on the bed, stripping off his shirt as he leans over me to kiss me full on the mouth, careful not to lean his full weight on me. He is ever-protective of me and the baby, my Santos.

After he's made long, slow love to me, and we lay on our sides lost in each other's eyes, he kisses me again and says those words again. *My love.*

And I know that we've fulfilled our destinies, that he and I have delivered each other from the grip of evil and made light out of darkness. Made love where there was only hate.

"I love you," I whisper before melting into his warm embrace.

"I love you," he says, wrapping his big, powerful and warm arms around me.

WHAT TO READ NEXT
RUINED KINGDOM

Amadeo
15 Years Ago

Hundred-dollar bills float to the peeling linoleum floor. Five. Ten. Fifteen. Fifteen-hundred dollars. It's what a life is worth to them.

My mother can't stop sobbing. She's going to choke on her tears. My father stands defiant, his hands fisted at his sides.

Fifteen-hundred dollars lie on the old green-and-yellow floor. Does he expect us to drop and rush to collect them? Thank him for his generosity? He's going to be disappointed if that's the case.

Lucien Russo moves to his father's side, inadvertently stepping on one of the bills with his polished, expensive shoes. Or maybe it's not so inadvertent. I ignore him, though. He doesn't matter. Not now. He is not the one in control.

He whispers something to his father while I take in the cut of the older man's suit. The scent of their combined cologne permeates the air in the small room as if syphoning out the oxygen. As my father instructed me to, I keep my gaze low and memorize the ring on Geno Russo's finger. The insignia. Lucien has one too. It looks out of place on his hand, though. Like a boy wearing a man's ring. He's new to his family's business with hands like that. His father's hands are dangerous. Violent. Although I know the damage Lucien can do. Today is evidence of it.

"No hard feelings, Roland," the older Russo says.

My father clenches and unclenches his hands. I shift my gaze up, just for a moment. I want to know if Russo has seen that fisting and flexing. That barely pent-up rage.

He has.

"You won't make trouble, Roland," Russo says, and I realize he hasn't missed my glance either because his eyes meet mine.

I step forward, flanking my father's right.

"Amadeo." My father says my name like a warning. He's still looking at the older man, who smiles a cunning, terrifying smile as he lays a heavy hand on my head.

"Amadeo," Russo repeats. "Your son is brave," he says to my father, then shifts his gaze to Bastian, who peers out from behind my father's back. "Tell me, are you as brave?" he asks my younger brother.

My mother swallows back a sob.

"They are children," my father responds, and it sounds like they're having a different, parallel conversation alongside the spoken words. The undercurrent of danger is undeniable.

"Two boys. Boys who will grow into men."

No one says a word for a long minute as the unspoken threat hangs between us. My mother's crying is the only sound in the room.

"We had a sister, too," Bastian says, his voice high. He's not yet a man.

They all turn their attention to my brother, and I know this is a fatal mistake. This moment.

Just then, the door opens, and we all turn to it, surprised when a little girl comes hopping into our small, ugly kitchen. She's softly singing a Disney tune and seems oblivious to the tension as her eyes quickly scan the room and land on Geno Russo. She smiles a huge smile.

"Daddy," she says. "Look what I picked. Daffodils." They're actually dandelions. She holds her bouquet up to her father.

Her father.

A man comes running in after her, expression hurried, frazzled. "I was... She..."

Russo gives him a deadly look that lasts an instant before he bends to scoop up his little girl. "So pretty. Go pick more for me, will you?"

She nods, but she's sensed something is off. I see it in her expression. And as he carries her toward the door, she catches my eyes on her before my mother's cry steals her attention. She tilts her head in confusion. "Daddy?" she starts, a dandelion dropping from her hand. But a moment later, she's gone, and the door closed.

My father pushes me backward with a heavy hand when Russo returns his full attention to us. Dad steps between the older man and me. And I know everything has changed. We're down to the real business of his visit now. I wonder if Bastian hadn't spoken, if I hadn't defiantly met the older man's gaze, what happened next would have gone differently. Would they simply have left? Hadn't they done enough damage?

"I won't make trouble," my father says tightly. "Neither will my boys."

Russo smiles, glances at us, then at his men. He nods almost imperceptibly, and my mother screams, throwing herself at his feet.

The rest happens so quickly. Someone drags my mother away. Her screams keep coming even after a bedroom door slams shut. Two men grab my father. Another takes my brother and me by the arm. Russo and his son step backward and watch as kitchen drawers are opened and rummaged through. Bastian cries beside me, and all I hear are my father's pleas telling him we're just boys. Children.

A soldier comes out of the back of the house. He's

been in my room. I know because he's carrying my baseball bat.

"Dad?" I find myself asking as one of the two men holding him snickers. It's the same time another soldier—how many did he bring into our small house—approaches my brother and me with the kitchen knife my mother uses to peel apples for pie. It's sharp. We're not allowed to touch it.

Bastian screams, and I don't know what is more terrifying, the sight of the bat being raised high then brought down on my father's knees, the sound of his scream, or my own as that razor-sharp knife carves a line into my face from my ear to the corner of my mouth. That of Bastian's as they slice him next. And blood. So much fucking blood soaking our socked feet. The money on the floor. Blood pooling around the tiny, wilting dandelion the little girl dropped. Blood dirtying expensive shoes as Russo and his son walk out, Russo adjusting his jacket, his diamond cuff link glinting as it catches the bright noon sun coming in from the open door.

And we're left lying in heaps, broken. All of us broken.

One-Click Ruined Kingdom Now!

THANK YOU

Thanks for reading The Augustine Brothers Duet. I hope you loved Santos and Madelena's story and would consider leaving a review at your favorite store!

ALSO BY NATASHA KNIGHT

The Augustine Brothers
Forgive Me My Sins
Deliver Me From Evil

Ruined Kingdom Duet
Ruined Kingdom
Broken Queen

The Devil's Pawn Duet
Devil's Pawn
Devil's Redemption

To Have and To Hold
With This Ring
I Thee Take
Stolen: Dante's Vow

The Society Trilogy
Requiem of the Soul
Reparation of Sin
Resurrection of the Heart

The Rite Trilogy

His Rule

Her Rebellion

Their Reign

Dark Legacy Trilogy

Taken (Dark Legacy, Book 1)

Torn (Dark Legacy, Book 2)

Twisted (Dark Legacy, Book 3)

Unholy Union Duet

Unholy Union

Unholy Intent

Collateral Damage Duet

Collateral: an Arranged Marriage Mafia Romance

Damage: an Arranged Marriage Mafia Romance

Ties that Bind Duet

Mine

His

MacLeod Brothers

Devil's Bargain

Benedetti Mafia World

Salvatore: a Dark Mafia Romance

Dominic: a Dark Mafia Romance

Sergio: a Dark Mafia Romance

The Benedetti Brothers Box Set (Contains Salvatore, Dominic and Sergio)

Killian: a Dark Mafia Romance

Giovanni: a Dark Mafia Romance

The Amado Brothers

Dishonorable

Disgraced

Unhinged

Standalone Dark Romance

Descent

Deviant

Beautiful Liar

Retribution

Theirs To Take

Captive, Mine

Alpha

Given to the Savage

Taken by the Beast

Claimed by the Beast

Captive's Desire

Protective Custody

Amy's Strict Doctor

Taming Emma

Taming Megan

Taming Naia

Reclaiming Sophie

The Firefighter's Girl

Dangerous Defiance

Her Rogue Knight

Taught To Kneel

Tamed: the Roark Brothers Trilogy

ABOUT THE AUTHOR

Natasha Knight is the *USA Today* Bestselling author of Romantic Suspense and Dark Romance Novels. She has sold over a million books and is translated into six languages. She currently lives in The Netherlands with her husband and two daughters and when she's not writing, she's walking in the woods listening to a book, sitting in a corner reading or off exploring the world as often as she can get away.

Contact Natasha here: natasha@natasha-knight.com

www.natasha-knight.com

Made in United States
Orlando, FL
13 May 2023